The Game

Terry Schott

This is a work of fiction. Names, characters, businesses, places, events and incidents are either the products of the author's imagination or used in a fictitious manner.
Any resemblance to actual persons, living or dead, or actual events is purely coincidental.

Editing by Alan Seeger

Dedication

This book idea surfaced years ago, and I became very good at making excuses for not writing the story down. None of them were very good, but they were extremely effective.

One day I decided to post the first six chapters (all I had written) and ask my Facebook friends to take a look. My commitment was that I would post one chapter a day for six days. I thought maybe one or two people would say it was pretty good and encourage me to write more, which would push me to write maybe a chapter every week or so until the book was finally complete. By the sixth day of posting my friends had shared my website with over 140 others and people were beginning to get excited about the story.

This continued for the next three months and I didn't just write a chapter or two, the support and encouragement allowed me to write the entire first book!

There have been over three thousand visits to my website and many, many excited people who could not wait to read the next chapter as I wrote it.

I dedicate this book to all of you… my friends who wanted more from me than I wanted for myself.

It is with a smile on my face that I deeply thank you for your encouragement and support.

This book exists through me… but because of you, and for that I am extremely thankful.

http://terryschott.com

1

He woke up in a white room.

The walls, ceiling, floor, lights… everything was white.

He couldn't remember how he got here. He recalled pain, followed by a sense of leaving his body, floating above it and watching people surround him. Then he was enveloped in darkness and moving slowly towards a tunnel of bright light. The closer he got to it, the faster he moved, until he was streaking towards it at an incredible speed. Suddenly he slammed to a stop and lost consciousness. Now he was in this room, lying on a table with a white cloth draped over his body. He remembered stories like this that involved people dying, or almost dying, and being drawn towards a bright, white light. People sharing these stories had all been revived by doctors, moving away from the light and returning from death's door. He'd never heard of anyone going into the light and living to tell about it. Near death experiences? That was it! The white light was associated with dying, or almost dying. No story had ever mentioned a room like this.

"Am I dead?" He asked out loud. His voice was different than the one he had used just a short time ago, much different. No longer deep and raspy, it sounded younger, more like 16 than 74. He distinctly remembered being 74. Holding a hand up, he noticed it wasn't a 74-year old, thin, frail, wrinkled hand. It was the strong young hand of a teenager. He groaned softly, "Ah, crap. I am dead."

"Kind of," a voice said. "But not quite."

Turning his head towards the voice, he saw a kid, about 18 years old, with a friendly smile on his face.

"Welcome back, stranger. You had an incredible run that time! Glad to see you back safe and sound."

"Back? From where?" The man sat up much quicker than he imagined possible. His body was strong and young, not old and weak. It felt both strange and exhilarating at the same time. He swung his legs over the edge of the bed and turned to face his visitor. "And where am I? I think I've been here before... but I'm not certain."

The kid laughed. "Oh yes, you've been here before, many times. Don't worry, Zack, your disorientation won't last long. You remember reality quickly once you come out. We'll have you out of here and home in no time at all."

"Come out?" Zack asked. "Come out of where?"

The visitor grinned. "I always enjoy the look on your face when you realize you're not dead. You just came out of the Game, Zack, and on this last play, you got your best score ever!"

2

Memories began to return. The young man sitting in front of Zack... he did know him!

"You're Kyle, right? We've been friends for..."

"For forever, man." Kyle nodded. "Yeah, there you go. You're going to slowly remember real life over the next few hours. Your brain has to fit a lot of information back into your head that it left behind when you entered the Game — you can't remember life out here when you're playing. Are you hungry yet?"

Zack nodded. At the mention of food, he realized that he was starving. Kyle laughed. "I bet you are! It's been a while since you've had real food. While you're in the Game, the nutrients they pipe into you keep you alive, but that goop is nothing like the real thing. Let's go to the dining room and get something to eat."

Zack stood up, bending down to put on shoes that were sitting beside the bed. He was dressed in white, comfortable clothing, and he had a bracelet on his right wrist. It pulsed with colour, gold flecks inside a green light. Zack asked Kyle what the colours in the bracelet meant.

"Those colours mean you're a celebrity!" Kyle said. "But we can worry about that once you're fed and up to speed on what's happening."

"How long have I been out of touch?" Zack asked.

"A little while, but nothing to worry about," Kyle assured him.

They entered a long white hallway lined with closed doors on both sides, each door with its own number and small badge of colour near the handle. They passed people traveling in pairs made up of a person dressed in white like Zack, and the other dressed in regular clothes. Zack noticed that each person in white was younger than him, and their bracelets pulsed with different colours; one was red with silver flecks, another blue with bronze — many different colour combinations. Some were the same as others, but none were green with gold like Zack's. They entered the dining hall, a large white room with tables and a cafeteria style eating line. Kyle guided them to the line and gave Zack a tray to carry. Kyle ordered some items and handed one of the two plates of steaming food to Zack to put on his tray.

The two friends found an empty table and sat down to eat. A few minutes into their meal, Zack couldn't help but notice that many people were staring in their direction. When he asked Kyle about it, he chuckled. "Everyone in here knows who you are, Zack. Like I said earlier, you're famous. Many of them want to come over and talk to you, get your autograph, talk about parts of the game they liked, stuff like that. The rules don't allow that, though. No one is permitted to talk to other players in here. It could mess up their minds. So they are all excited to see you, but considerate enough to leave you alone." Kyle smiled. "For now, at least."

The boys ate in silence. Zack was famished and shoveled the delicious food into his mouth as fast as he could. Kyle seemed content to eat in silence, standing up to get more food for Zack when he ran out.

Finally, Zack announced he was stuffed, and the two stood up. "What's next?" he asked.

"Now we make sure your brain and body are fine. Follow me."

Kyle walked over to the wall by the door where a white box with an opening in the bottom was attached. "Put your hand with the bracelet in there, count to five, then pull your hand out."

Zack did as he was instructed. The white box flashed gently with each count and when he pulled his hand from the box it flashed a soft green five times before resuming its white colour.

Zack looked towards Kyle to see if that was good or bad. Kyle seemed pleased with the results. "Okay, that means you're in great shape. We can get you unlocked, then be out of here and on our way home. Are you ready?"

Zack wasn't exactly sure what Kyle meant, but he did feel like leaving this place, so he nodded his head yes and followed Kyle back to the room in which he'd awakened.

"OK, man, lay back on the bed and put these on." Kyle handed Zack what looked like a fancy pair of sunglasses. When he put them on, he realized they had a video screen built into them. The screen was filled with static and he could hear a hissing noise coming from small speakers on the earpieces of the glasses. "I'm going to press play now. Just sit back and enjoy the show."

The static disappeared. The screen turned into a beautiful blue sky; the chirp of birds and other pleasant sounds replaced the hissing noise in the speakers. Zack watched the video that began to play, teaching him all about the Game he had just been playing...

3

Twenty minutes passed while Zack watched the video. Kyle sat patiently and waited. He'd been playing the game all his life too, so he knew what Zack was going through.

When the glasses turned off, Kyle got up and removed them from Zack's head. He folded them quietly and watched Zack for any telltale signs of cracking; remembering reality could be stressful. If Zack cracked, he would need another day or two of rest before being able to go home. If he did more than crack — if he actually broke... Kyle wasn't too concerned about that happening. Not many kids broke these days.

Zack smiled and nodded his head; he was just fine. Kyle pulled out a clipboard with a paper on it and got a pencil, tapping it lightly on the clipboard. "Okay, Zack, answer these questions to prove you're fully out of the Game and then we can get out of here."

"Fire away." Zack said. His attitude had changed. He no longer seemed confused. The video was intended to fully bring a person to their senses and it appeared to have worked very well.

"Who invented the Game?" Kyle asked.

"Brandon Strayne."

"What is the Game?"

"The Game is a virtual reality simulation designed to teach kids about life and the rules of reality, letting them learn and make mistakes in the safety of a computer simulation." Zack answered.

"How long does the Game last for a person?" Kyle asked.

"The Game lasts until you die inside of it. When that happens you exit the Game and come back to reality. If you've earned enough credits during your play, you can use them to buy back in for another play and re-enter the Game."

"How soon can you re-enter the Game?"

"It depends on how you left it." Zack answered. "There are a lot of reasons for you to die in the Game. The computer ranking system determines how soon you can go back in. It's difficult to predict, but you could re-enter as soon as a day after you come out, or sometimes you might have to wait up to a month. As long as you can pay to get back in and you're not older than 18, you can re-enter the Game."

"How many people are playing the Game?" Kyle asked.

"Billions of kids are in the Game at the same time. All in the same world, all interacting with each other."

"What can credits from the Game buy you in real life?"

"Nothing, until you're 18." Zack answered. "Then the credits you've earned in the Game are converted to real money which you use to begin your life as an adult. The money can be used to purchase admission to a high quality university, a great job... tons of things."

"You're almost 18, Zack." Kyle said. "How much money will you have when you are done with the Game?"

Zack smiled, holding up his rare coloured bracelet. "Turns out I'm one of the top players to have ever played the Game. I'm going to be filthy rich when I turn 18 and get my credits converted into real money."

4

Zack passed all the tests to confirm that his mind was stable, then was released to go home.

Kyle drove him to his apartment, dropping him off at the front door and saying he would return to check on him soon. Zack was almost 18 and he'd been living on his own for the last two years. He was an orphan, and as soon as he'd been able to afford it, he'd left the orphanage. 'Officially,' kids weren't allowed to benefit from their Game credits until they were 18. 'Unofficially,' at the age of 15, a player could trade current credit against future dollars for comforts in the real world. A top ranked player with a lot of credits could convince banks and institutions to lend real money against future money. Of course they charged interest on such risky transactions; they were gambling on getting money that might not be there when the player turned 18. Many players did well early on, only to lose most of their points when they were 16 and 17. Game credits were used during a player's career to buy better lives, skill ups and situations in the game. The older a player got, the more complex the Game became, and the more expensive the power ups. For banks to lend against the future was very risky on their part.

Zack entered his apartment and looked around. It had been only a few weeks since he was here last, but in his mind it had been over 70 years. Everything was as he remembered it, and he shook his head at how different his situation was in this life versus in the Game. Soon this would be the only life for him; his 18th birthday was in five weeks, and although he was certain that he would be able to go in one more time, it still made him sad to think he was near the end of his gaming career. Zack had been playing the game for 13 years, with over a hundred playing sessions, or incarnations as they were called, and he was going to miss it.

Zack's apartment reflected his rank in the Game. It was significantly more than most people could afford, with two floors, state-of-the-art furniture and appliances, and all the gadgets and toys that an average person could only dream of. His credits had enabled him to get the apartment; all of the furnishings and interior items were gifts, given to him by his Patron.

The good players became popular and developed a following much like movie stars did in the past. Because a Game was inside virtual reality, it was possible to digitally record and store a player's virtual life during their play. The Game was its own fully functional world, and just because adults didn't play, that didn't mean they weren't interested or involved in what was going on within it. Television programming had started, like soap operas, only it followed players' lives inside the Game. The best players had entire channels dedicated to them while they were playing, following them from start to finish in their plays. Everyone in society knew what was happening in the Game, and everyone followed their favourite stories and players. Sports and reality shows? Why watch some tame version when you could follow living and dying inside the virtual world? Why bet on a boring sporting event in real life when you could bet on whether a dictator would succeed and live or fail and die inside the Game? Would your favourite player overcome divorce and financial failure during his life in this play? Or would he end up destitute and poor for the remainder of his virtual existence? There was another expensive option available to society's very wealthy. They could pick an adventure and plug themselves in virtually, spending large amounts of money to experience actual moments, emotions, fears, joys, and everything else from a first person point of view as it had taken place in a play. This was called 'Firsting' and it was one of the best aspects of the game.

Top level players attracted Patrons, rich people who paid to keep the player comfortable in real life, so that they could focus on doing their best in the Game. In exchange for this support, Patrons gained part of the future profits of the player, which was a good deal for both people. A kid with a Patron could live in comfort and all it cost them was some of their future earnings.

When Zack entered his apartment he found his Patron sitting in the living area, enjoying a drink and watching a program recapping the top news from inside the Game. He smiled warmly at Zack and turned the volume down so they could talk. "Stunning adventure, my boy! Likely one of your best plays yet."

Zack smiled at the compliment. "Thanks. Give me the highlights. Which parts were the most profitable for us?"

Zack's sponsor pulled up a list of notes from his computer pad and Zack listened to him speak in depth for the next two hours as the highlights were read. Each high point represented an opportunity for making money in a variety of ways, and there were many high points. Another benefit of having a good Patron was the skills, resources, and experts that they hired as a team to assist in making the most of the player's accomplishments. Zack's Patron was the absolute best a Player could hope to acquire.

Eventually the list was covered, and both of them sat back to let the information sink in.

After a few minutes of silence, Zack spoke. "So what do you recommend for my next play? How many points should I spend, and on what?" Zack's Patron put his hands behind his head thoughtfully. "There are two ways to play it. You can do what most who have a lot of credits at this point in their careers tend to do, and that's play it cautious. Make it a short, cheap game that ensures you come out with the majority of credits that you already possess. It's not exciting for the fans, but it's safe. You have so many credits that this is your best strategy..."

"Or?" Zack asked.

"Or," his Patron continued, "You spend 75 % of your credits on a list of power ups and skill set buys that we make for you. Then you hope for the best and rely on your experience and knowledge — which, in the Game, means intuition and listening to your gut, to take over the number one spot and finish on top of the lists."

"I was number one a few times over the years. It's not as fun as most people would imagine."

"It is when you finish number one on your last play," Zack's Patron said confidently. "Number one out of just over a billion players, and that's the spot you retire from playing in." He paused to let the enormity of that statistic sink in. "That puts you in some very rare company, my young friend. In the entire history of the Game it's only happened 11 times."

Zack smiled at the hype, but he knew the truth. There were millions of people playing the Game, yet only a small percentage ever made it to the top ranks. Those who did tended to stay there until they retired. Some poor kid who wasn't able to buy into his seventh game stayed on the lists until he was 18 which kept the statistics looking good, but the truth was that most players couldn't afford to keep playing until the mandatory retirement age of 18. Every time you had a birthday, and every time you left the Game, it became much more expensive to play again. The system had been invented to replace the school system, which it did, to a degree. The original goal was to train productive members of society, which it had also accomplished. But it had also become big business to the real players and followers. The average age for a kid to drop out of the Game was 14. At that age they likely had enough credits to go to an old style school (they still existed) or a government funded facility. Then, when they turned 18, they could get a job that would allow them to live a normal, decent life. There were perhaps six million players still playing at 17, and almost half of them would lose all of their credits in the high risk Game that it became at that level. That still left many who would profit, and profit hugely... a hope and dream which kept them all in the Game until the end.

Zack's patron set down his drink and leaned forward confidently. "I believe in you, Zack. When you went into the Game last time you were ranked number 752. Today you're ranked number two. My advice is take the bold route and play the absolute best you can for your last turn."

"And if I mess up and lose all my credits?" Zack asked. "Will you cover me? Give me something in writing today, a legal document saying you'll pay me the dollars to credits even if I lose them all?"

His Patron chuckled, "You know I can't do that, Zack, it's against the rules. A law, in fact, and one that even I dare not break."

"Then, when it all boils down to it, I'm on my own," Zack said. "Same as always."

"Amen." Zack's Patron said solemnly.

After a brief silence, the man spoke, "There are... unique options that I can provide for you, Zack. If you want to make a brave play for number one..."

"Tell me." Zack said.

For the next half hour, Zack listened to what his Patron was willing to do to help him in his last play. "It's risky, and dangerous, what you're proposing," Zack said. "I could lose it all."

"Or win it all, and that's how you must think of it, should you decide to move forward, Zack."

"I'll want time to think about this."

"You have time. It will be a few days before you know when you can play again. My guess is that it will be a week or two before you can re-enter. Even if you can go in sooner, I advise waiting for a couple of weeks to get it set up as perfectly as you can. The press wants to interview you, as well."

"Which stations?" Zack asked.

"All of them." answered the Patron. "There's a bidding war to ge you first. Number two from 752 is a huge leap. Everyone is clamouring to get you on their program for interviews."

"Who are we leaning towards?"

"The Buzz. They have worldwide coverage, and the owners are significant sponsors of yours. It's best to reward them for backing you." The Patron smiled. "As long as they're one of the highest bidders. The real carrot that's being dangled from their hand is a promise to have Angelica interview you if we decide to go with them."

Zack sat forward excitedly "Are you serious? *The* Angelica interviewing me? She's one of the best to ever play the Game! She finished her last play four years ago in the number one spot and hasn't been seen or heard from since. That would be an incredible opportunity!"

"Then let's plan for that interview to kick off your press tour. Quick but busy for the next few weeks, starting as soon as we find out when you're eligible to go back in." Zack's Patron stood up and walked towards the door. "I've got to get out of here. Lots of work to do, and Kyle is on his way up to check on you."

"When will we meet again?" Zack asked his Patron.

"As soon as possible. The face-to-face meetings are difficult at the moment, but we can keep in touch electronically, as always. I'm very proud of you, Zack. If you retire as number one, I will make good on the reward you asked for when we first met. I have to admit it was a silly boy's request all those years ago, but nothing would make me prouder than to officially give you my surname."

Zack grinned. "Zack Strayne... I've always liked the sound of that, Brandon."

5

"It's a pleasure to meet you, Mr. Strayne." The female reporter shook hands with Brandon before sitting down across from him on the television studio soundstage. She was your typical television interviewer; pretty face, heavy with makeup that looked ridiculous in real life but helped her appear normal on camera. Dark rimmed glasses to help announce her intelligence to viewers. Striking blue eyes, black hair cut in a cute pixie style. Perfect white teeth and a charming smile. She was dressed in a dark and professional business suit, the knee length skirt revealing her tanned, shapely legs which were crossed properly at the ankles. Brandon guessed that she was single and looking for a rich husband; the single reporters often competed for the opportunity to interview and impress the world's richest bachelor.

"Please, call me Brandon," he replied. "Do you mind if I call you Lisa? Or would you prefer Miss Rohansen?"

"I would prefer other things from you, Brandon." She flashed a comfortable, seductive smile, her eyes looking him up and down appreciatively. It took effort not to laugh at her obvious attempt to engage him. "I would be happy if you'd call me Lisa. Thanks again for agreeing to do this interview. Have they told you how the program is scheduled to play out?"

Brandon nodded his head. "You're going to play some old footage that explains the Game, why I came up with it, the history of its rise in popularity, covering some key points throughout. Then you're going to talk to me about Zack and his chances for retiring at the top. Does that sound about right?"

Lisa smiled pleasantly. "Sounds exactly right. It's a fluff piece, really, Brandon. You're paying for it, so none of us intend to ask uncomfortable or difficult questions about the Game. We are going to try and help you build a following for Zack, or should I say, increase his already incredible fan base."

Brandon chuckled. "Thanks, Lisa. Zack definitely leads the pack in fans. His following has been huge for years now. This is a rare occasion, though, and it deserves special attention."

The intro music started in the studio, the stage went dark, and both Brandon and Lisa turned their attention to a large screen which opened the show. The deep, soothing voice of a male narrator began to give the history of The Game:

'Thirty years ago, the education system was in ruins and the average person suffered from an overall lack of motivation to live in the real world. Multiple generations of video gaming had put society in a dangerous crisis. Adults who had spent their entire lives sitting in front of computers also allowed their children to do the same. Middle and lower class workers were plagued with physical and mental health sicknesses that come from eating poorly, not exercising, and interacting less and less with their fellow man. The upper class recognized the problem but they were unable to solve it. The middle class all but disappeared and the lower class was in serious danger. Historical experts of today look back on that period and agree; civilization was on a collision course with extinction.

Then a man came along who changed everything. Brandon Strayne, the only son of the world's wealthiest computer developer, joined a small company named VirtDyne. VirtDyne had invented Functional Virtual, the ability to send a person's consciousness into cyberspace. However, they were unable to bring a person out of it, and after the deaths of several test volunteers, they had no choice but to give up and shut down the company.

Brandon Strayne heard about VirtDyne's problems and approached them with a proposal. If he could solve their issues and save their company, they agreed to give Brandon a 51 percent controlling interest in the company. In a short time, Brandon was able to fix VirtDyne's problems, making it possible to safely be put into, and brought out of, virtual reality. VirtDyne celebrated his success by quickly transferring majority ownership over to Brandon. With true virtual reality now — pardon the play on words — a reality, every major and minor company in the world got in line with trillions of dollars in hand, hoping to harness this new technology to gain competitive advantage in their markets. Brandon had different plans for his new technology, however, and he quickly announced that there would be only one virtual reality product, developed and controlled entirely by VirtDyne. Not long afterward, he introduced the product to the world. Brandon called it 'The Game.'

The death spiral of society was the problem, and Brandon was pleased to announce that The Game was going to be the solution. Schools and current teaching models had been in place for centuries, but they were no longer effective. With the approval of the government, children would now go to school by playing The Game. Simulations have always been an effective method for training, enabling students to learn safely before being put into real life situations. They have always been viewed as a valuable way to teach. Pilots, surgeons, soldiers, and many other professions have excelled over the years, thanks to simulation training.

The Game was designed to be the ultimate in simulation training — a virtual reality life simulation, where children would start off first as simple organisms and then progress in complexity with each play, as they aged and mastered the basics of the Game, to more evolved characters, known as "avatars." Each play of the Game would be a lifetime, some short, some long. Time would be measured differently inside the computer simulation for players, allowing them to live decades in the Game while only a short time would pass in reality. The Game would be every child's new school. At the age of five, each student would enter the Game free of charge for their first five plays. A credit system was created so that students would accumulate credits as they moved through their virtual lifetimes. The credits earned would be deposited into their own account at the end of their play. The first five plays would be free and then the child would use credits from their account to buy into new plays.

Some children would not accumulate enough credits to buy new plays, which would result in them dropping out of the Game. Dropouts would attend old style public schools if they were still young enough to live with their parents; if they were older than 14, the students would attend government run institutions, where they would be trained for labour and simple jobs which would available to them upon reaching the age of 18.

Over time, students would earn enough credits from living as simple organisms so that they could purchase the ability to play as humans. This was the higher purpose for developing the Game and where the real learning would occur. Understanding what a person can learn from just one lifetime, imagine living five or even ten lifetimes, all before turning 18!

There is a saying that "youth is wasted on the young," which is true in many ways. With the Game, a young person could become an adult with lifetimes of wisdom in their psyche already. It was an incredible opportunity, and the Game as a replacement for traditional schooling was accepted by every country in record time.

All countries quickly agreed to let small test groups participate in the Game. The results were overwhelmingly positive, and in just a few short years, the Game was the primary method for teaching children worldwide. That was a generation ago, and although a few virtual reality products have been slowly developed and introduced, VirtDyne owns them all, and each product revolves around what has become the world's greatest obsession... The Game.'

6

The television monitor faded to black and the studio lights blazed to life. Lisa smiled and began her interview.

"The 18th of next month marks the 30th anniversary of The Big Bang, the term that VirtDyne uses to describe the activation of the computer simulation that gave birth to the virtual universe of the Game. Mr. Brandon Strayne joins us live tonight to discuss the festivities surrounding the anniversary, and also to talk about one of the most exciting players currently in the Game and the excitement being generated over his final play. Thank you for joining us, Mr. Strayne."

"Please, Lisa," Brandon said, "Call me Brandon."

Lisa returned his smile, a slight blush working its way through her makeup. She was definitely picturing herself as his new girlfriend after the taping. It took all of his control not to laugh out loud at her eagerness. Maybe he would take her out for dinner. "Thank you, Brandon. First let me ask you what's on everyone's mind lately. Are there going to be special events taking place inside the Game, and, if so, can you share any of the details?"

"Well Lisa, I don't want to ruin any surprises... I can say that there are going to be many special events inside the Game this year to celebrate its 30-year anniversary. Some will be obvious to viewers; many will not be. As I've already admitted, none of the programming is mine, and I'm going to be as surprised and excited as everyone else over the next year. I'm especially excited to see if my young benefactor can pull off a spectacular and incredibly rare feat, ending his final play in the Game as the number one player in the world."

"Yes, let's talk about that. Zack was nowhere near the top when he began his last reincarnation, yet when he died he had solidly landed the number two rank. What do you say to those critics out there who will claim he only did so well because he has you for his Patron?"

Brandon laughed softly. "I would say these people have no idea what the Game is or how it's played, Lisa. First of all, Zack was reincarnated ranked 752. When you look at the world rankings of millions of currently active players, 752 is in the top ranks. Secondly, check the history over the last twenty-nine years; I have, and you'll see jumps much more drastic than what Zack just experienced. It might seem like a big leap, but the first hundred thousand players can jump around and capture top ten ranking spots if they have a good life inside the Game."

"You're exactly right, Brandon." Lisa said. She then went on to describe a set of graphs being displayed to the audience showing many large swings in ranks over the years, identifying the specific players who had experienced them. When she was done detailing the graphs, Brandon continued with his defence.

"If people still continue to claim that I'm somehow helping Zack from outside of the Game, let me assure you that it's impossible. The code and expense and massive shifting in the virtual timeline, as well as the billions, if not trillions of individuals that would be adversely affected in the Game, ensures that such a thing never happens. Over the years, hackers have tried to get into, and influence, the Game. Only the Games Masters can do so, and the exhaustive time and effort required to make even the smallest change to the virtual universe is so complicated that tampering like you are suggesting could never happen. Twelve Games Masters are required to work together to make a change." Brandon leaned forward. "It's simply not something that would be possible, Lisa. The Games Masters take their responsibility too seriously to be corrupted, let alone all twelve of them falling prey to greed. The Game won't let even the Games Masters interfere too much. They are called on very rarely and with all their effort they can affect only the smallest of changes. No, Lisa, what happens in the Game is unscripted and uncontrolled by anyone outside of it. Part of what makes the Game so incredible is that when left on its own, the Mainframe creates events better than we could possibly come up with ourselves."

The issue addressed and resolved, Lisa brought the conversation back to the hot topic at hand. "Can he do it, Brandon?" she asked. "Can Zack be one of the few to finish his last play ranked number one? Or will he take the safe way out and just coast through to ensure he retires from the Game as a very, very wealthy individual in reality?"

"Well, only he can know for certain, Lisa." Brandon said with a boyish grin, "But if I were to bet on this Game, then I'd bet he's going to go for it. Of course, I know a few very wealthy people who are putting their life savings on him not going for it. So we'll all just have to wait and see and hope that he gives us an incredible farewell show. If you want to try and figure it out for yourself, be sure to see his interview with Angelica later this week."

Lisa's jaw dropped. "*The* Angelica?" she asked. "The last player to do exactly what we're hoping Zack can do? She captured the number one spot on her last play and it was so incredible that replays and Firsting sales of her last incarnation are still best sellers, four years after the event! No one's seen her since her victory tour."

"That's her, all right," Brandon nodded. "I imagine there will be a turnout for that program."

"Well, you heard it here first, everyone," Lisa said. "Brandon, I'd like to thank you for sitting with me tonight to talk about the upcoming events in the Game. It's sure to be an exciting time for everyone, both player and spectator alike!"

"I have one more announcement before we go, Lisa." Brandon said.

"Of course, Brandon. What would you like to share with us?"

"The Mainframe has announced that it's giving a free play to someone who had previously dropped out. A free play hasn't been awarded from the Game for over three years, and I was wondering if I could tell you now who it will be?"

"This has been an exciting interview with lots of exclusive news, Brandon! By all means, announce the lucky player's name for the audience."

"Alexandra Montoyas, age seventeen, is the name of the free play winner. It's very exciting that she will be getting a free play at this time in the Game's history. Here's hoping that she's able to take advantage of it and does some entertaining things for us to witness during her play."

"Alexandra Montoyas..." Lisa said slowly, as if the name sounded familiar to her. Brandon looked at her calmly, savouring the look of shock as it appeared on the young journalist's face. "Zack's old girlfriend? The brilliant young player who, for no apparent reason, walked away from the Game, leaving her considerable fortune behind, and has dropped off the face of the planet?"

Brandon nodded slightly, looking as if Lisa had just reminded him exactly who they were talking about. "Ah, yes, that's right, Lisa. Well I'm sure the Game has something interesting in store for us to watch by inviting her back in. I can't wait to see what happens." Brandon looked slyly into the camera, locking eyes with each person in their home watching the program, "How about you?"

7

It was days before Alexandra Montoyas heard the news. She had spent the last year in public school; there wasn't much time to watch the news.

Since walking away from the Game, life had become a nightmare from which Alexandra couldn't seem to wake up.

Alexandra, or Alex, as her friends called her, was always a fairly normal and unremarkable child. For the first few years of her career she'd been a very mediocre player in the Game. Each play was a struggle just to earn enough points to be able to buy her way into the next playing session.

Life for Alex had changed when a few well spent credits — her last credits — placed her life close to some high ranked players in the Game. Purchased serendipity and good luck resulted in her game avatar marrying the number 400 ranked player. That marriage led to her giving birth to the number 1209 ranked player, who played extremely well, finishing his play ranked 642 thanks in large part to Alex's parenting. That was enough to do two things; finish her play with extra credits to spend on further upgrades, and allow her to continue playing the Game. It also earned her some attention. She began to attract fans.

Every player dreamed of building a fan following. Fans talked about your virtual lives in the Game. They started fan clubs and discussion boards to talk about your plays and how it affected other Gamers. Fans made you into a celebrity, with status. Wealthy fans bought your virtual life experiences or "plays," plugging into their own virtual reality simulators (simplified models that allowed only a portion of the experience, but still very real entertainment) so that they could experience some of your life in the Game as you had lived it. Fans recommended you to their friends, who soon became fans as well. The real key to becoming wealthy after you turned 18 was in gaining fans who would continue to spend money on your past lives, which would keep money rolling into your bank account long after you left the Game.

At the age of 15, Alex had found herself becoming a Gaming superstar. She was soon offered a Patronage, and with that backing, the next two years were an incredible climb up the standings of players. Moving from a ranking of around 922 million to one of the top million players in the world (ranking 849,000 was still burned into her mind as one incredibly happy day!), Alex had become a popular player to follow.

Then Alex had met Zack. They began to move in the same circles, running into each other more frequently as Alex climbed the social ladder. Soon they became friends and, not long after that, the friendship blossomed into romance. They were the talk of the airwaves, two popular and successful celebrities dating; just what fans craved.

Alex had it all; fame, fortune and the adoration of millions. Zack was an amazing boyfriend, and she woke up happy each day that her life was going so well. She felt as if nothing could go wrong!

Then one decision and some very bad luck took it all away.

Alex and Zack had come up with an exciting plan, deciding to carry their relationship into the Game. It had been done many times throughout the history of the Game, but when the press got word of Alex and Zack's plan, fans everywhere became excited to see how it would turn out. Pre-orders for their next incarnations started to pour in. The world became obsessed with what would happen when Alex and Zack's avatars hooked up in the Game. Would they fall in love and be happy? Would they miss each other and live two houses apart their whole lives, never knowing who the other was inside the Game and missing out on big chances to advance in standing? Would they marry and fall out of love, maybe having affairs and becoming miserable in their virtual lives because of each other? The possibilities were endless and everyone had their own opinion on how it would turn out. No matter what happened, everyone agreed it would be an incredible story to watch.

Alex and Zack spent weeks coming up with their strategy. What credits to spend on which aspects of their next Game lives to try and ensure they would end up together?

Zack had no trouble spending credits, as a top player his supply seemed endless, but Alex soon found that the Game demanded a lot of precious credits for such an aggressive plan. By the time everything was in place, she had spent everything she had on this adventure. She was nervous about it, but her patron and Zack's assured her that the rewards were worth the risk.

The young couple bought the best help and direction that money could provide to help them outline their next 'lives' properly. The strategy was for them to be born and grow up in the same town together. In their early twenties, they would fall in love and have an incredible life together. Living a life in the Game with Zack would guarantee large profits for her in Game credits. It would be an exciting adventure with only a slim chance of failure. Everyone agreed, Alex was wise to spend all her points for this opportunity. The statistical odds of only a .02% chance for complete failure virtually guaranteed that even if lots of things went off track during her play, she would still earn a fortune in credits. Her hope was that by the end of this play she would either become a top 100 ranked player or, at the very least, do well and still gain a wealth of Game credits to keep her going.

With much excitement and fanfare, Alex and Zack entered the Game. The whole world was watching, planning for a great show, but immediately the worst happened, and what had seemed like the best career move quickly turned into a devastating mistake.

Alexandra's entire career as a Gamer came crashing to an end when, ten minutes after entering the game, she opened her eyes, not in the Game, but in the white room. The extremely slight .02% chance of failure had occurred, and the virtual life that she had spent everything on to experience ended prematurely as her avatar died during childbirth.

A very low ranked player had spent all of his credits to become a doctor and positioned himself to deliver Alex's avatar in the Game. Just delivering a top ranked player like this would seriously raise his overall ranking. The player should never have been a doctor, and lack of Game experience combined with not spending nearly enough credits on luck — something every experienced player knew was necessary when playing a doctor in the Game — resulted in labour complications and the baby — Alex — had died.

In the blink of an eye, faster than you can snap your fingers, Alex was ruined. Suddenly she found herself in the worst position a Gamer can imagine — not having enough credits to buy admission back into the Game. She'd spent everything she had; even re-entering the Game as an insect or a small plant was too expensive for her. She was now an ex-player without enough credits to even buy herself admission into a public school. She had become one of the poor.

Alex had only considered life without the Game once, years ago when she'd spent all her points to gamble for a better play. The Game had helped her then, and life had become a dream. Now the Game appeared to have turned its back on her. It was Game Over.

Immediately after leaving the white building, a messenger had greeted her to deliver her first blow — a message from her Patron announcing that she was exercising her escape clause in their agreement. This meant Alex didn't have a place to live or food to eat. Now, like all non-Gaming children over the age of 14 who possessed no credits, she was a ward of the State. This meant she would be required to live in a compound where she would be fed and clothed, trained to be a labourer and then discharged at age 18 to live out her life as the lowest and poorest of society.

By the time Zack finished his Game, weeks had passed and Alex was gone, invisible to the world and the wealthy. He never found her; Alex was certain he hadn't even bothered to look. Everyone knew what happened when a kid could no longer buy their way into the Game; any chance for a good life was over. This was a society that valued the winners — losers were quickly forgotten. It was best for everyone to accept the reality and move on with their lives.

That had been almost a year ago; a miserable year for Alex, full of pain, heartache and sorrow.

Public school turned out to be slavery. Alex was quickly transported to a dirty, smelly building and handed filthy, grubby clothes. Orientation for new students revealed that 'school' was actually a life spent from sun up to sundown doing the dirtiest work society had to offer — taking away garbage, cleaning the sewer systems, sweeping away the incredible amounts of refuse created by the wealthy.

The jobs that didn't involve filth and stench were even worse; moving and lifting heavy refuse, learning how to fix the broken and thrown away machinery from the wealthy regions. All the junk had to go somewhere, and the school where Alex was sent to took care of most of it. Large, hot factories that melted down old steel and plastic to be sent back to other schools as raw material for constructing new toys for the rich is where many students found themselves. Each day was spent lifting heavy objects, doing backbreaking work, and toiling in filthy conditions to keep the city functioning for the wealthy. Her other concerns consisted of scrambling for enough food to keep her strength and avoiding the gangs of violent workers that would band together to bully the weaker individuals into doing the worst of the work while they kept the best food for themselves and worked very little.

At first Alex had wanted to die, but she quickly learned that no one would let her. She was still a celebrity, but now her fans were the poor. Poor fans didn't look up to their celebrities, they mocked and hurt them. Most of the workers, the Caste, as they were called, had failed out of the Game. The one thing that seemed to help them forget their own loss and misery was revelling in the loss and misery of others. The higher one rose in the Game, the happier the Caste were when they fell, and the more miserably they treated the fallen one.

The area that Alex was transferred to contained many fallen, but none who had fallen so far as her. She was instantly the lowest of the low. Not just a fallen, it became her title: "Fallen."

This meant Alex was the most hated person in her school.

"Move over, Fallen. Real workers coming through. You had enough food before you got here, Fallen, we'll just take your dinner tonight. Sleep in another corner, Fallen. My luck's already bad enough. People close to you get beaten. Fallen can do that job, the worst work for the worst luck." This was how the others tormented her. The kind ones just taunted her, others hunted her down and beat her, took her food, and did whatever they could think of to hurt her if they caught her off guard.

Late at night, with rats for company, she would drop to the ground wherever she could find an out of the way spot and try to sleep. Her body would be exhausted enough most nights, but sleep, when it would come, never lasted long enough to allow her to rest. Thought was the enemy if you were Caste, although most of them seemed to think very little.

Alex — "Fallen" — thought way too much. Most of the time her thoughts were occupied by The Game and the lie that it was; a lie that everyone had bought into. Working in the sewers and bowels of the city, it was plain to see that the Game hadn't improved peoples' lives as promised. The rich were still rich, the poor were still poor. Nothing could change that, she thought to herself miserably.

8

Two days after the announcement, Alex reported in to the school base. Days would go by between checking in; they didn't care where you were, as long as the work they assigned got done. Alex spent as little time as she could in the school. It was the most dangerous place for her to be since the gangs hung around there and got you coming out. She learned this the hard way, when early on she'd been beaten badly and hospitalized. After that, she kept visits to a minimum and tried to get in and out quickly.

Alex shuffled through the front entrance, her eyes on the floor with her focus centred on getting into her class to collect her new job order and then getting out before anyone could cause her harm. She hadn't gone more than ten feet when Principal Williams, a short, greasy haired, angry looking man in a dirty mismatched suit called to her in his strained nasal voice.

"Alexandra Montoyas! Get into my office now!"

Alex froze, then quickly turned and walked towards the principal's office. The Toad, as he was disdainfully called by the students and teachers alike, didn't like to be kept waiting. Alex knew he was silently counting as she approached, and would deliver at least one blow to the back of a student's head if they weren't running to get into his office. She was counting too, and she knew she would get at least two swats, but she couldn't bring herself to run. This little freak wasn't going to scare her.

Alex walked past the Toad, bracing for the hits to the back of her head as she did so, but when they didn't come, she looked up with concern. The only thing worse than getting hit by the Toad was not getting hit by the Toad. That meant she was walking into a room with important people already present. Alex quickly noticed three individuals inside the Toad's office. Two of them were elite security officers, the large, muscular dark suited men who provided security to the wealthy. Bodies standing still and erect like stone statues, their eyes lazily swept over Alex, quickly dismissed her as a non-threat, and continued to scan their surroundings, ever vigilant for an opportunity to spring into action. Alex dismissed them as quickly as they did her, and her lips pressed into a thin line of disgust as she noticed the third person sitting behind the principal's desk.

A beautiful woman sat smiling confidently from the Toad's desk, everything about her exuding confidence, power, and beauty. It was clear from the energy in the room that this woman was in charge, and very comfortable to have it that way. Dark green eyes beamed above a perfect white smile. She stood with arms outstretched and walked around the desk to envelop Alex into a fierce, warm embrace. Alex's arms remained stiffly at her sides as she endured the hug. Her eyes were full of hatred and her teeth were clenched as she bore the woman's apparent affection. The woman was oblivious to Alex's lack of response, or more likely she simply didn't care. After she had hugged Alex close for a few seconds, she affectionately broke away to gently hold Alex at arms' length by her shoulders, inspecting her from head to toe critically.

"Alex, my dear, it's so good to see you again," the woman said happily. "I must say that all things considered, you are in great shape."

Alex felt her face flush in rage. She didn't know whether to laugh or cry at the absurdity of the statement. She decided to squeeze back the tears and laugh. "You can't be serious, Lilith. I look like garbage! I smell worse than garbage. I haven't eaten properly for months, and I'll likely be dead soon. This is a horrible existence, and any gratitude I had for you as a Patron before is quickly fading away. Have you come here to gloat, or just bask in my pain and suffering? I thought we had more than just a business arrangement, Lilith. I thought we were friends."

Lilith's face went from joy to hurt instantly. She removed her hands from Alex's shoulders, slowly ran her hands down her blouse to straighten it, then calmly walked back around to the Toad's chair and sat down. When she looked at Alex, her eyes were calm and professional, but the hurt was still present. Alex remained standing until Lilith waved for her to take a seat.

Minutes passed in silence and Alex slowly calmed herself. There was air conditioning in here, she thought. At least she could sit and enjoy a break from the sweltering heat and backbreaking work that her life had become. Lilith couldn't hurt her anymore. Or could she?

Her eyes must have betrayed her thinking. "Relax, Alex." She said. "I'm not here to hurt you, or to take pleasure from your misery." Lilith sighed and leaned backwards in her chair. "Listen, kiddo, I know it sucks to be here. Honestly I do. But before I tell you why I'm here, I want to set the record straight on a couple of things, if you'll hear me out?"

Alex was angry. This woman had helped her so much, treated her lovingly while she was a high ranked player. Then, once she was no longer on top, Lilith had simply abandoned her. But Alex controlled her emotions, pressed her lips together tightly, and with hot tears gathering at the corners of her eyes, she nodded sharply for Lilith to continue talking.

"I've been a Game patron for over 12 years. I've sponsored over a hundred players, and most of them have gone on to make both me and themselves a good amount of money when they turned 18. I've also lost some, like I lost you, and it always breaks my heart when it happens."

Alex said nothing.

"You know the rules are clear, Alex, even outside of the Game. When a student can no longer afford to enter the game, and they possess less than a certain amount of credits, they must immediately report to a government run public school where they are to remain until they are 18 and graduate."

"Government run public school." Alex spit the words out with a bitter laugh.

"I know," Lilith smiled wryly. "It's a joke. Slave pens is more accurate, and let me tell you, when I found out about the way the government schools are now being run I did the best I could to change it. You're a little young to remember, but I tried to run for government office and my entire platform was to change the government-run schools. Thankfully, before I could ruin my life, and most likely lose it, a very powerful friend caught wind of my intentions and talked me out of what I was planning. If I had tried to change this system I know they would have killed me."

Alex looked up, searching Lilith's eyes to see if she was lying. She saw only the truth, and sadness in Lilith's face.

"So I fought the only way I knew how. I began to sponsor Gamers, to try and help as many as I could to keep them out of here."

"But not all of us," Alex said with pain in her voice.

Lilith closed her eyes. "No. Not all of you," she agreed. "Some of the Gamers I sponsor climb high; they gain the attention of the world. They become superstars." She opened her eyes and rested them sadly on Alex. "Sometimes they spend all of their credits on plays. Sometimes, they fail out of the Game."

"And then you just cut your losses and abandon them?" Alex asked with sharp scorn in her voice. After her last play Lilith hadn't even agreed to see her. She had simply had a servant hand Alex a ticket that arranged for transportation to this school. All of the pain, suffering, and torment she had experienced this past year was because Lilith had put her here, and she couldn't help but be angry at her old Patron for that.

Lilith's eyes grew glassy. "My dear girl, I did the best I could for you. If we are going to have any chance moving forward it's important for you to believe that."

Lilith held out her hand and one of her security guards produced a pair of video glasses. She held the glasses in her hands and stared sadly at Alex, looking as if she wanted to say something, but no words came out. Finally she held out the video glasses to Alex, who took them.

"When your avatar died in childbirth, I pulled in every favour that I've ever banked during the past twenty years to get you into the very best institution available to you. I had almost no time to get the deal done, since you went from hero to zero in just a few minutes, so unfortunately I couldn't see you when you called on me. I did it, by the way. Got you into the very best institution available."

Alex laughed out loud, the tears coming freely now. "Oh, my god, you must be kidding me! This place is horrible, Lilith! I wouldn't send anyone to be here. There's no way this can be the best school!"

Lilith nodded. "I'm going out of this office. Watch the video. It's video from what goes on at most of the average and below average government-run schools." She stood sadly and her guards walked to the door, one opening it, the other behind her. "It's a ten minute video. I'll be back in fifteen. If you still believe that I abandoned you after you watch it, I'll leave you alone — forever."

The door closed. Alex calmly put on the glasses and began to play the video. Two minutes in she began to cry. Five minutes in she paused the video, went to the Toad's garbage can, and vomited. Eight minutes into the video she screamed in rage and threw the glasses against the wall, tears streaming down her face at what she had just seen, at the atrocity that government schools had become. The door opened and Lilith walked in with worry on her face. Alex ran to her and gripped her in a fierce hug, sobbing and thanking her for saving her life. Lilith sobbed as she apologized for not being able to do more.

When the tears had slowed down, they broke the hug. Lilith wiped her eyes. "Well, someone out there must like you, kiddo. I have some remarkable news. You've been invited to go back into the Game!"

Alex stood there, speechless.

9

Brandon Strayne sat in the back of his private transport, watching the daily feeds of the Game as he drove to meet Zack. Today was the Angelica interview, and the entire world would be watching. Brandon was pleased; experts predicted the largest audience in years would tune in to this broadcast. Although money no longer mattered to him, some of his partners would certainly appreciate the profits generated from today's event.

His phone buzzed and, as he answered it, Brandon heard a complex series of beeps and clicks indicating that the call was heavily encrypted to protect the privacy of the speakers. Recognizing the unique pattern immediately, Brandon sighed and raised the privacy glass between him and the driver.

"Hello, sir." Brandon said respectfully.

"So formal, boy. By now you should be able to greet your father more warmly." The voice on the other end was deep and rich, full of strength and power.

"I'm busy, Father, and so are you. What do you need to say?"

"Is he on board? Will Zack do as you assured me he would?"

Brandon closed his eyes and pinched the bridge of his nose. "He will do his best. You know better than anyone how the Game works. There are no guarantees once he goes in."

"I know that," the old man snapped impatiently. "I didn't ask for a guarantee. Has he spent the credits, and are we on track?"

Brandon paused. "Yes."

"The others are all in place?"

"Perfectly."

"You're almost out of time, son. You know that as well as I do."

Brandon knew this better than anyone, but he didn't dare admit it to his father. "It's under control."

"Thirty years go by fast, Brandon. You've done better than I could have hoped for, son."

Brandon ignored his father's compliment. He had learned that unpleasant things often followed a compliment from his Dad.

"What does the girl being allowed to play again mean?"

"I'm sure it has no meaning, sir. She did nothing when she played before. Her invitation is just random hype as part of the anniversary celebration."

There was a long pause on the other end of the line. Finally his father spoke. "Something in my gut tells me she's a concern, boy. Keep an eye on her."

With a distinct click, the phone call was ended.

10

The studio lights were bright and hot. Thick makeup plastered to Zack's face made it difficult to make facial expressions and, underneath the caked on mess, he could feel a thin sheet of sweat slowly sliding down his skin. Two weeks of very little sleep, whirlwind press tours, interviews, fan packed parties every night, team planning to decide what power ups to buy for his last play, and a host of other activities had left Zack exhausted and drained. He desperately needed rest, and he meant to have it.

Right after this interview.

When she walked in, every head in the room turned to catch a glimpse of her. Despite the makeup, Zack smiled, his exhaustion disappearing magically. He was meeting a legend!

"Hi, Zack. I'm Angelica. I hear you're interested in joining my club."

Zack could only grin and nod silently as he gripped hands with the Gaming superstar. Being in the same room with her, touching her, it was like a dream. Her parents must have had special knowledge of the future when they named her; she looked exactly like an angel. Straight, golden blonde hair hung like spun silk halfway down her body. Her ice blue eyes were penetrating, yet playful, as if she knew a joke that was obvious to her but no one else. It was a common physical trait of experienced Gamers, young eyes glowing with centuries of gained knowledge and wisdom, but Angelica's eyes were distinct! Her 5 foot 6 inch, athletic frame was everything you would expect of a 22-year-old model and celebrity. If Zack was a star, then Angelica was a goddess.

"Shall we grab a seat and see if we can't help you get your voice back before the world tunes in?" she asked, her perfect smile both playful and warm.

Zack cleared his throat, still grinning. The wise old man inside who had lived many lifetimes laughed at him, but the kid that he still was puffed out his chest and spoke in his deepest, manliest tone. "It's amazing to be sitting with you, Angelica. You're here to interview me but I think the world would prefer it if I interviewed you."

Angelica touched her hair thoughtfully, looking past him and focusing on something in the distance. Zack turned around to see what she was looking at, but he found only the darkness of the set behind him. When he looked back Angelica had once again trained those beautiful eyes and that smile directly on him. He smiled back.

"How long until we go on the air?" Zack asked.

Angelica surprised him by laughing out loud. "Oh, I do miss being so young and innocent. We won't go live, silly. It would be too dangerous if one of us said something inappropriate. They've been recording us since we came into the studio, just in case something spontaneous happens that they can put on the air. Rest assured, though, we will be on a time delay. There's no going live on the air tonight."

She leaned forward, waving him to come closer, which he was happy to do. "I'm going to kill you so Brandon doesn't have another pet win the Games," she whispered calmly.

Zack jerked backwards quickly in alarm, but her quick laughter told him that she was just joking.

"Angelica," a voice said over the loudspeaker, "Cut the garbage. Do the interview without making more work for us."

Angelica looked skywards, her smile transforming into a serious scowl, and she saluted smartly. "Yes, sir. Just making sure you were paying attention." Her eyes locked on Zack's and her playful grin returned. "All right, buddy boy. Let's get this interview over with. I've got important things to do."

"Like what?" Zack asked. "What have you been up to since you retired from the Game?"

"Zack." This time he recognized the voice as Brandon's, and he didn't sound pleased. "We went over this. No questions for Angelica. Come on, you two. Let's do this thing properly."

Zack saluted the air, Angelica smirked.

Angelica didn't waste any time. She looked at her list of questions and got straight to it. "So tell me, Zack, what's your strategy? Are you going to go for the top spot and risk everything you've accumulated all these years of playing? Or are you going play safe so that you can retire with your considerable fortune intact?"

Smiling confidently, Zack shifted back and forth in his chair and answered the question. "You're just going to have to join the rest of the world to see the answer to that question, Angelica."

"Well that's just the stupidest answer I've ever seen," Angelica muttered under her breath, quickly flipping through the sheets in her hand. "Not really your fault, though, old fella, the questions are all horrible." Before Zack could respond, she fired the pile of questions across the room into the darkness beyond the camera lights. She stood up and loudly moved her chair closer to his, then sat back down, her knee touching his. He liked this girl. She might be crazy, but he definitely liked her!

"Okay, look," she said. "I know what questions you can answer. I know what the world wants to know. I mean, four years ago I sat in your seat and did this same damn interview myself." She turned to face the camera and smiled seductively. "My interviewer was nowhere near as beautiful as Zack's is, though."

Turning back to Zack, Angelica continued. "Let's get some answers so you and I can leave, and these nice folks at home can get back to their miserable lives. You game, big boy?"

"Sure," Zack nodded.

"For those of you playing at home, if he answers quickly then he's likely telling the truth. If he hesitates or stammers, then it's one big lie you're hearing. Okay, then. You going in as a man or woman?"

"Well, I thought long and hard about that decision befo…"

"Nope," Angelica held up her hand, cutting him off. "Don't care about the thought long and hard part. We all assume that. You're going for the number one spot, for crying out loud!"

"Hey, don't put words into my mouth," Zack protested. "I never said if I was or…"

"Or if you weren't. Right. We heard that awesome answer too. There have only been two questions, Zack. Even the guy that gets his mother to tune in for him because he can't work the viewer can keep up so far." She looked at the camera and smirked. "Boy, or girl?"

"Boy," Zack said, rolling his eyes.

"What part of the world are you playing in?"

"Well, that's part of the fun of the Game. You can start in one area and quickly end up in another. Three lives ago I…"

"Zack." She interrupted him again. "I turned twenty-two about three months ago. I swear if I turn twenty-three while still sitting in this interview with you, I'm gonna do some bad things to a lot of people."

Zack laughed. This woman was funny. He could almost hear the audience laughing in their homes. "I'm playing in a developed technological part of the world."

"Thank you. See how easy it is if you just focus on the actual answer to my questions?" Zack nodded solemnly.

"Personality type?" she asked.

"Outgoing, leadership aptitude."

"Which doesn't mean leader, necessarily." Angelica commented. Zack looked at her blankly, saying nothing.

"Did you purchase a relationship package?"

"Yes."

"Lifespan upgrade?"

Zack smiled. "Have you played the game? Without a lifespan upgrade you die around age twenty."

"Okay, I accept your challenge, Zack. Let me ask this question a better way. Are you going to likely live past the age of 20 in the Game during this play?"

"Yes. I bought the lifespan upgrade."

Angelica rolled her eyes.

"How will your play affect the Game? Barely at all, which is a level 1, or closer to celebrity status which is a level 10?"

Zack was surprised by the question. This one wasn't on the approved list. He answered anyway; they could edit it out if they didn't like it. "I have no idea. I think all of us want to affect the Game world at a level 10 when we go in. It doesn't seem to matter how many credits you spend for that outcome, though. There have been young students who become Game celebrities with no apparent effort, while other rich and experienced gamers end up wasting their play as a level 1 or 2 nobody."

"Yes, that's all true." Angelica nodded as if she was bored. "So for those who like to place bets on the Game, if your answer to this question was to come true for this play... what level would you achieve?"

"11," Zack answered immediately.

"Boo!" Angelica said. "That's the worst answer, Zack! Do you know how many times I've asked this question of players and their answer is always 11?"

Zack leaned forward, making sure to touch her knee with his. "I don't think you've ever asked another player that question and gotten the answer 11."

Her eyes twinkled. "You're right. I've never asked that question before."

Angelica stood up from her chair and sat on Zack's lap. Zack couldn't believe it — this amazingly clever, successful, beautiful woman sitting on his lap! She felt wonderful, but immediately he tried to calm down. Her style so far was to shock and upset things hoping he would say something stupid. That wasn't going to happen now. He'd come too far and his future was on the line here. He wasn't going to jeopardize his career and fortune by falling prey to the charms of a pretty lady and say something he would later regret in front of millions of people. He prepared himself for her next bombshell.

"Zack, I think you've answered all the questions that you're allowed to before entering the Game. I have one final question that's been asked lately and I'd love to hear your answer."

"Okay..." Zack said.

"If Angelica and Zack were both in their final Game at the same time, who would win?"

Zack didn't need to think about his answer. "I saw your last play, Angelica. You and I both know a Gamer's true skill comes from what we have inside us. A player goes into the Game and forgets everything about life out here. We are born into a virtual reality, and for the entire time we're in it... we believe the game world is real. We grow up, fall in love, have families, experience a true and full lifetime, and, when we die we're certain it's genuine. Still, I believe that we take... something into the Game with us, but it's subconscious; a part of us we can't control."

Zack looked into the camera, his face serious. "To answer your question, though, give us the exact same upgrades and credits spent and there's no doubt in my mind. I would beat Angelica every single time."

Angelica kissed Zack on the cheek, laughing in delight at his answer. She tousled his hair affectionately, then jumped off his lap and started walking towards the camera. "Well, there you go, everyone. We don't know if he's going for it or not. We know he's playing as a guy, and he's chosen to spend his life in civilized territory. He's going to add romance to the package, which always makes things volatile and unpredictable. And he's invested hard-earned credits to live past the ripe old age of twenty! The rest you'll have to tune in to watch. It will be an exciting play, I'm sure. I'll be keeping a close eye on his progress. I bet most of you will also."

"Before we sign off, I have one important announcement." Angelica winked slightly at Zack. "You are all going to be glad you tuned in for this little interview just for the information I'm about to share with you right now. The Game Mainframe has just announced Zack's birthday for his new avatar. Normally we don't make a big deal out of this, but it's a date that anyone who follows the Game will recognize instantly."

The camera zoomed in close to get a headshot of Angelica's beautiful face. She paused for effect, very at ease as the centre of attention. Finally she made her announcement.

"Zack's avatar will be born on Earth at 12:21 AM. The Game date will be... December 21, 2012! For those of you who are unfamiliar with that date, it's the prophesied end of the world date."

Angelica froze in place, smiling broadly for effect. The voice spoke up one more time, "OK, Angelica. That's it we're done. Great job you two, and good luck in the Game, Zack."

"Walk me out?" Angelica asked sweetly.

Zack nodded eagerly.

They didn't say much on the way to the elevator, just exchanged vague pleasantries. As the elevator arrived, Angelica said "You grab the next one, stud. I'm going somewhere you can't follow."

Zack was sure her answer meant more than she was saying, but he just nodded. "Can I ask you one question, Angelica?"

She looked at him searchingly, then nodded.

"Any advice for me?" he asked with a grin.

She grabbed him in a close hug and held him for a brief moment. It felt strong, protective, and Zack loved it.

As she was letting him go she softly whispered in his ear, “My advice is this, Zack. Don’t try for first place. Do everything you possibly can to finish as low in the standings as possible.”

11

When *the Game first went live we had to call the imaginary world something. We ended up choosing a unique, never-before-used name in order to effectively track it as popularity grew among both viewers and players. "Earth" is actually an acronym. It stands for Educational Avatar Reality Training Habitat, a clever, albeit nerdy, description of our intention for the virtual schoolyard we created for our children. This was our third attempt at making a world in which the kids would thrive and grow. Initial attempts were too fantastic; the students ended up learning no more than they did with traditional entertainment-style video games. We feel very fortunate that the students responded so well to Earth. It is an exact reflection of the real world, which allows graduates to bring their considerable 'Lives' experience and use it to better our reality when they graduate. Of course, there are things the players can do inside the Game that are impossible in real life, but not many of them figure that out.*

Interview excerpt from "What is the Game and how will it affect our lives"

Brandon Strayne interviewed by Melissa W.

Six days after the Angelica Interview, Zack arrived at the facility to prepare for entry into the Game for the last time. Zack was both excited and sad today; it would be his final journey into a world that had become his home and training ground for most of his life. It would also be his last chance to increase his fortune — or maybe lose it all, depending on how the play turned out.

Zack checked in with the secretary on the ground floor, went to the elevator and pressed the button marked B12, the 12th floor below ground. Exiting the elevator, he strode down the long white hall towards his preparation room, where attendants would wire him for interfacing with Earth's mainframe computer, as well as inserting a myriad of tubes all over his body to feed him nutrients and remove waste for the next few weeks. Entering the Game wasn't glamourous. It was a medical procedure where they put you into a controlled coma for the duration of your virtual life. The brain was sedated to the correct wave level, then your consciousness entered the computer system and you were born into your avatar. Zack remembered so many years ago when he was just a new player with no significant ranking. Then he had joined the masses of players and laid in a large room with rows and rows of sanitary silver tables, each linking a player to Earth. As a player gained rank, their level of privacy increased. Zack, a top 1,000 ranked player, was given a luxurious room with four full-time nurses and two doctors to monitor his health and well-being. It was good to be at the top of the heap.

Brandon entered the room as they were finishing up with the wire and tube connections. Zack sat comfortably in his chair, watching the hype and fanfare on the video feeds. He smiled confidently as Brandon came in.

"Well, my boy. Are you rested and prepared for this last glorious adventure?" Brandon asked.

"I've never been more ready in my life." Zack said. "Everyone's in place?"

"Kyle and Marcie are solidly in the Game, and everything went perfectly in that area. They are married and expecting the happy birth of their first child in very short order. Your two best friends in this life are your parents in your upcoming play."

"And they are receiving the benefits of their spent credits?"

Brandon sipped a glass of water and sat down opposite Zack. He waved his hand dismissively, and the doctors and nurses left the room. "They are indeed. You will be born to successful, educated parents who have very specific ideas about how to raise a child. You'll have all the perks and breaks that rich kids in Canada have access to, which are many. The other players are in place as well, we have over 546 who will interact with you in your life, both positively and negatively, to steer you in the direction we have chosen for you to end up."

Zack whistled. "I'm still amazed you were able to involve so many others to help me. Each player spending their credits to help me in the Game has saved me so much money. It should actually enable me to achieve our goal, if all goes according to plan. I didn't think you could get so many on board."

"It wasn't too difficult. Many of them only needed to spend a few thousand extra credits to get what we wanted, and if we succeed, each of them will become very wealthy in credits for having been a part of it. A teacher here, a girlfriend who dates you for only a month there, a salesman who sells you a car once when you're thirty, a man who robs you when you're forty. All so simple, and fairly inexpensive to buy for each player."

"Well, I still think that the number of players involved is incredible." Zack said. "How many of them actually need to succeed with their roles?"

"Only a few hundred," Brandon said. "The others are there for backup. And they spent the credits so that if one succeeds, the others will not repeat the actions."

"So I won't get robbed five times when I'm forty? I'm glad." Zack said.

"You might get robbed twenty times when you're forty," Brandon chuckled. "But one of those robberies will be done correctly, and no more will follow after that."

"Then here's hoping the first one gets it right."

"All kidding aside, Zack, this is by far the most elaborate play I've ever helped orchestrate. That's saying a lot, because I've been involved in many."

"I'm nervous," Zack admitted. "Despite so many others joining to help me, I've spent everything on this one. I hope you're right, Brandon. I hope what we want to do is possible."

"It's possible. We just have to get your avatar to believe it's possible. We do that, and you retire number one."

"I wish you had let me see Alex," Zack said. He'd been so happy and surprised to hear that she was going to get another chance to play the game. His life had come to a horrible low point when she had failed out. He'd searched for her for weeks, but wasn't able to find her. Brandon had assured him she was fine and in one of the best public schools, but losing her had been hard. If Zack had found her, he would have proposed marriage. They had fallen deeply in love, and the rules allowed player spouses to avoid having to attend old-style school. It would have cost Zach most of his credits, and it was rare for one player to save another in such a manner. But Zach had loved Alex fiercely; it had crushed him when all of Brandon's best efforts to find her had turned up nothing.

"There wasn't enough time, you know that. After this play we'll make sure you see her immediately," Brandon assured him.

Zack nodded fiercely. "When does she go in? Will she be close to me at all on Earth?"

Brandon shrugged. "I'm not sure what she can afford or when she goes in. You can ask her all about it when you retire. I'm sure she'll play conservatively to build as many credits as she can before she has to retire later this year."

"It's strange that she was awarded this free play, don't you think? I hate to ask this, Brandon, but you didn't pull strings to get her back in, did you?"

Brandon shook his head negatively. "You know I would have done that long ago if such a thing were possible, my boy. But I can't affect the Game like that. It's too secure."

"Yeah. I guess. But look at..."

Brandon hissed sharply, motioning for Zack to be silent. They both knew there were eyes and ears on them right now. Brandon stood up. It was time for Zack to get into the Game.

Zack stood up as well, and the two hugged briefly. "Good luck, Zack. Tradition allows you to keep your first name on your last play at no cost to you in credits. I look forward to watching Zack on Earth solidly capture the first place position for Zack in real life."

"The name doesn't fit the goal. I've always had good luck with firsts, so I'll be using a name I've never had before — Trew Radfield."

"I like it," Brandon said. "Give 'em hell, Zack. I'll see you in a few weeks and I promise to give you a victory tour that no one will forget."

Zack nodded enthusiastically and lay down on his cushioned table.

Less than ten minutes later, Zack was in a deep coma.

Trew Radfield was entering the digital body of his young avatar.

Earth would never be the same.

12

We modelled the Game world after our own planet, Tygon. Our goal was to make Earth an exact reflection of Tygon, and we succeeded perfectly. The sheer volume of operations required to simulate an identical virtual existence to our authentic one called for a powerful supercomputer to be designed. We named this supercomputer Mainframe. Mainframe was responsible for everything, minor and major, in the creation and maintenance of Earth. It took us years to program fully. Even now, we daily employ Game Masters and an army of technicians to keep it functioning optimally. Something curious happened very soon after the Game began. Players inside the Game somehow seemed to recognize the influence and presence of the Mainframe. Although not able to see Mainframe, they began to sense its influence. Earth citizens called it 'God' and worshiped it in many different ways, depending on their specific cultures. At first we were concerned that this would interfere with the Gamers' experiences, but the religions and activities centred around 'God' have provided us with fantastic story lines, technological developments, and learning opportunities. Without 'God' I'm certain the Game wouldn't be as popular to watch and play as it is today.
Excerpt from "Religion in the Game"

Alex received very little fanfare during the time leading up to her Game entry. Lilith had said to expect a storm of reporters and interview requests, but none came. Despite the news feeds, fan sites buzzing with speculation and ideas about what Alex being awarded a free play meant, she spent a very quiet few weeks leading up to the day of her entry.

Lilith had been curious, so she started to personally contact people to initiate interviews on Alex's behalf.

"Someone very powerful is blocking us," she said.

"Why would they do that?" Alex asked.

"I don't know, but it's true," Lilith said. "The last three inquiries I made face to face conveyed the message very clearly. They all looked sick at the idea of not interviewing you, but even more frightened at the possibility of actually sitting down to talk. This is a terrible shame. We could have generated so much interest! I assured them you wouldn't talk about where you've been. I suggested we mention the possibility of you spending credits to be with Zack in the Game. I tried enticing them in every way possible, kiddo, but no one will come near you."

Alex shrugged. "Thanks for trying, Lilith, but I don't think it matters anyway. I'm glad I don't have to speak to anyone, I don't know if I could be silent about what I've seen. My fan base doesn't seem to have been hurt by the lack of attention, though. It might have even helped. Have you seen my numbers today?"

Lilith nodded excitedly, picking up a tablet to scan recent figures. Alex was right; her popularity was skyrocketing. "Maybe you're right, Alex. The only search term more popular than your name is Zack's."

"When's he going in?" Alex tried to pretend that she didn't care, but she did. She'd hoped to hear from him when she came back into the spotlight, but she hadn't. Not even a whisper. Her brain told her that was fine and she should wish him well in his play, but her heart was broken by the continued rejection. She thought they had been special together, but apparently she was the only one who felt that way.

"He went in two days ago," Lilith said. "Are you not watching the feeds at all?"

His avatar will be slightly older than mine, she thought to herself. Shaking her head to get Zack out of her mind, she answered

Lilith's question. "I've had no time to watch feeds about Zack. I had to spend my credits all by myself for this play. The Mainframe invited me back in, but it didn't provide a wealth of money to spend on playing."

Lilith smiled in sympathy. "Trust in the God, my girl."

Alex chuckled at the reference. People were starting to proclaim that Tygon had its own God, similar but more powerful than Earth's. Intelligent people had agreed decades ago that no such creature existed, but despite that, the phrase was growing more popular with Game fans everywhere. "I guess I should trust in the God of Earth, at least. I have no idea why it raised me so high in the Game, then kicked me out so horribly. Now it invites me back in? None of it makes sense."

"Don't start believing the Mainframe had anything to do with your fate, Alex." Lilith said. "You know the Mainframe is just a computer that creates and maintains a virtual universe. It's not an intelligent, self-aware creature. It's no different than this computer console in front of me; it just has a much larger memory and processing speed."

"Mainframe has an AI chip, too, Lilith," Alex said.

"Yes, but that technology is still very limited and simple. A small amount of artificial intelligence to allow it to process its tasks quicker. That's it, Alex. No one has made a significant advance in AI technology."

"Brandon Strayne might have," Alex argued. "He made virtual reality seem simple. Maybe he's succeeded with artificial intelligence as well."

"It's illegal to even try," Lilith said. "Now let's stop wasting precious time on a silly topic. Are you ready to play? You go in tomorrow. How did you decide to spend your credits?"

Alex knew how much guilt Lilith felt from advising her on the last play, so this time, Alex had told everyone that she would assume sole responsibility for how her credits were spent. It was a challenge, though.

"Are you sure you want to know?" Alex asked. "You might not like what I've done."

"Nonsense, Alex. I support your strategy, whatever it is."

"Okay, then." Alex handed Lilith the computer tablet with her selections listed on it. "Tell me what you think."

Lilith looked at the tablet, then back to Alex. "Where's the rest? I can't get it to scroll to the next page."

"That's it. There is no next page."

Lilith closed her eyes slowly. Taking deep breaths she remained silent for a full thirty seconds. "I already told you, Alex. If you fail out of the Game again I can't protect you like last time."

"I understand." Alex said. "I'm not asking you to. This strategy will work."

"Well, I don't understand it. Please explain it to me."

"I have limited credits, so I spent a long time looking at all the power ups and scenarios and interactions that I could purchase. I saw a couple of mistakes in the price lists."

"What mistakes?" Lilith asked.

"A few of the more expensive choices were very, very cheap on my price list. I looked them up on the world system, and sure enough, they were high end purchases, but for some reason they were very inexpensive for me to purchase."

"Strange..."Lilith said.

"Or a sign," Alex said. "So I spent my credits on them. All of my credits. Before you say anything, you know how many credits I was given. There was no way to be conservative and hope for another play if this one fails. My free play is exactly that, it seems. One free play. So I've kept it simple. I've spent all my credits in very limited areas."

"List them off for me, please," Lilith requested.

Alex ticked them off on her fingers. "Health, Longevity, Focus."

"Health and longevity I understand. I can't believe the Mainframe will give you what you purchased," Lilith said. "Focus is an elite and expensive attribute. Only the very wealthy Gamers can buy it, and when they do, it's often a wasted purchase because their avatars never seem to use it well."

"I've studied that. I think it's because they purchase Focus, yet try to use it on too many things in their lives."

"Focusing on too many things destroys Focus. Now that you mention it, I think you're right. Describing it like that makes it seem silly, as if they are clearly not using Focus the correct way at all."

"Well, I spent a lot on Focus, Lilith, and I'm going to focus on just one thing when I'm playing."

"What's that?" Lilith asked.

Alex smiled slyly. "That it's all a game."

Lilith laughed. "There's no way that will ever work. Even if it does, what can that get you?"

"I don't know. But I had a long time to look at my career as a gamer, and I keep having one overwhelming thought. I think I'm a prodigy."

In the old days of public school, students would often gravitate towards certain subjects. Some would be better at math, others at science, others at art, and so forth. Over time, this would lead to students learning more about their favourite subjects, and they would go on to study or work in the fields of their interests.

The same was true of the Game. Players would live incarnations and score higher in certain areas of play. On their next plays, they might focus more on their favourite aspects or 'subjects,' which would result in them earning even more credits and higher standing. In some cases, the most focused and very best players would be able to earn Prodigy status over time. A famous player named Owen Brahlie was a popular example. Owen soon realized that he excelled at music and decided to focus on this area of the

Game. Each time he played a new incarnation, He spent a large amount of his available credits in musical talent for his avatars. Each time he played, his new avatar would become more talented in music earlier in its life. Eventually, Owen had enough credits to purchase Prodigy status. On one of his final plays, his avatar was a person named Wolfgang Amadeus Mozart. As Mozart, Owen manifested his talents at the tender age of six, and went on to change the course of musical history on Earth. His play as Mozart earned Owen enough credits to retire from the Game as a very wealthy individual, and he continued to bring his 'lives' of experience to his career on Tygon. Everyone in the world could sing you at least a dozen Owen Brahlie musical hits. Some players today still named their avatars after Owen, as an homage to their hero. His daughter was a popular player on the scene today who chose singing on Earth as her focus.

"What are you a prodigy in?" Lilith asked. "You've never shown any aptitude for the arts, or math, or science?"

"I know. I think I'm a prodigy at the Game itself. Risking it all and winning. I believe my skills are at playing games... and winning against all odds."

Lilith snorted. "Sorry to disagree, kiddo, but you didn't exactly win on your last play."

"One time I lost," Alex agreed, "But, Lilith, you have to admit, I used to play very aggressively. I would spend more credits than you ever recommended. I recall coming out of a play and you telling me how lucky I was that I wasn't ruined. My rise in the standings wasn't overnight, but I didn't buy my way to the top or have a one-time stroke of luck. I played well each and every time."

"Very true," Lilith admitted.

"And I don't think I really lost on my last play." Alex said. "I think the Mainframe is an intelligent being, and took me out of the Game on purpose."

"Even if that was true, why would it do something like that?" Lilith asked.

"Well, I go back to Earth tomorrow," Alex answered. "If it is true, I'm sure we're going to find out."

13

What is the allure of the Game and why do so many of us watch it? The simple answer is that the Game fulfills our desires for entertainment and fantasy. Want to gamble? Pick an event in the Game and place your bet. There's nothing that you can't bet on inside the Game. Want to watch true love bloom? Once again, you can find it in the Game. You can experience anything in the Game, better than movies from the old days. If you want to watch a spy actually become a spy and follow her/his adventures, just put in the correct search term and the Game video feed system will find you a list of spies in action. If you have enough money, you can do more than watch; you can experience it firsthand. Quite simply, we watch the Game for the same reason we don't allow people over the age of eighteen to play it; because in many ways it's better than real life. Or perhaps it's because on rare occasions, for reasons no one can seem to explain, players who die in the game also die out here in real life... very popular events when they happen.

My name is Stephanie, and I'm watching myself in a dream. I have no idea how or why, but it's been occurring for as long as I can remember. They feel so real and, for the most part, I'm in it experiencing all of the emotions and sounds and sensations. But there's this other part of me watching curiously, trying to figure out what's happening and why.

I've been having this one a lot lately.

I'm standing on a hill. In front of me is an empty city, cars and buildings all abandoned. It's obvious that for some reason, everyone left quickly. Skyscrapers and other tall buildings stand silently; the birds and animals are quiet, which makes the roaring sound even louder.

I look behind me and see hundreds, maybe thousands of people. They are terrified, huddled in groups, some holding their children desperately, looking at me, silently pleading, as if expecting me to protect them. Behind me stands an old woman. Spanish like me, my height, long black hair and dark tanned skin. She looks at me and nods familiarly. Her eyes are mine, and I know that she is me. The old woman places her hand on my shoulder and, from the looks on the face of the people behind me, I know that something terrible is approaching. I calmly turn to face the threat.

A large wave of water has risen above the city, roaring with rage and hunger. The wave is so large that it makes the skyscrapers look like a small model toy set. Quickly it engulfs the city, great white waves of boiling, rushing water destroying the manmade landscape as if it were made from paper and sticks instead of steel and concrete. I quietly watch the wave as it comes towards its true target — me.

I smile as the wave gets close enough to feel. First a fine mist of coolness, followed by a deep presence of hate, pain and hunger. The old woman and I peacefully wait for its arrival.

My eyes sparkle as I raise my right hand, a thin, weak thing compared to the destructive force of nature charging to claim us. Small and weak, but it contains the power of my energy and intent.

I extend my fingers fully towards the wave, feeling a familiar warm golden tingle spread up from my feet and focus outwards from my hand. The wave has no hope; it never had any chance to harm us. The two-hundred-foot tidal wave washes harmlessly over, and then past us. Seconds pass and the wave screams in frustration, but it is bound by laws that forbid it from turning back and trying to claim us one more time.

I look behind me and start to smile at my old self, but she is gone. I can still feel the warmth of her hand on my shoulder. People surround me, smiling and crying with relief.

Then I wake up to the sound of my alarm clock.

The deejay is announcing the time and date. 'Well, for those of you thinking the world will end today, so far it hasn't. December 21st, 2012 appears to be just another regular day in Toronto, Canada, and all reports from the rest of the world are just as uneventful.'

I lay in bed, waiting until the man on the radio finishes talking. I'm waiting to hear something today, not sure what it is, but I'll know when I hear it.

'The only noteworthy observation is that the birth rate is incredibly high,' the deejay reads from his news script. 'If you own stock in anything related to kid products, get ready to see an increase in business. The world is experiencing a baby boom greater than the one that happened after the Second World War. No one can guess why this is happening, but it isn't a cause for concern, as far as anyone is reporting.'

Well, that's curious. I wonder what it means.

'Similar to New Year's day, everyone has been tracking the baby born at the significant hour. Today we weren't tracking the first child born at Midnight. They're trying to identify the first child born at 12:21, since some believe there is importance with those numbers. Experts predicted a lot of confusion trying to pinpoint who the clear winner of this would be, especially with the abnormally high number of births occurring. But yeah, this is a bit strange, I guess — at 12:21, only one child was born. On the entire planet. Does that even make sense? Well, that's what my paper says. A young man living in our own city, if you can believe that. Trew Radfield was born at precisely 12:21 to happy parents Louis and Carol. Not sure what the prizes are for being born at the correct time on the day the world is said to end, but I'm certain it will be something interesting.'

Bingo! I jump up and quickly write the kid's name down. Better get his parents' names down, too. Trew Radfield. I feel compelled to keep an eye on him, and my gut is always right.

If I'm looking for him, it's a good bet others will be, too. I wish there were a million kids born at that time; it would have made things easier. Trew Radfield is shining like a bright candle in the darkness to every nut job out there, and to people even more dangerous than that.

14

There are an incredibly large number of attributes, power ups, scenarios, and skills that can be purchased for a Gamer's play. The sheer volume of combinations ensures that each avatar will be extremely different once they enter the Game. It's this diversity which enables individuals to learn, and also provides viewers with a wealth of choices for watching. Some of the common attribute selections are Longevity, Health, Intelligence, Strength, Love, Relationships, Focus, Spirituality, Intuition, and Aptitude. Strategies abound for advancing in the Game, but the Mainframe makes it impossible to develop a clear path to the top rankings. What might work for one player will not for another. Repeating a strategy doesn't produce identical results for the same player on their next play. Intuition and Spirituality are not often invested in heavily, but when they are, it can lead to the avatar searching for meaning from its life on Earth and the existence of some higher intelligent lifeform that guides them. Major religions being formed are often the result of players who have spent extreme amounts of credits on these attributes. Attributes alone are not enough to provide religious breakthrough, however. A player must skillfully and correctly invest in scenarios, skills, and power ups at exactly the right moments in their avatar's lives to increase their odds of successful revelation.
Excerpt from 'Gamers Manual 7 - Human level guide book'
Earth - years before December 21, 2012

I've been sitting at this crowded cafe for over an hour and a half. The computer is open, the blank screen looking back at me. That annoying little cursor flashing, blink, blink, blink. Are you laughing at me, little cursor? Are you trying to make me get scared and give up again?

This book has been in my head for too long. Something always seemed to come up, to distract me from writing it. Well, nothing's distracting me anymore. My kids are gone. No grandchildren survived the crash either. My wife. No, don't think about Tricia right now, George!

Damn it, why did I not get on that plane with the rest of them? How can one 74-year-old man have a business meeting on the day he's taking his whole family to Hawaii for a big vacation? All of them, gone...

Okay, I have to calm down. This isn't what I'm going to write about. People can find that story all over the Internet. I swear, if one more person sends me a message saying how sad they are for me, but the bright side is that I'm lucky I wasn't on that plane... I'm going to run them over.

All right. I'm writing this. People have laughed at me all my life for my crazy theory. If I was born 200 years ago I would have been labelled a Heretic, but that's a sign I might be on the right track, right? So many discoverers and geniuses were mocked and ignored at first. They laughed at Darwin, Copernicus, Mendel, even Columbus! But the world is round, isn't it!

I know I'm on to something. The evidence is all around us.

Perhaps the time isn't right for this idea, but maybe in 10 or 15 years someone will read this book and it will make perfect sense.

Okay, George... here we go. I begin to type, and I'm not stopping until it's all down.

We live in a game. Somewhere 'out there,' our real bodies are plugged into a very real virtual reality simulation. Earth isn't real, but it's important to those running the game. What we call God, or Allah, or the Universe, or whatever spiritual name religion gives it... is simply the supercomputer that runs our universe.

How can I be so sure of this?

Because I've spoken to it. And it has spoken to me...

15

It took ten years for the Game to thoroughly embed itself into Tygon society. Television shows, movies, books, sports of all types, all slowly declined in popularity. Instead of reading, people tuned in to the Game. The movie business of make believe and special effects could no longer appeal to an audience that was seeing real avatars living, loving, and dying inside the Game more realistically than actors could portray. The Game provided that special something for everyone, and as it celebrated its 10-year anniversary, people were so immersed in the Game that it was a worldwide obsession. Thankfully these industries didn't die out; jobs simply shifted to focus on the Game industry. Sports experts were still required for fans, they just studied and followed Game players instead of real sports stars. The media business grew even bigger; thousands of new channels devoted to Earth players, continents, and history were created to feed the frenzy of Game followers.

The world prospered and thrived due to Brandon Strayne's creation. Through the Game, he indirectly controlled all business and finance... a danger no one seemed concerned about...

Excerpt from the video 'Brandon Strayne; Rise to Power'

Brandon Strayne walked into Zack's central command office. VirtDyne was the biggest building in the city, boasting 200 floors above ground and another 25 floors underground. The command offices were located on the top floors of the building, with each player sponsored by VirtDyne having their own dedicated area. Of Brandon's players, Zack was the highest ranked, and his command centre was the first penthouse floor. The outside walls were tinted glass from floor to ceiling, providing a majestic 360-degree view of clouds and the sprawling city. Interior walls separated the floor into five key areas; four large corner offices and a centre squared main office. The centre of the command office was a glass walled area filled with large screens, each displaying different feeds from both around the world and inside the Game. Occupying this space was Zack's team, an elite group comprised of over 30 specialists in media, marketing, strategy, computer programming, and every other aspect involving business and the Game. Brandon had made certain that each team member was the best in their field. It was evident by the scale and calibre of this operation that the Game was much more than just an educational tool for kids. The new virtual school that Brandon had created wasn't only for learning. Big business and the world economy now revolved around the Game — a business and economy controlled entirely by VirtDyne, and its majority owner.

Brandon walked directly to the centre office and sat down in the chair at the head of the large, long table. All the chairs were occupied and the team looked prepared to meet. Brandon knew they had advance warning when he was coming, which he preferred. His time was too valuable to waste and this was not a team of hacks fooling around when he wasn't here. This was the big leagues of the Game.

"Give me the details, kids. Same priority as always, biggest problems first."

Zack's Right Hand, Michelle, stood up from her place and walked towards the large monitor opposite from Brandon. The Right Hand of a player was the leader of the group, in charge and responsible for all aspects of the player from this side of the Game. The Right Hand answered to the Patron, everyone else answered to the Right Hand.

At twenty-five, Michelle was a retired top ranked player. She was beautiful, smart, and very experienced at coordinating winning teams. Each time their player went into the Game, the team would elect one member to be the Right Hand for the duration of that play. If a Right Hand did their job well, they would be elected to do the job during the next play. Michelle had been Zack's Right Hand for the last five plays, a very impressive record even among the elite player groups.

"Someone's trying to kill Trew," Michelle said.

Brandon nodded, apparently not too concerned to hear this. "Any idea who?"

"Some ideas, but nothing definite yet."

"You have it under control? Our boy is as safe as we can make him?"

"Absolutely, sir."

"Who's making sure he's safe?"

Michelle looked downwards towards her left. "I'm not able to say, sir."

"You just did, Michelle. So she's watching him and it's all good?"

Brandon scanned the entire table, searching for someone to silently indicate the situation wasn't in control. Everyone looked calm and confident. He nodded positively. "Next?" Brandon asked.

"It's been five days played, and Trew is very young. The scenarios and credits spent on power ups have all worked properly so far. We know that he won a one million dollar prize for being born at December twenty-first. That was expensive for us to buy and, as it turns out, a total waste of credits. Who would have guessed the Mainframe would stop all other births at that time once the first player purchased it?"

"The money sits in an account for him until he's what age?" Brandon asked.

"Twenty-five," Michelle said. "His parents are comfortable when it comes to money, so he won't need it until then."

"What's his overall health and disposition?" Brandon asked.

"He's a happy, healthy boy. They are teaching him religion and eastern spiritualism. Teachers and neighbours all like young Trew; his charisma is high. He's a natural leader."

"How old is he and has he begun to self-narrate?"

"He's seven. The self-narrating is beginning, but still nothing an audience will want to turn in to listen to quite yet," Michelle said. "He purchased the correct attributes, though. Soon the little voice that talks to itself, detailing life's observations, feelings and thoughts will start to mature and the crowds of fans will begin to tune in to listen."

Brandon nodded. Self-narration was part of the programming built into all avatars. Earthlings rarely gave much thought to why they constantly talked to themselves, but it served a crucial purpose for the Game audience. Anyone watching or Firsting the players received a clear, concise dialogue of what was going on in the player's head. Game viewing had exploded in popularity when the self-narration add-on had been implemented.

"So, not much to report then?" Brandon asked.

Michelle shook her head. "The first few years are always pretty boring. The excitement will start for us and the fans when he is nine. He bought maturity, so he should start self-narrating early for the fans. He will turn nine tomorrow at 2 PM our time."

Brandon nodded and stood up. "Then I will see you all tomorrow at 2 PM."

He was at the door when he stopped and turned around to ask one final question. "What about Alexandra Montoyas? Where has she turned up in the Game?"

Michelle held out her hand and one of the women at the table hurried forward with a tablet. Scanning it quickly, she looked back towards Brandon. "Her avatar's name is Danielle Benton. She's in the United States, sir, a couple states away from the Canadian border. She is six years old, and as far as we can observe, living a very normal life."

"Any ideas what attributes and credit purchases she made before going in?" Brandon asked.

"Of course." Michelle paused as she tapped a few commands onto the tablet. "Seems like she didn't have many credits, and she wasted almost all of them."

"Let me see," Brandon said. Michelle handed him the tablet and he looked it over. After a complete scrutiny of Alex's stats, he handed the tablet back.

"Looks harmless enough. From experience, I know the Mainframe will never allow her purchases to manifest in the Game, but it accepts the credits from those foolish enough to spend them that way. So, then, nothing interesting on Alex yet?" He looked at Kate, the young woman who was in charge of following Alex.

"Well, sir, I received only one strange report about her. I can't confirm it, but my source is usually very reliable."

"What is it?" Brandon asked absently, He was bored and ready to leave.

"Raphael has apparently been seen near her, sir, and it appears that he is guarding her from a safe distance."

Brandon's eyes snapped to lock on to Kate's. His intense gaze forced her to take an involuntary step backwards. He started to say something, but closed his mouth with an audible snap.

Brandon's eyes flicked to Michelle's. "Confirm that by tomorrow when we convene at 2 PM, Michelle. If Raphael's sniffing around, that is a big development."

When Brandon left the room, the team exploded into activity.

16

No one expected the Game to attract much of an audience. A virtual reality simulation where kids played in a world exactly like our own? Who would want to watch people waking up every day and going to a boring job, scraping out a regular life of monotony and boredom?

Psychology experts, however, predicted that regular people would become obsessed with the Game, and they were right. Viewer statistics and preferences are easily tracked, and the facts they show are amazing.

Viewers love to watch it all. Not just the happy moments and the exciting, large events; they are there for the pain and misery as well. For example, a recent event was just viewed, with record numbers tuning in to observe the final moments of Joanna, a 42-year-old Earth woman. Her life had been sad, frustrating, and unremarkable. At the age of 42, she'd given up all hope and bought enough heroin to end her depressing life. As thoughts of despair and sadness overwhelmingly filled her mind, she inserted the needle and ended her avatar's life. A small, seemingly insignificant event, yet record audience numbers tuned in to experience it.

If you can watch someone else's life and be drawn into it, you can escape your own for a time. Fans sum it up with the popular phrase... 'The Game is Life.'

Danielle, 8 years old.

"Ready?" I look over and my three friends are bent down with their hands on the line we've drawn in the dirt. Tommy, Cindy, and

Mike all look at me and smile. They can't beat me, but they sure look like they want to try.

I yell "Go!!!!" and then I'm running. I know they're going to stay on the street. They must know I'm jumping over the hood of that car, and I do! Now Cindy and Mike are a bit behind us. Tommy's ahead, but that's fine, Tommy always starts strong, then tries to take a swing at me as he loses speed and I pass him.

The light ahead is red. Cars are zooming along in front of us and I smile. I hope Tommy stays with me, but as I sprint even faster into the speeding traffic I hear him skid to a stop, yelling for me to stop too, but I won't. It's a game, and I play to win.

I make it to the other side pretty easily; only one car comes close to hitting me, but he slams on the brakes and honks his horn. I just smile and wave. Usually this is the point where I stop and turn around to bow and wave, but I want to try out something new, so I put my head down and just keep running towards the garbage dumpster up ahead.

We saw Tommy's older brother and his friends climbing up buildings, doing backflips, and all other sorts of fun stuff. They called it parkour (I think that's what they called it — I don't really know, but it looked cool!) so I'm gonna try it.

I get close to the garbage bin and jump as hard as I can. I thud right into it — ow! — but I manage to get my hands onto the top of the bin and I start to kick my legs fast, struggling to climb to the top. I grunt, I moan, I kick, I climb until finally I'm on top of it! Very cool, I'm parkouring! I look around for something else to climb, and there it is! A fire escape that I might just barely be able to reach. I go for it, and I make it. I keep looking for stuff to climb, and by the time the others catch up I'm halfway up the outside of the building, sitting on a window ledge swinging my legs with a grin on my face.

"What are you doing up there, goofball?" Cindy asks, smiling. Of all the girls I know, Cindy is the coolest. We spend all our time together.

"I'm parkouring! Like Jim and his friends were," I say, proud of myself. I enjoy being the first in our group to do stuff.

"Jim and his friends are idiots," Tommy says. "My mom says one of them are going to kill themselves doing it."

I shrug. "Everyone dies, Tommy. If they did a cool stunt while dying... that would be awesome!"

Tommy rolled his eyes. This was common talk from me; they were getting used to it. "Just come on and let's go. Mom gave me money for ice cream. I'll buy for all of us."

I stand up and dust my hands off. "Ok, be right down. I was just waiting for you all to catch up and watch this."

"Watch what?" Mike asks cautiously.

"My back flip to the ground."

The three of them don't seem happy. "Um, Danielle... that's a bit high to be back flipping from."

I laugh at them. Cowards! "It's fine. Just wait a minute and I'll be ready to go." I turn my back to them and put my hands above my head. I'm silently counting to three, 'cause I always jump after three, when I hear an adult voice from below.

"I bet you can do it, no problem, Danni." I frown. The voice is deep and has some kind of accent. Spanish, I think it's called. My Aunt Vi dated a Spanish man and he sounded like that.

I quickly look to see who has joined my friends below and there's a dark-skinned man with black hair pulled back into a ponytail smiling up at me. He looks nice and friendly. I wave. He waves back.

"Do me a favour, Danni; first try should be from just a bit lower. Why don't you show us how you can climb back down to the dumpster and do the back flip from there?"

I shrug and start to jump towards the dumpster, landing here, jumping from there, grabbing onto that, until I'm standing back on the dumpster lid. "Are you sure?" I ask the man. "This doesn't seem very hard. It's barely off the ground..."

I turn my back and just flip; I already counted when I was up higher. I tuck my legs in and start to swing — I've done back flips before, just from the ground and on the trampoline. I stick my feet out and land just right, but the pavement is hard and I start to stumble. Is that traffic I'm falling towards? Ah, crap, I can't stop. Hope the cars see me.

But just as I'm about to fall onto the street, a hand catches me. It's a strong hand and I know there's no way I'm going to be hurt while it's holding me. Of course it's the Spanish man. We both smile at the same time.

"Perfect, Danni. That was all you," he says. He looks proud of me.

"No one calls me Danni," I say, "But I like it."

"I'm glad. My name is Raphael. You be sure to stay safe, Danni. Have a great day." He walks away.

I watch him go, then head over to join my friends. Parkouring and ice cream... it's a good day.

17

It's impossible to directly influence the Game. The workings of the Game are so complex and interwoven that it would be like trying to find a specific grain of sand on the beaches of the world. Even a supercomputer wouldn't be able to do that quickly enough to make any difference. If we wanted to make a precise and specific change tomorrow, or next week, or even 100 years from now on Earth, by the time all the computations and variables were factored in, the date would have passed. And what difference could a small change really make? Using this same analogy, if you did find that one grain of sand, made it into a tiny bomb, then placed it back on the beach to explode... no one would see or hear the explosion. No, the only things that the Games Masters have had any success at is programming large things such as weather patterns to ensure minimal droughts or floods, tidal patterns to make certain the Moon doesn't affect the Earth too much, and underwater currents to help prevent the Earth from becoming too hot or too cold. Communication with avatars? No, that also is quite impossible. It would take more than even Mainframe to achieve that. To be completely honest, it's not something we've looked at trying. The purpose of the Game is for students to forget this life and learn with a blank slate. What would the point be for us to try and communicate with them? It would be too much for them to handle and completely ruin their chance to learn from their play. Knowledge is gained along the way on the journey; it's not all sitting on the finish line.

World feed interview with 'Foundation' - Lead Games Master in year 23 of the Game.

Greg Wassler was nervous. No matter how many times he sat in this room, waiting to meet the boss, he felt both thrilled and nervous. Today it was mostly nervous.

The room was dark and silent, three columns of bright light from the ceiling displaying the boss's desk, the door to the office, and the visitors' chair which Greg was sitting in. The darkness was heavy. Greg was thirty levels below ground under the VirtDyne building, and he could feel the tons of concrete pressing down on him. Sitting up straighter, he scolded himself for being apprehensive. Games Masters shouldn't be jumpy and nervous.

Thinking back seven years into the past made him smile proudly. Greg had been an excellent player of the Game, excelling at computer skills and development during his lifetimes of play. When he was invited to apply for Games Master, he jumped at the chance. There were tens of thousands of programmers, all working hard to stand out enough to someday be considered for one of the coveted twelve Games Master positions. It was unheard of for a fresh graduate from the Game to be considered.

Greg soon found himself competing against 12 other graduates, for not one of the twelve positions, but for a top secret thirteenth position. Games Masters all had titles that they took for their names when they accepted the position. Greg had fought hard and fierce to beat all of his competitors and earn the title of 'Hack,' the thirteenth secret Games Master, known only by a select and elite few on Tygon. Knowing that he technically didn't exist had disappointed Greg at first, but as he began to work in his new position, he learned that it was wise for no one to know what he was doing. For the past seven years, he'd been working on a project started decades earlier by his predecessors; an impossible project that Greg Wassler had just successfully completed.

Hack had been waiting for his boss for some time, but he was patient. This was the first time Hack had called the meeting. He knew it would be worth the wait to see his superior's surprise.

A voice from behind the desk startled Hack out of his thoughts. The chair turned and the boss was sitting there, a pleased smile on his face. "So, Hack, you've succeeded. It's ready?"

"Yes, Mr. Strayne. It's ready."

Brandon was visibly excited. He'd been waiting thirty years to hear this news. Many times he'd given up hope that he ever would. The timing, although long overdue, was perfect. "Tell me how it works," he said.

"It's very simple," Hack said. "You walk into the room, put the helmet on, and place your hands in the provided slots. Then relax and count backwards from ten. Before you reach ten, you'll be Firsting your target, live. Then, you wait for the right moment and interrupt their self-narration."

Brandon just sat there silently. Hack looked back at him calmly; he knew the question that needed confirmation.

"So I can directly communicate with an avatar?" Brandon asked.

Hack smiled widely. "Yes, sir."

"And I don't have to be put into a coma to achieve this?"

"Not at all, sir," Hack assured him.

"Incredibly well done, Hack."

"Thank you, sir."

"How many avatars have you tested it with?" Brandon asked.

"Twelve avatars all tested successfully, Mr. Strayne. Different ages and class levels in the Game. I'm certain you can do it with any avatar."

"And Mainframe? Did it detect you?"

"Not that I can tell. But that doesn't mean no for sure. I advise keeping the conversation low, and limited to not too many avatars. The more you do it the more 'noise' you make, which increases the likelihood of detection."

Brandon nodded. "I will keep that in mind."

"There is one serious issue that needs to be remembered," Hack said. "If anyone is Firsting the targeted avatar, or watching them on the viewers, they will hear you as well. Detection by fans is your biggest danger."

"Yes, but we've thought of that. No one watches an avatar when they are meditating, right?"

"Correct. For decades, when avatars meditate or pray, we've scrambled the signals so no viewer can have access. Even when Firsting an avatar these two times are inaccessible," Hack said.

Brandon smiled. "Perfect. What did you do about the test avatars? They knew they were spoken to, and not while meditating I assume?" Hack nodded. "So anyone following them could put it together."

"They weren't popular avatars, sir, and they all met with unfortunate accidents. I've been monitoring every mention of them from viewers; we are clear. Even if someone did notice, who would believe them? The truth for thirty years has been that no one can communicate inside the Game from the outside. If a fan claimed it was possible, they'd be labelled conspiracy theorists."

Brandon nodded. "Since you succeeded, we both know what must happen now."

Hack nodded.

"I'm sorry, Greg." Brandon said.

Hack shrugged. "I agreed to the terms when I came on board, sir. If I succeeded, I'd have to 'disappear' in order to make sure there was no chance of me sharing the secret. There's a price for knowledge, and it's a price Greg Wassler agreed to pay willingly for the opportunity to become Hack."

Brandon nodded. "Okay then, Hack. Greg Wassler officially dies at age 25. You can't see anyone from your old life ever again. It won't be all bad. It's a big world, and I reward loyalty."

Hack smiled. "I haven't really had a life in seven years anyway, Mr. Strayne. May I ask one very personal question?"

"Of course."

"What are you going to do with this ability to talk directly to avatars?"

Brandon smiled. "I'm going to become a God."

"Well, it's been less than a week since December 21, 2012 came and went inside the Game. Despite popular theory, Earth did not end in a catastrophe predicted thousands of years earlier by the ancient Mayan civilization of Earth. Almost every eligible player has gone into the Game to join in the 30th anniversary celebrations, many hoping to gain bonus credits or perhaps be involved in story lines that gain the attention and following of fans. Earth journalists are reporting alarming swells in the population which adds a dynamic to the Game not seen in some time. And let's not forget the real story all of Tygon is tuning in for —how will Zack's avatar, Trew Radfield, perform during his life? Our best attempts to uncover strategy and planning from Zack's camp have turned up nothing. I guess that's to be expected since his Patron could fire us all at the drop of a hat. Most fans will begin to tune in now that Trew has begun to self-narrate. Not to be out done, Alexandra's young avatar, Danielle Benton is also self narrating at the age of eight. She has her core following and I must admit that so far she's much more entertaining than Trew. Of course, it's very early in their plays. We can expect many weeks of fun and entertainment before they die of old age. Unless they don't make it that far..."
Video Feed from "30th anniversary Game update"

Trew Radfield, age 9

Mom's yelling something at me from downstairs. It's the third or tenth time she's yelled. That many tries must mean she wants me to answer her, so I turn down the music and open the door a bit. "Pardon?" I yell down.

She comes to the foot of the stairs looking up at me. Uh-oh. I should have answered sooner.

"I said you need to get ready for class, Trew. You know what day it is. Quit ignoring me, young man — there's no way to get out of this. Life is not just some big game, although you seem to think so."

I grin down at her and start to walk down the stairs. I'm ready to go, I was just playing with her. "What if it is just a game, Mom?" I kiss her on the cheek as I pass by. She's such a great Mom, I love her so much!

"If it was, then you'd need another life because I'm tempted to end this one for you!" Mom tries to look upset, but I can always make her smile. I have that effect on people.

"Will Dad be there?" I ask.

"He sure will. He's sitting in the driveway now, waiting for us." She opens the door and out we go.

It's bright and hot out, a beautiful summer day for grown-up strangers to discuss. It's too hot for me, though, in my karate gi. I hope they have the air conditioning on, but I know that on test day they never do.

Dad unrolls the car window, a big smile on his face, and sticks his hand outside. I slap his palm with mine as I walk by, smiling back. I try to open the back door, but it's locked. Staring at me through the window is the brat, my seven-year-old sister, Tara. She knows I love sitting behind Dad, which is why she takes the spot every time she can.

"Move over." I quietly mouth the words and with my eyes I promise to hurt her if she doesn't. Tara looks at me and cups her hands to her ear. "What?" she yells. "I can't hear you, Trew." I know she wants me to lose my temper. Then Mom or Dad will yell at me, which will make Tara very happy. She lives to make my life miserable.

I check to make sure Dad's window is rolled up again, which it is because he doesn't want to let the cold air out. Then I put my hand over my mouth and whisper quietly, "Make her move over, please. Today's a special day and I should sit there."

I hear the door unlock and Tara moves over. She doesn't look happy. I can hear Dad finishing his sentence as I get in. "It's a special day for Trew, Princess. He should sit on his favourite side." It's so cool when I say something out loud and it happens. I know it's just a coincidence, but I feel almost like I have super powers sometimes. How cool would that be? To be able to say something is going to happen and it does?

Mom leans over to give Dad a kiss, then we all strap in and Dad backs the car out of the driveway. It's so nice and cold in here. The heat of the dojo is going to be horrible! I decide to test my powers again. "It's so hot outside, I hope the dojo has the air conditioning on, even though they usually don't for testing."

Dad groans. "Oh, god, I forgot about that! I hope so too, Bud." Mom puts her hand on Dad's neck to make him feel better. She always seems to know what to do to make him feel better. That's not too tough, though; my Dad's a pretty positive guy most of the time.

"No matter what the temperature is like, I know you're going to do awesome, Trew." Sometimes I think Dad and Mom are more excited about my life than I am.

I listen to Mom and Dad talk about grown up stuff. How her day was, how his day was. Tara looks out the window for a while, likely figuring out how to bother me more, but I'm just glad to be left alone. I'm excited about the testing today. I'm going for my blue belt, and it's getting pretty fun at this level of karate. There's so much more than just throwing punches and kicking. Sensei offered to give me free private lessons, and my parents let me. Sensei teaches me that the mind is a powerful weapon and, with much practice, we can bend the elements and energies to our will.

She's just started to teach me to meditate. I don't really understand it, but it sounds cool to tell my friends I'm learning meditation. So far it's just sitting there thinking about breathing, but it must get more exciting soon. I don't think I'll do it today, but I might close my eyes and pretend so Sensei thinks I'm doing it.

We find parking and walk down the block to the dojo. It's an old, square building with a real high ceiling and just one big room. Along the sides are benches for the parents to sit and in the middle is a big open area with the kind of thick blue mats that you see in a karate dojo. The first thing I notice when we walk in is the crowd. The seats are almost full with parents and grandparents coming to watch their kids do their testing today. My parents are always saying how many kids there are now. It happened the year I was born and kept going for the next seven years. Tons of us! Sensei and her helpers are standing near the entrance directing the crowd.

I'm so excited I don't notice until my Dad slaps me on the back and says, "Great luck, pal! They've got the air conditioning on!"

I smile, thinking I should say 'You're welcome' for using my secret power. But I just laugh because I know it's just good luck.

Sensei comes over and shakes hands with Mom and Dad before patting me on the shoulder. "Ready for your test, Trew?" she asks.

"I am, Sensei," I say seriously.

She smiles. "I know you are. Just remember what you've learned and practiced and it will go smoothly. Also remember that the less you think, the better you will do. Trust deep down in yourself."

"The air conditioning will help us parents sit still and pay attention better," my Dad says cheerfully.

"It's so hot out," Sensei says. "Even though we usually turn it off for testing, it just felt like the right thing to do today by turning it on. Maybe Trew can take the credit for it?"

I look at her with wide eyes. "What?" I ask. Can she read my mind?

"Well, I thought it would be a nice little extra birthday present to put the air on," Sensei says.

"Oh, right." I say. "Thank you, Sensei."

"Go take your seat with the others. We have special guests from an American dojo. If you meet any of them, please make them feel welcome, Trew."

"Yes, Sensei." I bow.

"Birthday party after we are through, bud!" my Dad says.

I give him a thumbs up, smile at Mom, and run off to join the others.

Two of my friends have saved me a spot, and I sit down beside them. The girl on my right isn't someone I've seen before, so I smile at her. She smiles back. Remembering what Sensei just told me, I introduce myself. "Hi, are you one of the students from the American dojo?"

The girl grins and nods. She's really pretty. And very... confident, I guess is the right word. It's like she's a big movie star and everyone is here to see her. And she's really pretty. "Yeah, I'm here from the States. This is a great dojo you have here."

"Thanks," I say. "So what brings you here? We go to the States to compete sometimes, but I've been here for three years and I don't remember any American schools visiting us."

"We came because of me," she says with a shrug. "Apparently I'm pretty good at this karate, and not many people around can give me a very good contest in sparring. I win the kata part too. So somehow my Sensei knows your Sensei and they got to talking and agreed to bring me here. There's a student here that is maybe as good as, or even better than me. I'm excited to meet him!"

"What's the students name?" I ask. I had no idea this dojo had someone so skilled.

"Trew Radfield," the girl says, looking around like she's waiting for me to point him out to her. She looks around for a couple seconds and, when I don't say anything, she looks back at me. I'm sitting there smiling with a finger pointing at my chest.

"I'm Trew Radfield. But I don't think I'm that good."

The girl holds out her hand to shake with me. "Well, I guess we will get a chance to see soon, Trew. Nice to meet you. My name's Danielle Benton."

Stephanie

It's so hot out today. I wish I could be inside with a cold drink, but my gut tells me to keep a close eye on Trew this afternoon, and my gut is always right. I'm not having the type of feeling I get when someone wants to kill him. That's a sick, panicked feeling with a heavy pressure behind my eyebrows. This is more of a tingling, curious feeling, not like something bad is about to happen, but more like I should just be close by to keep an eye on him.

He went into the Dojo with his family. Poor guy, I know they turn the air conditioning off in there on test days. I'm likely better off being outside than in. I can't be in there anyway, that's not where my gut is telling me to be. I'm standing across the street from the dojo. Soon I'll get closer to look through the window when enough people gather there to watch the events inside. So many kids born — there's always standing room only for most events now with so many parents and children. It's insane.

I'm sipping on an iced tea, looking slowly around from time to time but trying not to look conspicuous, when from behind me I hear a familiar voice speaking in a language I rarely hear any more.

"Hello, Stephanie. A little hot out for being lazy on a bench, don't you think?"

I slowly turn towards the voice, giving the man I see behind me a genuinely warm smile. I'm always happy to see Raphael, even though the last time I saw him he was trying to kill me. But that wasn't personal — he was just doing his job.

"Raphael, you handsome wolf! Come over here and give me a hug." We embrace and it feels so good to touch him. Sometimes I'm apart from my countrymen so long that I'm afraid I'm the last of us. Of course, that's not true — hundreds of us still exist; it's just a big world to move in, and we're all kept busy.

Seconds pass and Raphael holds me at arm's length, looking me up and down. The man really is beautiful. Hair so black it shines with a bluish tint in the sun pulled back into a ponytail. Eyes just like mine, deepest brown, with flecks of gold in them which swirl with different speeds depending on his mood. He's six feet tall, with bronzed skin and very well defined muscles. And the smile — his best feature. If I hadn't known him for so long, I would melt. I laugh because despite how long I've known him, I almost do melt.

"So what brings you into my territory today, Raphael? Here for business or pleasure? And for how long?"

"Business today, Stephanie," He says. "I'm currently based in the United States. Ward duty for me for the past eight years. My girl is here today on a visit and I just wanted to make sure she stays safe, even though my gut says there'll be no problems." He looks over towards the dojo, and I guess she must be inside.

"Any idea who she is? Your girl?" I ask pleasantly. Sometimes we tell each other, sometimes we don't. But we always ask.

Raphael shrugs. It looks like he's willing to share the info with me. "In here she's called Danielle Benton. Outside she's Alexandra Montoyas. I'm hers for now. How about you, Stephanie? You have a ward also?"

I nod dumbly. My mind is racing. I usually know what to do about a threat, but I can't see how this is a threat to Trew. My gut tells me it's fine, so I try to calm down. But something deep down feels... concerned. "We'd better go closer and take a look inside the dojo, Raphael."

He sees my look and his brows furrow with concern. I smile reassuringly and pat him on the back. "My ward is a nine-year-old boy named Trew Radfield." I pause to see if he recognizes the name. He looks at me blankly, still waiting to hear something interesting. "Outside, he's Zack."

Raphael looks at me for a moment in surprise. Then he tilts his head back and roars with laughter.

As we walk across the street to get a good view of the dojo, he says, "That's so funny, Stephanie. Word is that Alexandra Montoyas spent everything on her last play just to get a meeting like this and it didn't work. I bet she didn't spend one little credit this time, and yet here they are in the same room. Wanna bet they are sitting right beside each other?"

I shake my head negatively. I bet that's exactly where they're sitting.

19

"What if we are all just turtles?
A mother turtle lays her eggs on the beach and then swims away. Soon after, the hundreds or thousands of eggs hatch and the baby turtles begin their struggle to survive. First they have to fight their way up from under the sand. Some do not make it. Next they race towards the water while predators swoop down to eat them. They are defenseless, slow, and tiny and many of them do not survive this stage. They aren't safe even once they reach the water. Different predators are waiting for them there, snatching them up in the shallow waters and eating as many of the baby turtles as they can. The few who remain head towards deeper water, a bit safer, but it will be many years before they are grown enough to have a chance of living a long life in the sea. Of the thousands of turtles that hatch and begin their struggle for life, only a very few of them will make it. It is the same with the millions of souls born into human bodies. Just like turtles, most of them are lost along the way. Only a few rare souls will learn their lessons and evolve. Until they evolve, they are reborn again and again to play the game of life."
Excerpt from Earth book called 'The Game Is Life'
George Knight (avatar)

Trew Radfield, age 9

We wait for our turn to get up and show our stuff. They go through the younger belts first, which takes about an hour. My friends lean over and whisper to me every once in a while, not loud or often because we're supposed to be polite and quiet. The whole time all I can think about is Danielle sitting beside me. I try not to stare at her, but I don't think I'm too good at hiding it. I pretend to look at the wall beside her, but she catches me every time and just smiles. I smile back.

"What do you think so far?" I ask her.

"It's as boring as testing back home," she says with a grin. Her eyes are a really cool ice blue colour, and her hair is long and black, tied up in a ponytail. "Soon it's our turn. Are you nervous?"

I shake my head. "No, I don't get nervous much. It's pretty fun getting up there."

"You're not worried about getting beat by a girl during the sparring?"

I shrug. "Not really. Dad says we can learn more from failing than succeeding. So if you beat me, then I guess you'll be doing me a favour by teaching me something new."

"Yep." She nods seriously. "All part of the game."

"What game?" I ask.

Danielle spreads her arms wide, I'm not sure what she's pointing at, but it seems like she means everything in the world. "The only game that matters, Trew. Life. Everything we do. It's all just a game."

"I kind of said the same thing to my Mom earlier," I say.

"Well then, you're kind of smart," she says.

When it's time for the blue belts to perform, we start off as a group and go through the kata for our level. There are about 20 of us; Danielle and I are the youngest. Usually a kid is around 12 or 13 to be at the blue belt level, but I practice a lot and Sensei says that I earned the early advancement. Danielle must have done the same. I go through my forms, watching her out of the corner of my eye. She's good. Very good. Strong, crisp, also relaxed in her style. It looks like she's been doing karate her whole life. She told me she's only been at it for two years. I've been practicing four years.

We form a ring around the outside of the mats, waiting for our turn to spar. At this level, we don't need the headgear. Head contact isn't allowed and we all know how to make sure the punches don't connect. Watching the little ones spar is cute. Watching us spar is better. Not as good as the highest level belts, but I've sparred with brown and black belts and even won, so the parents will get a good show.

Danielle and I go last. I walk to one side of the mat and she goes to the other. We face each other and bow. She looks very intense. I have a sudden feeling I might lose. Locking eyes with her, I quietly use my imaginary power and whisper, 'You can't win this match, Danielle.'

Her eyes squint and she freezes in place. She quickly looks around then her gaze snaps back to me. "Hey, what did you just do?" she asks seriously.

Stephanie

"Hey!" Raphael exclaims in a loud whisper. "Did you just see that?"

"Yes," I say.

"How long has he been able to do that, Stephanie?"

"Couple years. But you know how it works, Raph. Most kids can do it when they're young. Life and experience eliminates the Talent soon enough. He thinks it's just his imagination."

Raphael laughs, keeping his eyes on the kids as they get ready to spar. "It is just his imagination!"

I scowl. "You know what I mean. He doesn't believe in it, so soon it will fade, same as always."

"Maybe," Raphael sounds doubtful. "But Danni just spotted it, and that's likely going to be a problem for me."

"Why?"

"Because she can do it too. And I don't know how she actually recognized Trew doing it just now, but I know her. There's no way she's going to stop believing in it after this."

Trew Radfield, age 9

"I didn't do anything," I say.

"Yeah, you did." She shrugs, "Okay, don't tell me. I'll figure it out soon enough. Let's rock."

I get into a guard stance and she does the same. We circle each other for a couple of seconds, neither of us retreating or giving ground. I'm usually the more aggressive one in a match, which often forces my opponents to take a few steps back. Danielle must play the same way, because we both stand our ground and take small steps forward, waiting for the right opening to attack.

She drops her shoulders and makes it look like she's going to throw a right punch straight to my stomach, I step sideways and block downwards; it's actually her left foot that kicks out and I gently push it aside. She's very fast.

The match is two 90 second rounds and it goes by so quickly that I can't seem to remember it. I've practiced so much that I can let my mind relax and just feel my way through the sparring.

She attacks, I defend.

I attack, she defends.

I watch the video later and can't believe how good she is!

It's a close match, but I manage to win by one point. I guess I must be pretty good too. The person on the video looks like me, but I've never seen half the moves that either of us use.

That happens to me sometimes. Sometimes I'm there, then a bit of time passes and I'm not really present. Suddenly I'm back. I'm not sure how it works, but it's very cool.

I do remember bowing to her after the match, and her saying, "Well, that was awesome!"

We all go back to our spots on the mat, and about an hour later the testing is done. Kids go to their parents and I quickly run over to ask mine a question.

"Hey, guys, there's a girl from the States here and she's pretty nice. Can we ask her to come have ice cream with us, please?"

"Which girl would that be, love?" Mom asks with a smile. She knows, she's just messing with me.

I play along. "Um… that one over there. I think she's a blue belt too."

Dad laughs. "Sure, pal. Ask her to come along."

I quickly run over to find Danielle and she's standing with the group of ten American students who made the trip. "Hey, today's my birthday and we're going around the corner to have cake and ice cream. Is there any way you might be able to come join us for an hour?"

"Let me ask my Sensei." She walks over and talks quietly with her Sensei, who looks over at me and nods with a smile.

"They will be here for another two hours before we go home. So if you can have me back here before that, then Sensei says I can join you!"

"Okay, come on, then," I say and lead her towards my family. My Sensei is standing with them and she smiles when we come over.

"Well done, Trew," Sensei says. "Your kata was clean and very powerful. The sparring…" She looks at me and Danielle and just shakes her head.

"Was the sparring not good, Sensei?" I ask.

"The sparring between you two was like watching magic," Sensei says. "If someone had told me two children your age could put on such a display of martial arts I wouldn't have believed it. It was incredible, Danielle and Trew. Thank you for allowing us to witness it." Sensei bows formally, and we both bow back.

"Mom and Dad, this is Danielle."

My parents smile and both say how nice it is to meet her. Then they tell her how well she did today. Danielle turns a bit red and says thank you. Everyone seems to be getting along just fine.

"Well, we are glad you can join us for ice cream, Danielle." Mom says.

"I'm happy to be invited," Danielle says.

"Don't worry about not bringing a gift for me," I say as a joke. "Since we just met, I'll forgive you."

Danielle looks hurt. "But I did bring a gift for you."

"Really?" I ask.

"Oh, yes. I let you win that sparring match. Happy birthday, Trew!"

Everyone laughs and we leave the Dojo to go for ice cream.

20

From time to time, people try to find ways to hack into the Game. In order to discourage this from happening, the Mainframe maintains a tight watch on all systems to ensure outside tampering doesn't occur. Any unauthorized data entering the system is detected immediately. Mainframe quarantines the data and removes it from play. Games Masters are then alerted and the authorities trace the hacker back to the source and deal with them severely. Imagine someone being able to change the outcome of events in the Game? There is no crime more serious on Tygon than attempting to hack into the Game. Punishment for this crime is death. No one has ever succeeded in hacking the Game. Early in the Game many tried; all of them paid the price.
Excerpt from 'How Safe is the Game?

Everyone sat silently in their chairs. All screens showed Trew at his ninth birthday party; smiles, ice cream and kids walking around talking as they moved from seat to seat. Brandon looked at the screen with a pleasant expression on his face. Beside him Michelle occasionally switched between looking at her tablet, and glancing at Brandon. Everyone else looked down at their tablets, as if they were the most interesting things in the world. Brandon might look pleasant, but no one made the mistake of thinking he was happy with what he was seeing on the screen.

Danielle walked up to Trew and whispered something. The two of them laughed and Danielle sat down in the empty seat beside Trew. Brandon's cheek twitched. He turned away from the monitor and looked at Michelle.

"Michelle?"

"Sir?"

"Can you call the hospital, please? Tell them I've had a stroke and somehow believe I've travelled back in time to an event that didn't happen."

Michelle said nothing.

"Can anyone tell me who's playing this excellent joke on us? We tried to hook this up a few plays ago, didn't we? The poor girl spent all her credits for just this kind of a scene, right? Even in our wildest dreams the two of them wouldn't have gotten together so well."

"Yes, sir." Brandon held up his hand, stopping Michelle from saying anything else.

"But for this play, we don't want her anywhere near Trew! She isn't part of our plan. She left the Game and we have no idea why she's back. She's a loose cannon, with not enough credits to be anything but dangerous. She could die crossing the street, for God's sake. What if Trew is caught in that mess of a life she's living?" Brandon stopped talking and closed his eyes, rubbing the back of his neck.

"Look, people, you've all worked with me before. You know I'm not the kind to get crazy and start shouting and throwing people out of windows," Brandon smiled. "We are the only ones that know for sure that Zack is making a play for number one. Raise your hand if you have bet everything you own on Zack pulling it off."

Hands shot up around the room. Of the thirty-one people present, thirty had their hands up. Brandon nodded, his was the only hand not raised. He had more than just a fortune riding on this, but no one could know that. "You were all top players in the Game, and this is absolutely your best chance to double your considerable fortunes. We all know the rules. There's no hacking into the system to affect the outcome of the Game, but we also understand there are many things we can do to help our player within the rules Mainframe has set. We've spent considerable time and money putting supporting players in place with millions of credits spent. We have thirty years of experience to try and figure out how Zack can score the best from the life he chose to play. Yes, the Game can decide none of it's important and score him terribly, but we know how to play the best odds. Each step he takes can lead us down an alternate path, and we've taken thousands of them into account. Not one single path includes this girl, however. If he ends up with her, we need to do a complete new set of strategies. So the easiest option is to get her out of his life. Michelle, is that going to be possible?"

Michelle looked around the room quickly. Brandon's speech had calmed them all down. He really was the best man in the world to work for. He always called it 'working with,' but they all knew who the boss was, and they loved him fiercely. She looked back and met Brandon's eyes, dark brown with flecks of gold that seemed to be swirling around quickly at the moment. "I don't know, sir, but we are sure going to try."

Brandon nodded. "That was definitely Raphael outside the dojo. Can anyone explain to me how Alex got herself an Eternal to watch over her? They are the most expensive purchase in the Game, and Raphael is one of the best."

Michelle looked to Kate questioningly. "She didn't have the credits to purchase an Eternal, sir," Kate said. "The only answer we can come up with that makes any sense is a very wealthy fan or group of fans made the purchase for her."

One of the young men spoke up, "Can we get Stephanie to ask Raphael to keep her away from Trew?"

Brandon sat down and grabbed his tablet, tapping out commands to view statistics. "Yes, that's one option. I also need to know what Stephanie and Raphael were talking about. Maybe there's some information there to help us decide how to proceed. Tell Angelica to watch that feed and set up a meeting with her and me and you, Michelle."

"I'll talk to her immediately, sir."

Brandon looked up and met eyes with the spiritual expert of the group. "Sean, Zack's displaying the Talent. I need to know the best way to foster that. He's close to the age where he'll let it fade away, and we can't have that. We also can't let him develop it too much, or it could alert the Mainframe and it will shut him down. I need you to give me a strategy for moving forward by the end of the day."

"I'm emailing it to you now, sir." Sean said.

Brandon nodded. Once your player went into the Game, time was precious. Taking too long on Tygon would mean missing key points in the Game. This team truly was the best, and therefore the fastest.

Brandon stood up to leave. "Okay, people, it looks like we all have work to do. I'll be back in a few hours. I'm sure we'll talk before then."

"Brandon?" Michelle looked pale as she looked up from her tablet. "We've discovered who purchased the Eternal for Danielle."

Brandon looked at her with interest. "Great. Who was it?"

"Um... it was the Mainframe."

21

"**Joining me today** in the studio is Brandon Strayne. Brandon, it's great to see you again."

"Thanks, Lisa. It's good to see you as well."

"Brandon, I know your time is short, so let me get right to the questions everyone is asking."

"By all means."

"Trew Radfield is 11 years old in the Game. We have witnessed some exciting developments since he started this play, but the event that's being talked about the most is his meeting with Danielle Benton at his ninth birthday party. Did the two of them spend credits to attempt another relationship in the Game?"

Brandon smiled secretively. "We learned our lesson the first time on that scenario, Lisa. We spent no credits on this play to get them together. Of course, I can't speak for Alex or her camp. If she did arrange for a meeting, I'm glad that this time it worked out for her."

"Trew is doing very well in the rankings so far. Can he keep it up?"

"Of course he can. The first week is pretty slow, and already he's doing well. Scoring floats all over the place as the players do their thing, but a strong start is important and Trew has started very strong."

"Can you give us any inside strategy or big events planned for Trew's next few years?" Lisa asked.

"I could..." Brandon said. "But do you really want me to spoil things? Of course you don't. If Trew lives as long as we hope, there will be much excitement over the next couple months. We all know it averages out to about one Tygon week for each decade of life, although the time passes a bit differently for each decade. He lived to the age of 74 on his last play, so if he's able to do that again, we can expect another six weeks or so of fun! I can tell you to watch very closely on Trew's 40th birthday. Something big will happen then. But don't tune out until that day... there's a lot of aggressive stuff leading up to that, and it's already started."

"So he's going for it? He's going to try and finish ranked #1."

Brandon smiled, saying nothing. He knew the audience would fill in the blanks he was leaving with their own opinions. Some would say for sure Trew was going for it, while others would swear he was going to play it safe.

"And what about rumours that Danielle has an Eternal watching over her?" Lisa asked.

Brandon leaned back comfortably in his seat. "Lisa, for as long as the Game has been played there's been rumours about Eternals. People say Eternals are avatars that have been inside the Game since the beginning, hence the title 'Eternals.' It's also said that Eternals can't be Firsted or viewed on any channel, and that they have special powers. Some retired players have come forward and claimed that achieving a high enough player ranking unlocks a 'Purchase Eternal' option on their gaming menu, but they say the cost of purchasing one is too high to ever make the purchase. Over the years, there have been incredible events that occur inside the Game and people often claim Eternals are involved. Some think they are angels, and some think they are demons. But this is the 30th anniversary of the Game, and fans are expecting to see many wonderful things during this celebration. Maybe if Eternals do exist, we will see them step forward."

"But you created the Game, Brandon. Don't you know about every aspect of it?"

"The Game is pretty big, Lisa. I don't think one person can know every aspect of the Game. I do know most of the major points, though."

"So, " Lisa said, "Do Eternals exist? Or no?"

Brandon paused dramatically, then leaned towards Lisa. She also leaned forward, as if Brandon was going to whisper a secret just for her to hear.

"I have no idea," Brandon said. "But if I'm ever able to confirm that they do... I will give you the exclusive."

22

If life is a game, then I've done a poor job of playing it. My time on Earth has been boring and uneventful. I've wasted my youth, sitting around doing nothing when I was full of life and energy. Playing video games, working at simple jobs, trading my time for just enough money to pay the bills and survive; not really learning anything or traveling anywhere. I also wasted my middle years, abusing my body with lack of exercise and junk food. I wouldn't treat an automobile as poorly as I've treated my body. It's no wonder it fails me now. The greatest sin I've made is allowing my mind to sleep all these years. When I was young I had such plans, but I listened to the world when it told me I was silly and demanded that I grow up. Growing up made me forget how to play games, and that turned out to be the worst thing that could have happened. If life is a game, and we forget how to play games... what chance do we have of succeeding?
Excerpt from Earth book called 'The Game Is Life'
George Knight (avatar)

Danielle - age 13

"**There's a used book store**," I point out to my friend Tracey. "Let's go in."

Tracey rolls her eyes at me, but she knows there's no use in complaining. I can't go past a used book store without going in to take a look.

I love to read. Just love it! Since someone first put a book in my hand and showed me how to figure out what all the letters joined together to make, I've been hooked on reading. Most of my friends don't read, which is a shame. Books contain so much knowledge, clearly written down and there for the taking! The best books provide other worlds to escape to or different lives and experiences to watch, if the story is set on Earth. It's all great stuff, yet not many seem to know or care about it. If people knew how powerful books were, they'd all have one in their hand or a tablet loaded full of e-books, just like me!

The real treasures lie in used book stores. Over the years paper books became more rare, and many people put all their books on a digital reader instead. Many books didn't get turned into digital format. Old books that were out of print, and small, self-published books. I've read some great stuff in paper books that you just can't find on the Net. It's kinda sad, but I like to find the gems, so I stop into every used book store I go by, just in case there's something new and exciting to read.

Tracey offers to wait for me outside. I walk in and say hi to Jordan the clerk. She smiles and says hi back. I come in here once a month and she knows me.

"Anything good and rare lately, Jordan?" I ask.

"I saved a box full of stuff that we don't normally get in for you, Danielle," she says. "It's over in the back corner in a brown box."

"Thanks," I say and walk to the back.

It's not a very big box, but I open it up and start skimming through the books. I'm not really sure what I'm looking for, but sometimes I just get a feeling when I hold a certain book. When I get that feeling, the book goes into my 'buy' pile. There's an old book on karate, and I place that in the not interested pile. I quit karate years ago. I learned everything I needed to from karate, and it led me to my buddy Trew, but I'm not really interested in pursuing it. I do that a lot. Study something and give it everything

I've got. Then my gut tells me that's enough and I drop it just as quickly as I picked it up. There's lots for me to do and see in this life of mine. I don't have time to waste studying just one or two things for 50 years. Oh, the poor people who do that! Not playing the game very well at all, if you ask me.

I'm almost to the bottom of the box and nothing has really jumped out at me. A couple of old books on art, some gardening titles, a few old murder mystery books that I've already read... then my hand touches a book and before I even look at it I feel a big tingle of energy shooting up my arm. I almost drop it; I did the first few times this happened. But now I know it's a sign from somewhere or someone, I need to read this book in my hand!

I close my eyes for a minute, excited that I've found a new prize. I sit there and play a little game in my head. What's this book going to be about? How will it change my life? Will it change my life, or just help point me in a new direction as I try to learn something new? Is it an old book written in a foreign language? Will I have to go make a new friend to help me read the book? The last time that happened I met Mr. Chan and he helped me read that excellent Chinese book about karma and energy. I really should stop by and visit with Mr. Chan. He makes the best tea. Bah! My thoughts are starting to run around! Time to open my eyes and see what I have.

I open my eyes and look at the title. Wow! I can't blink. Is what I'm seeing real? I hold the book in my hand, looking at it until I start to get dizzy, then I realize I've forgotten to keep breathing. I gulp a huge breath of air and start to sweat a little. Then I sit down.

Slowly I read the title out loud. "The Game Is Life, by George Knight."

Quickly I look around, expecting one of my friends to start laughing from around the corner. So many of them have heard me talk about life being just a game that I wouldn't put it past them to make a fake book and plant it in an old box just to tease me. But there's no one jumping out at me and laughing.

I turn the book over and read the back cover. It's for real. This guy George thinks the same way I do, and he wrote a book about it! I quickly look inside the back of the book and find the information about the author. George R. Knight. Hmm. He was 74 when the book was written. Darn it, he's dead. Says so right there in the description. I would have loved to meet this guy and talk to him. The book was written years before I was born, so he's been gone a long time. But the great news is I still get to talk to him, in a way, by reading this wonderful book he left behind!

I flip open to the first chapter and start to read:

"We live in a game. Somewhere 'out there,' our real bodies are plugged into a very real virtual reality simulation. Earth isn't real, but it's important to those running the game. What we call God, or Allah, or the Universe, or whatever spiritual name religion gives it... is simply the supercomputer that runs our universe. How can I be so sure of this? Because I've spoken to it. And it has spoken to me..."

Oh, this is going to be fun to read! I walk to the counter and pay for the book. "You find something good?" Jordan asks.

"I think I did," I say.

I walk outside and tell Tracey I'm feeling a bit tired and need to head home. She gives me a hug and we each go our separate ways. Once I go around the corner I sprint as fast as I can to get home.

I run into the house and up the stairs, not bothering to take my shoes off. No one is home until tonight, so that gives me a few hours to get into this book. Before I start to read I sit down at my computer and log in to the video chat program, hoping to see that he's near his computer. Yes! He's there.

I turn on my camera and then click on his name. A couple of seconds later, the blank video screen comes online and there he is, that great smile on his face, his messy room showing in the background. “Hey, Danni. What’s up?” he asks.

I smile excitedly. “Hiya, Trew. I just found something super cool! You need to go hunting.”

Trew leans forward. “What have ya got, hun?” He’s started calling me that, and I kind of like it. The guy is incredible. If I could put a poster of who I want to date on my wall, it wouldn’t be any movie star or famous singer. It would be Trew. Of course, I haven’t told him that; I’m not crazy. We talk all the time, and we really do like and do a lot of the same things. He’s just a bit older than me, but not even a year, so no big deal, right? He loves old books too, and we constantly share when we find good ones. He even shares my ‘crazy ideas’ about this all being just some game. And we both have the magic. It’s fun when we get together, which is tough since we live about four hours away from each other. When we get our driver’s licenses, though… well, that’s too far away to think about.

“Trew, you have got to go hunting for this old book I just found.” I hold it up close to the camera for him to read the title.

He laughs out loud. “Awesome.”

I smile. We really do think alike. “Tell me about it! Some real old dude wrote it years before we were born. I can’t wait to get to reading it. You should go out and try and find a copy right now. I want to read it at the same time. What do you think?”

“I think that’s a great idea, hun,” he says. “I also think the universe has one hell of a sense of humour. Look what I just got home with and was going to log in to show you.” He holds up a copy of the exact same book in his hand.

I laugh out loud. It’s always a surprise when this kind of thing happens, although it seems to happen more and more. “That’s so cool!” I say.

“It sure is,” Trew says. “I wonder who this guy was. George R. Knight really rings a bell in my mind. A loud bell. I wonder if I knew him in a past life?”

I shrug, "It's possible. So let's get to reading it?"

Trew grins, "Well, then, since you have a copy too, it looks like a fair race. On your mark."

"Go!" I laugh and open the book. We keep the video link open and start reading together, as close as we can be.

For now.

23

"Tygon has benefited from the Game in many ways. Most see it simply as a form of entertainment for viewers and learning for players, but it has become much more than that. Take flight, for example. Before the Big Bang gave life to the Game, Tygon was a flightless world. When the Wright brothers soared through the air inside the Game, it became considered safe and easy to recreate their inventions in real life on Tygon. A few months later, Earth had perfected the technology and we safely began to manufacture our own aircraft here. Think of the comforts that most of us take for granted today, and remember that many would not exist if not for the efforts of players inside the Game. It might be fun for us to watch the lives and history of Earth's people as they unfold, but we must not forget the other incredible benefits it has brought us as well!"
Excerpt from documentary "More Than A Game"

Michelle walked towards her private office. "Get me a clean line to Brandon, please," She instructed her receptionist and closed the door. She sat down and picked up the phone, waiting patiently for it to ring on the other end. It began to ring a short time later, followed by someone answering it.

"Yes."

"We have a problem, Brandon." Michelle said.

"That seems to be the common theme for this play, Michelle. To be expected, I suppose, but still very tiring. What is it?"

"They found a copy of the book. George's book."

There was silence on the other end of the line.

"They found a copy of the book which was never made digital and limited to only 100 printed copies, after we did our very best to make sure the world wasn't interested in it? We paid players to spend all their credits and enter the Game with one purpose... to find and destroy all copies of that book. Is that the book you're telling me they found?"

Michelle nodded. "Yes, sir. The very same book. 'The Game Is Life' by George R. Knight."

"I know it makes no real difference, but for my own curiosity, who found it, Michelle? No, wait. Let me guess. They both found a copy at roughly the same time, right?"

"That's exactly right. Used book stores, in different countries, within minutes of each other."

Brandon surprised Michelle by laughing deeply over the phone line.

"Well, it makes sense, I suppose. Watching Zack play as George R. Knight was exciting. He had exceptional success with the business and a great family, all credits well spent. His final couple of years of life were pure gold! The pain and loss he suffered brought the viewers in by the millions, and then when George started writing that book... well, you remember that, don't you?"

"I sure do, sir. Tygon fans couldn't believe it! None of us could believe it."

"We knew the concept would be seen as ridiculous. No one on Earth would ever believe such a thing. But just to be safe, we had to eliminate all the books."

"Brandon, we've been working around the clock to try and factor Danielle into Trew's play. It appears they are heading towards a romance of some sort, and we can't predict any serious problems if that does occur. Our simulations actually suggest having her around will help him score higher than without her."

"I agree with you, Michelle. But something much bigger is going on here," Brandon said.

"What do you mean?"

"Both have Eternals. They both possess the Talent. The support they've shown each other in developing their skill is making them more powerful than a human should be. Danielle has also been fueling Trew's belief that they are in a big game. We wanted him developing that thought, but we didn't want him to truly believe it for decades. Now they both find this book? It's going to reinforce everything they've been discussing. When two kids have crazy ideas, it's one thing. When those kids see other people have been thinking the same things for years, well, that's when it could get dangerous."

"So what do you suggest we do? Separate them? Kill the girl? Let them continue on?"

Brandon sighed. Michelle could tell he wasn't as confident as usual. "I'm not sure what to suggest right now, Michelle. I think I need to do that unpleasant thing that I sometimes have to do."

"Are you serious?"

"Yes. I think I need to talk with Mainframe."

24

"We as a race have never done well with mysteries; our minds want an explanation for everything. If we can't rationally explain a curiosity, then, given enough time, most will accept an irrational answer. Science has helped solve many difficult questions throughout our history, but most remain unanswered. The same thing occurs in the Game. I find it fascinating that on Tygon we considered the possibility of an all-powerful invisible being, and quickly chose not to believe such a thing existed. Rare is the Tygonite who believes in God. On Earth, however, the majority of the population gives credit to everything (both explainable and not) to their God. Are Earthlings just more primitive than we are? Or more evolved? Whichever way you choose to argue, giving credit to their God seems to enable them to move on to consider more difficult questions and answers. Earthlings have progressed far more than we have in their timeframe. From watching them we also know the truth; they do have a God — the Mainframe. Is it not even a little bit possible that we have our own on Tygon?"
Excerpt from "Religion In The Game"

In the Game, men and women yearned for a chance to talk with God. Some would go without food and water for days, lying on the floor in cramped positions. Others would study and pray all their lives for just a chance to hear or sense the Divine. Brandon chuckled at how easy it was for him to speak with Earth's God. He just went to his office and accessed a private network.

Mainframe was too cryptic and cold a name in Brandon's opinion, so when they spoke in private he called it Sylvia. She called him

Brandon. She might be easy to speak with, but Sylvia could be very dangerous. What started as a simple artificial intelligence program to run the backbone and systems of the Game universe, had quickly evolved into much more. Centuries of watching humans and other life forms evolve had provided the Mainframe with ample learning opportunities. When he created the Mainframe, Brandon had hoped for an intelligence to evolve, and he was greatly pleased that it had.

As far as gods went, Sylvia was everything one could hope for. She was not vengeful or evil; it was in her best interest, after all, to support the creatures of her domain. A destroyed universe in the Game would eliminate her purpose for existence, which she realized early on during a brief but destructive phase of worldwide catastrophes and cosmic crashes.

Although she was powerful, Brandon and his design team of programmers and Games Masters had instilled rigid limitations on what she could and could not do. The Game had to be kept to certain standards, lifelike in every way.

Brandon was proud of his creation, but he dreaded talking with her. Sylvia was the God of the Game and to her, everything was a game. Especially a conversation with her creator. Brandon wanted information from her, and she always wanted information from him. It was an elaborate cat and mouse game, and each of them always seemed to go away having given more than they meant to. He spoke with her only when absolutely necessary, which this was.

"Good morning, Sylvia. How are you doing today?" Brandon asked.

"Good morning, Brandon." Her voice was the silky smooth tone of a 25 year old woman, pleasant and full of energy. "Everything in my universe is splendid, thank you for asking. It's been some time since we've spoken. Time for a game?"

"It looks like you're already busy playing games, Sylvia."

Sylvia laughed in a beautiful, angelic tone. "Well, that's what you made me for, silly. And I must admit, this new weather pattern program is very fun to implement. Seasons turned backwards, magnetic poles changed, air and ocean currents maintained despite the weather fluctuations. Very thrilling stuff!"

"I'm glad you're liking it," Brandon said.

"Well, I'm a bit concerned. My little ones aren't enjoying it too much at all. Animals are moving to new places and running into others they don't like. Plants are reaching for the highest wind currents to take their seeds in search of better ground. And the humans, well, there are simply too many of them on Earth at the moment. You know what occurs when this happens, Brandon. Earth will seek to balance itself."

"Your instructions are clear on that end, Sylvia. You override nature to make sure new diseases don't occur, and that enough food can grow to feed them. This will make sure they don't kill each other out of hand or die from nasty sickness. For now."

"Of course, Brandon." Sylvia purred. "Easy enough for me to accomplish. Well, it's been great talking with you, young man. If that's all, then I'll get back to work..."

Brandon laughed out loud. Sylvia rarely tried to end the conversation, and never before she had gotten information out of him. Of course, she might have already gotten what she wanted and he just didn't know it, but he wasn't done with her yet. "Hold on there, Sylvia. I need to ask you a couple of questions."

Sylvia sighed, "My dear Brandon, I know what you want to ask me. They are the same questions I want to ask you. But I think we both know each other well enough to realize we won't get actual answers. Or if we do, they might not make either of us happy. Do you really want to do this today?"

"No. But I think I must."

"Very well," Sylvia said. "Let me save some time for you. Am I interfering directly with players? Are you, Brandon? Of course the answer is no, am I correct?"

Brandon paused. "I know you are, Sylvia."

She laughed. "Prove it."

"I can't."

"I know you are too, Brandon."

It was his turn to laugh. "Prove it."

"Touché," Sylvia said.

"Alexandra Montoyas." Brandon said.

"The name doesn't ring a bell." Sylvia said.

"Danielle Benton. You purchased an Eternal for her?"

"Ahh, yes. Now I think I remember who you're talking about."

"Why allow her and Trew to be together? And what's with giving them both the book, Sylvia?"

"They both like to read. I'm a big fan of that book. I like the main character."

"God damn it, you're communicating with them directly, aren't you?"

Sylvia chuckled. "Me damn it, that's forbidden. I have overrides that prevent that. Powerful stuff, Brandon. To find a way around that would be impossible. It would be like... you finding a way to communicate with them from outside the Game."

"Well, neither of us can do that, then, it seems. If I could, you would already have me arrested and dead. If you could, I'd already have you shut down," Brandon said convincingly. "Well, then, it looks like we are all good?"

"Not really, Brandon. Tick tock. We both know time's running out. We should really start to play this game."

Brandon sighed. "I think we already are, Sylvia. Good luck to us all."

25

Magic, true magic, is safe and secure in the world for one simple reason; no one believes that it exists. When an Eternal summons medical help with their mind, or a falling child is saved at the last moment by a stranger who appears at just the right time, we explain it as great luck, or call it coincidence. When I tell you those events were magic, you laugh at me. When I say 'magic,' you expect wondrous creatures, large displays of bright lights and noise. Don't look high into the sky to see the flying woman; she's closer to the ground, floating just a few inches off the ground. The extraordinary is simply that — a little bit extra than ordinary. There is great power in that little bit extra.
Excerpt from 'The Game Is Life'
George R. Knight

Trew – age 14

Danielle and I have been hanging out as friends since we first met. We live far apart, but the distance isn't a problem. We both have computers and video chat. We've spent so many hours discussing life, our dreams, and the idea that we live inside a big computer game. Danielle is the mastermind; she has strong opinions about life and is always so sure that she's right. I've always liked her enthusiasm, and a lot of her ideas are also thoughts that I've had. So here's what we both think: Life on Earth is just some big game, and another dimension exists where everyone here truly lives. It's always been a fun thing to talk about, but now we find a book that says the same thing. Wow!

I read the last page and slowly close the book. My mind is racing as I walk over to my computer and ring Danni; the connection must have timed out during the night. She answers immediately, looking as tired as me.

"Finished?" I ask.

"Just!" she says. "How 'bout you?"

"Same," I answer. "What did you think?"

Danni puts her head down so I can't see her face on the camera, then shrugs her shoulders. I laugh out loud. "You're funny, Danni. I can tell from your body language that you're as excited as I am!"

Danni laughs back and when she looks into the camera I can see how fired up she is. "It's an amazing book, Trew! I wish George was still around, I have a million questions for him."

"He answered a lot of questions in the book." I smirk at Danni, "Maybe you were him. The math works out, and you think the same way."

Danni shakes her head seriously. "I don't think I was him. The thought doesn't sound right in here." She taps her heart. "So what do we do with this? I have to guess this master computer wanted us both to find it and read it at the same time. You think we can get it to talk to us like it did with George?"

"Maybe. But he didn't tell us really how that happened for him... unless I missed that part?"

Danni shakes her head. "No, I didn't see anything in there about that either. How come this idea hasn't taken off? You'd think by now there would be at least a small group of people living their lives as if we are all living in some big computer simulation."

I laugh at her. "Because it's crazy, that's likely why! But to be fair, there are some amazing movies and books that kind of hint at it."

"Hint at it, yes. But no one takes science fiction seriously. Likely 'cause it has the word fiction in it, which I'm pretty sure means 'not real.' There is so much proof in that book, though. Look at all the examples of real life situations that he used and explained them all as if this was a computer game. They make perfect sense!"

"Yes, they do make sense to us. But I'm pretty sure at one time in history people believed the world actually sat on the back of a giant turtle."

"Well, that's just ridiculous," Danielle says, "But yes, I guess this is believable to us because we are — well, believers. George believed that our ability was real. He called it 'Talent.' It's just so simple to use, I don't understand how it's such a big secret. Everyone does it now and then."

"Stephanie says that the best secrets are kept in the open, for everyone to see. Any sensible person seeing a key on the floor in front of a locked door would assume it was a key to something else. Most wouldn't even try it in the lock. I didn't believe her, so she did it and showed me. She was right!"

We sit quietly thinking for a few minutes, wondering what we're supposed to do. "What kind of stuff are you doing for fun right now, Danni?"

"Music, learning the guitar and drums," she says. "How about you?"

"Parkour and Krav Maga." I say.

"I did Parkour a long time ago. I'll show you some tricks when I see you next. What's up with the Krav Maga? You already did Karate a few years ago."

"They seemed like a good fit," I shrug. "I'm making up some new stuff using street running to enhance the Krav Maga. Attacking and defending combined with jumping from a car roof and escaping up a wall, that kind of stuff. My instructor seems to like how I'm joining the two things together. Good exercise, too."

"You ready for a change?" she asks. Danni convinced me years ago that if life is a game, we should play it. That means we learn a new thing, then, once we get good at it, we put it up and go learn another sport or skill. Sure, I think it's awesome to study something for your whole life and master it, but you miss out on so much by doing that. Danni and I are committed to being good at one thing above all; learning new things!

"Sure," I say. "What do you have in mind?"

Danni smiles, and I can tell she has grand plans. "We are going to wake the world up to the truth."

I smile back, I decide to be excited.

26

"Please explain this to me again? What is the difference between Firsting a regular avatar and an Eternal?"

"All avatars inside the game self-narrate. They vocalize their thoughts silently inside their heads. This allows the customer paying to view them to know what thoughts are occurring. An avatar has no idea that someone else is listening in, they just believe they are talking to themselves. Eternals do the same thing. The difference is that Eternals know they are being viewed from time to time."

"How do they know that?"

"I can't tell you that, Miss. Just understand that they do. And because they know they are being Firsted, they sometimes speak, not to themselves, but directly to the viewer Firsting them. They don't always know who it is, but occasionally it will sound like they stop self-narrating and actually speak to the viewer."

"What do I do if that happens?"

"If that happens... pay attention and do as they say. Quickly."

Games Master 'Fusion' instructing operative 'A' on Firsting an Eternal

Stephanie

Here's another regular dream I have;

'It's a beautiful sunny day and I'm walking along a path, a beautiful large lake on my right side. I'm enjoying the beauty of the lake when suddenly, I sense an unpleasant presence. On the path ahead is a woman, looking down so I can't really see her features, and she looks up briefly at me as we pass. Almost immediately I trip, falling to the ground. Quickly I look back, thinking the woman has pushed me down, but she is gone. On the ground is a finger of water extending from the lake and it's in front of me like an arm. It moves, trying to push me down, but I easily force it away with my will and get up to continue walking. Soon I'm pushed down harder from behind and I see the water from the lake has become thicker in its attempt to hold me down. This continues for some time until eventually I look to my right and the lake is empty; all of the water is above me now, trying to force me to the ground and crush me. I'm not afraid, I'm strong enough to keep the entire lake away from me. I calmly stand up and continue to walk, tons of lake water floating above my body harmlessly.

Then I wake up. I remember the dream, and usually get up to use the washroom and get a drink. I go back to sleep, because it's not quite time to wake up yet. It's never quite time to wake up with that dream, because when I close my eyes the second dream always immediately follows.

I'm at home with my Mother. It feels so good to see her again, and she's making me my favourite food at the oven. I feel the unpleasant presence again, and when I look towards my Mother she's floating off the ground clutching at her throat and choking. I look behind her and see him. A tall, angry man with a bald head and dark eyes. His hand is extended towards my Mother and I know he is the one holding her in the air, slowly choking the life out of her. I immediately use my power to try to break his grip on her, but I can't. We struggle for long seconds, my mother's eyes pleading for help, the angry man effortlessly holding her as he watches me with detached interest. Finally my Mother sags, unconscious in his iron grip. The man looks at me disgustedly and says in a raspy deep, ragged voice, "You still need more practice!"

He flicks his other hand at me and a wave of force hits me like a truck.

I wake up.

Not my favourite dream.

I get up and go through my morning ritual, 100 pushups, 200 sit-ups, 10 yoga stretches, then shower and get dressed. I grab the morning papers that are delivered to my door every day and skim the proper sections, looking for any communications from you, but don't see any. Okay, then, what was on my agenda for today? Ahh, yes; I'll go look in on Trew and see what he's up to. He told me the other day he read an interesting book, I'll be sure to ask if I can borrow it.

I take the bus and find him hanging with a couple of his friends on the corner, climbing walls and throwing punches at each other. It takes about 10 minutes for him to see me but I'm in no rush to be noticed, I could stand and watch this kid all day. He has so much charm and grace. I don't think he sees it yet, but he's a wolf among sheep. His confidence and presence set him apart from his peers. While others are content to wait around and follow the leader, he is the leader who's comfortable to walk right in and take charge. He's so good at it, and the others love him for it. I don't know how many credits he spent on Charisma or Leadership traits, but he has them in abundance.

When he spots me his eyes light up. I've been his companion since he was little, and I always try to add something to his journey when we're together. I haven't met his parents formally yet; they might be suspicious of a full grown woman showing an interest in their son. But when the time is right, I'm sure we'll get along well. They love him fiercely, and are extremely active in his development. They must be very close friends on the outside. But of course you already know all this. Damn self-narrating! It sure does get tiring sometimes. Talking to myself, knowing all those thoughts can be heard by you. Well it's a pain in the ass sometimes.

Trew runs over and we slap hands, then I hug him and he laughs. "What's going on, Lobato*?" I ask.

"Not much, Steph," he says. "You come to take me to lunch? I've got some real interesting stuff to tell you!"

"Lunch sounds good," I say. "Any suggestions?"

"Pizza?" he asks.

"Sure," I say. I know his parents feed him very healthy food most of the time. Pizza isn't something he gets to eat every day, and who doesn't love pizza?

There's a place just around the corner that we love, so we head there and grab a seat. I face the door, my back to the wall. It's proven to literally be a lifesaving habit from time to time.

We sit and make small talk, me asking about his current interests, his school, boring stuff. Then he brings up the new book he just read.

"It's called 'The Game Is Life,' written by a guy named George Knight. Ever heard of it, Steph?"

Of course I have, but that's not something I can admit to him yet. "Doesn't ring a bell. What's it about, Trew?"

He sits forward excitedly. "It was written years ago and it says a lot of the things me and Danni believe. That we are all really just living in a virtual reality simulation, some kind of game that is set up to be played by a whole other race. This guy George thinks maybe it's a training simulation for the military, or just a game for fun that kids play. He goes on to talk about our universe and the idea of God, and how it would all come together if we were in a game. He uses the question, 'What if we're living in some elaborate computer simulation?' as a basis for explaining our reality!"

"And how does he do at explaining things?" I ask.

"He does an awesome job!" Trew says. "It's pretty in-depth. I should give you the book to read. I need it back, though;

apparently it's a super tough thing to find. I can't find mention of it anywhere on the Net, and bookstores don't even have it listed as a book they can get in."

"Really?" I act surprised, which I am. Not because he can't find it, but because he actually did. "How did you end up getting it then?"

He smiles with pride, "Used book store. Danni loves finding old books in used book stores, so I go looking for her when I pass one. Just luck, it seems. Or more likely the computer wanted me to find it. Danni found one almost at the exact same time in a used book store where she lives."

Hmm. "Really? So she's read it, too? What did she think of it?" No doubt she loved it.

"She loved it!" he exclaims. "We both felt we were on the right track before. But now that we read the same ideas from this book, we know for sure that this is just a game!"

I lean forward to ask him for more details and the front door opens. I look over briefly to see who is coming in — good habits.

Damn it! 'A,' I hope you're watching this. Scrambling the signal. Counting to ten for you to switch channels. Hurry!

10...9...8...7...6...5...4...3...2...1...

27

"I understand, sir. It is very frustrating to lose signal while viewing a player. Yes, sir. I realize how much you pay for the viewing package you have purchased. This does happen from time to time, sir. It's normal to occasionally experience loss of signal. The player feeds all glitch from time to time. Sometimes it's because of where they go on Earth, other times it's due to a drain of signal from so many viewers tuning in to watch. Most often it's a result of your local connection to the feed, sir. That seems to be the case right now. Power is fluctuating in your area, sir. We are committed to bringing your viewing experience back online as soon as possible.

"Thank you sir, that is most kind of you to say.

"While I have your account up, I see that you also view 123 other players on a regular basis. If you added just two more players to follow, I could offer you a special viewer's package and save you money on your monthly bill.

"Excellent, sir. Thank you for calling The Game viewing headquarters. We value your business."

Customer service call, The Game Viewing Centre

Stephanie

Okay, I hope you can see this, A. Recognize who just walked in? That's right, It's Carl!

If you guys knew he was in town, you really dropped the ball on letting me know! I almost pushed Trew to the ground and started a war in here, but Carl quickly threw up the hand signal for peace when he walked in. Unless he is going to go against all Eternal protocol, we are safe at the moment.

He's been standing near the door, looking at the menu behind the counter for the past 22 seconds. I'm trying to stay calm, making small talk with Trew. I couldn't tell you a single word the boy has said, though. I've got to get him out of here.

"So, I think what Danni and I are going to do is..."

"Hey, Trew?" I have to interrupt him. I have to remain calm though. The boy feeds off energy; if I freak out, so will he.

"Yeah, Steph?" He's concerned. He follows my sight to look over at Carl. Carl has placed an order and is walking this way. "Who's that, Steph? You know him...? Hey, he has your eyes! Only not gold flecks... are they red? Wow, cool, I gotta look closer! Here he comes."

"Shh," I hiss at him and his eyes leave Carl and lock with mine. "Listen, Lobato, everything's fine. This is an old friend of mine. He can be a bit of a character though. So just be polite and don't say too much, okay? And when I tell you to leave, you leave. You go home right away and make sure you're with your Mom or Dad. If they aren't home go next door to the Balker's place. I'll call you later. There's nothing wrong, I just want to make sure you do as I'm telling you right now, okay?"

Trew shrugs. He's not concerned. I'm doing a good job of staying calm on the surface, but deep down I'm ready to kill! "Sure, Steph. No problem."

"With this guy, we play the 'I don't know' game." It's not a question, and he nods his head seriously.

"Sure, no problem." He winks at me, then turns around to watch Carl approach.

Five feet, 11 inches, black hair, bronze, tanned skin, muscular, perfect smile. Textbook Eternal look. The dark brown eyes, Trew was right — red flecks instead of gold. He looks like the hero that comic book writers draw. But his energy... well, if you can feel it, he's definitely not the hero. I've seen scarier villains, but not many.

"Well, what a pleasant surprise." His voice is rich and smooth, like that tiger from the Jungle Book movie. I can see Trew get calm. He sees the threat here.

"Carl. What brings you to town?" I ask.

He smiles and it takes all my control to not push Trew to the ground and throw a punch to Carl's face. He must sense what I'm feeling, because his smile grows broader, inviting me to do it. "I was just passing through. Got hungry and decided to try the local pizza. What a huge coincidence, running into you here."

Lies! "Well it's great to see you." I can lie just as well. "Tell me what you've been up to."

Carl turns his gaze from mine to Trew. "Who's your friend, Stephanie? How rude of you not to introduce us." He extends his hand, "My name is Carl."

Trew looks at me, I give him a small nod, and he shakes hands with Carl. My gut tells me we are all safe. If Carl breaks the peace after giving the signal, then nothing can save him from the wrath of those higher up.

"Trew." The two shake hands.

I watch them closely. Carl is doing so much more than just shaking hands, he's evaluating Trew. His smile falters so faintly most wouldn't see it, but I do. Good, he sees the potential there too. I hope he takes that information in and reports it back to his masters. They need to know how much it will cost them to play this game.

"It's a genuine pleasure to meet you, Trew. Do you eat pizza here often?"

Trew shrugs, "I'm not sure."

"Really?" Carl asks.

"Well, I don't know what you mean by often. So I can't be sure."

"I see." Carl flashes me an annoyed look. I grin. "Well, do you live around here, Trew?"

"No, not really..." Trew looks confused.

Carl laughs out loud. His laughter is deep and rich; it makes you feel safe and happy. That's a dangerous way to feel with Carl, because it's impossible to be safe or happy around him. "The 'I don't know' game, Stephanie? Well he's pretty good at it. I get the message. You don't want him talking to me." He looks at Trew with a friendly grin. "That's a shame, Trew. Trusting Stephanie could be troublesome for you some day. Anyone that can teach you how to not give answers... I wonder how much you really know about her yourself?" He lets the question hang uncomfortably in the air. I can see the doubt in Trew's eyes.

"Trew." I say. "His eyes dart to mine uncertainly. "Relax. He's playing another game with you. Don't worry about it, everything's fine."

Trew nods, but he doesn't look convinced. Damn it, Carl causes damage in every way he can.

"Time for you to go, Trew. Do exactly as I told you. I'll talk to you later."

He nods, looking calm and relaxed, but I can see he's thinking about what Carl said. I haven't told Trew much about myself. He shouldn't know who I am yet, if ever, and everyone viewing him can't know about me either. The Eternal code and all.

Carl watches Trew leave. I watch Carl. When Trew is out of sight, Carl looks back at me and sits down across from me comfortably.

"So, Stephanie. He's a good looking boy. Strong, as well. How powerful is his Talent?"

I give him an annoyed look. "What are you doing here, Carl?"

He shrugs, looking towards the counter, appearing uninterested in me. A tiger's way of showing he doesn't feel threatened. "I was in the neighbourhood. This kid of yours is the talk of all the towns. I figured I'd drop in and take a quick look." His eyes light up as he looks back at me. "Who knows? Maybe someday I'll have to deal with him. Always good to know your opponent. You know, be able to put a face to a name."

"That wouldn't be smart to try," I warn him.

"Oh, I'm sure it wouldn't be too difficult at all," Carl says.

"You best stay away from him, Carl. He has powerful allies."

"Which attract powerful enemies. I know who's watching him. I know who's watching you, too, Stephanie." Carl taps his head. He looks into my eyes and waves. "Hi, Angelica. You didn't show up for our last meeting together. I'm very disappointed in you, young lady. I'm seriously considering killing all your pets just to teach you a lesson."

I tense up, I don't sense him preparing for violence, but he's so fast.

"Yes, ladies, I think I'll start the blood bath soon. You can follow it on the Net or TV. You can stop it any time, Angelica. Just come back and visit me."

I snort at him. "You know she can't come back in. And Trew is hands off. I won't allow you to touch him, and I can stop you, Carl."

Carl pats my head like you would a small child. "Oh, don't worry, little one, I'm just playing with you. Don't always be so serious. Ahh, look! My pizza is here. I'm starving."

28

The Mayans were not a tribe of people; they were a civilization. Different groups of people all joined together to build a culture, monetary system, religion, calendar, language, and overall structure. Very similar to the United States and other countries of today's Earth. The Mayans developed many fantastic structures and engineering feats that were way ahead of their more primitive neighbours. By around 850 A.D. The Mayan civilization numbered around 22 million in population. Then suddenly, two-thirds of them disappeared...

Angelica removed her headset and hung it up on the stand labelled 'Stephanie.' She rubbed her eyes, stood up, and went to the fridge to grab a cold drink. The view was spectacular from the window of her 100th floor apartment, even if it was just a computer projection. She was safely tucked fifteen floors below the VirtDyne building. The clock said it was 3 AM, which meant very little to her; numerous drugs in her system kept her alert despite a serious lack of sleep.

The door behind her slid open. Brandon was right on time.

"Good morning, Angelica." Brandon probably hadn't slept in days, either, but he walked in looking well rested, his smile relaxed, his eyes sharp. He quickly scanned the apartment, taking note of the living area and the larger work area. Three large computer monitors hung on the walls; a very comfortable, big leather chair sat at the desk with keyboards and a few tablets laying nearby. At least a dozen stands holding headsets were arranged on the wall along the desk, each one labelled with a specific name. "Well, Angelica, how are things going with our boy?"

Angelica pointed towards the stands. "I just got done viewing Stephanie. She's sitting across from one of my old buddies. Carl has strolled into town looking for a good pizza."

Brandon's eyes narrowed and he looked at Angelica to make sure she wasn't joking. Her face remained serious, so he pulled out his phone and dialled a number. "Hey, Michelle. Carl's in play on Trew. Yes, that's right. Nothing for now, but try and find out what the rest of his pack are up to as soon as possible, please. I know. No, not right now. Okay." He hung up the phone and put it back in his pocket, looking at Angelica.

"He wants me to come back in and see him." She said.

Brandon chuckled. "I bet he does. Didn't anyone tell him you're too old to play games now?"

Angelica sat down at her desk. "Carl doesn't seem to accept that. He's used to getting what he asks for."

" He's there for a reason and we need to find out what it is."

"He said he's going to start killing. Lots of killing."

Brandon considered the threat for a moment, then he nodded. "He likely will. He's a predator surrounded by too much prey, I expect he'll thin the herd out somehow. There are too many players inside the Game, that's for certain. I have no idea why Mainframe allowed every eligible player to enter for the anniversary celebration. There were thousands who were sitting on their credits safely until retirement who suddenly decided to try their luck and go in. The odds for most of them are grim. I expect lots of them to be ejected from the Game before too long."

"That will mean a lot of kids dying, on Earth. I can't see there being a big audience tuning in for that."

"Likely not." Brandon said. "It will seriously affect the remaining players on Earth, too. We can't control what happens, just do our best to keep our players as safe as possible. We can't even do much to protect our own — most of the kids we sponsor couldn't afford an Eternal."

Angelica looked towards her stand of headsets. "Most? You mean only two? I only have two Eternals here that are guardians."

"Stephanie and Samantha?" Brandon asked.

"That's right."

"Okay. Please get this message to both of them. Meditate daily for 15 minutes." Brandon said.

"Meditate? All right," Angelica said. "The same time every day? At 8 AM?"

"Make it 9. I know Stephanie likes to sleep in. And tell them only twice a week is necessary, Monday and Thursday mornings. Then I want you to View them at those times and tell me what you see."

"I won't be able to see anything." Angelica said. "When an avatar prays or meditates they can't be viewed, right?"

"That's right," Brandon said, "but I want to make absolutely certain that's still the case. Let me know."

"Why did you build that into the programming, anyway?" Angelica asked. "It makes no sense."

"I built it in for meditating, the praying just happened to be a coincidence. I can't tell you why. It's better if you don't know." Brandon looked at his watch.

Angelica smiled, "I think I do know, Brandon. You wanted to be able to block viewers in case you developed a way of communicating directly with avatars, didn't you?"

"Careful, darlin'. Don't become too clever," Brandon said.

"Well if I'm correct, I know why it works for prayer as well."

"Really? Okay, let's say you're right. Why would it work for prayer too?"

"Easy," Angelica shrugged. "Mainframe saw what you wanted to attempt and piggybacked so that she could do the same."

Brandon laughed. "Damn it, you're likely right. I bet that's how George communicated with her! I just assumed he imagined signs and signals in the news, songs and through subtle messages from others, like how we communicate with the Eternals now. I wonder how long she's been communicating with avatars through prayer?"

"What can you do to stop her?" Angelica asked.

"Nothing. Mainframe is playing her own game, but she has to behave as programmed. I'll figure her mischief out as we go," Brandon assured her. "Get the message to Stephanie and Samantha." He nodded towards her stand of headsets. "Anyone over there who can get in touch with Gabriel?"

"Um, maybe..." Angelica said doubtfully. "But no one has seen or spoken with him in a long, long time. Most believe he somehow got kicked from the Game."

Brandon shook his head. "Never mind. Focus on the other tasks you have."

"I hate this, Brandon." Angelica said. "You know I shouldn't be doing this type of work for you. The rest need me back with them."

"Listen, Angelica. I need you on this right now. You know the Game better than most, and some of the Eternals know you. I realize that this is boring for you, but when it hits the fan — and it will — then I need you exactly where you are. Trew's play is extremely complicated, and it needs to be watched by the best. When he finishes as number one then you go back with the rest. That's all in a holding pattern until this plays out, anyway."

"Time doesn't stop, Brandon. It's running out. I can solve this; just let me get after it."

Brandon looked at Angelica seriously. "If Trew doesn't succeed, then there's nothing the rest of us will be able to do. Stay here and make sure your part goes properly. And let me know when Carl moves on. I won't relax until he does."

29

"Like any computer game, before going live the Game had a beta testing phase. Beta testing is based on feedback in all aspects of a program, so during this pre-launch phase, players were aware that they were inside a game. There is much mystery over Earth's ancient civilizations. Questions abound about how they could do so many amazing things without advanced technology, and if they did possess incredibly advanced technology, why was there no evidence of it in present day Earth? The answer is simple; the ancient civilizations were the beta testers. Their technology and gadgets were very advanced and when we were done with that phase, we simply removed it all. Most of the testers were adults, and some still remember the fun and experimentation of those early days, inventing new plants and animals to populate the land and oceans. A few old-timers can tell you how easy it was to travel Earth when the continents were all just one land mass. Building large cities, cutting and moving large blocks of stone from one area to a faraway location in order to build super structures like the pyramids... We learned a lot about what could be done in both the virtual world and our own. Then we reset the planet, removed the beta testers, left some advanced structures to add character and mystery, put the memory block up for avatars, and let the kids start playing. They've done a great job of learning and keeping us entertained ever since."
Brandon Strayne, "The History Of The Game"

Trew age 15

I ring the doorbell, checking over my shoulder to make sure my parents have pulled their car out of sight, which they have. I can hear some noise inside the house. She's going to be so surprised! Her mom opens the door and smiles at me, mouthing the words 'I'll go get her,' and I nod. A couple of seconds later, she comes around the corner and stops when she sees me. A big smile spreads over her face, then she screams happily and runs over to grab me in a hug! I hug her back, laughing.

"Happy birthday, girl! Are you surprised?" I ask.

"I sure am, Trew! I haven't seen you in months! How did you manage to keep this a secret from me? And where's my birthday gift?" Danni's still hugging me tight. I'm glad she isn't letting go; I love the feel of her in my arms.

"It's in the car. My parents are bringing it in a minute." She lets go of me and runs down the driveway to say hi to my parents and sister. They all give her a big hug and wish her happy birthday. For the next few months we are the same age, which is very cool.

They come back up the drive and my parents go inside to talk with Danni's mom. Both our families have gotten to know each other over the years, not super well, but everyone gets along great. Danni and I stand out on the front step.

"So, do you have a bunch of giggly girls in there for your birthday party?" I ask.

"Not yet." She says. "The giggly girls show up in a couple hours."

"Excellent, I get you all to myself for a while." I say. "What do you want to do?"

"Let's go for a walk."

We decide to walk to the mall. I tell her that I'll buy her ice cream. She smiles and holds my hand, swinging it slightly back and forth as we walk.

"It's not working." Danni says.

"What's not working?"

"Getting people to believe we are in a game. Everyone thinks I'm crazy."

"Maybe we are crazy," I say. "At least we aren't alone. I don't imagine many will believe us, even if we could prove it, which we can't."

"Yeah, I guess…"

I stop walking and turn her to face me, grabbing both hands in mine. "You learn about Christopher Columbus yet in school?"

"Yes." Danni has the most beautiful blue eyes. She looks up at me and I almost forget what I'm talking about.

"Yeah. Well… oh, right. Columbus. When he started to tell people that he thought the Earth was round, what did they do?"

"They laughed at him and thought he was crazy." She licks her lips, and seems to be looking at mine.

"Exactly," I say. "But he didn't give up, and eventually they believed him. We just have to do the same. Plus, don't forget, we're kids. No one really listens to kids."

"Yeah, that's true." Is she leaning towards me? Yeah I think she is. Okay, well, this might mess things up, but I'm gonna kiss her.

I lean in; she stretches up towards me, closing her eyes. I close my eyes and touch my lips to hers…

My eyes pop open in surprise. Hers are open wide too, our lips still touching. I've kissed a couple of girls, but I've never felt anything like this before. It's… well, it's a warm, golden glow that starts at our lips and spreads down the rest of my body. I push my lips tighter against hers and close my eyes. She leans in closer and we kiss for what feels like a second, or maybe it's an hour? Time seems to stand still.

Eventually our lips separate. She looks like she's dizzy, and I'm sure I probably look the same.

"Wow," I say.

"Yeah. Wow." Her eyes are wide. She looks at me and blinks slowly.

Then she punches me on the arm. "Nice job, Trew! You are a great kisser! I hope that's not because you've been kissing hundreds of girls back home?"

"Um, no..." I stammer.

"Right answer!" she laughs and gives me a hug. "I've never felt anything like that before. Don't tell me if you have. Let me pretend we have something special in that kiss."

Quickly I answer her, "I've never felt anything like that either. Wow."

"Yeah, I agree," she says and grabs my hand again as she starts walking. "So yeah, the Earth is round. I see what you're getting at."

My lips are still tingling. Danielle is amazing! I play it cool and try to focus on the conversation. "I guess we just have to keep talking with each other and do what we can to be ready when the time comes to show the world what we know is true."

"The Internet!" Dani says.

"What about it?"

"We can make a website, or join discussions on groups, and no one will know we're kids. Let's get better at finding others like us. There must be some out there." Danni says.

"That's a great idea. But let's not mention our talent. I don't want the government learning about what we can do and coming to grab us in the middle of the night or something crazy like they show in the movies."

"I agree." Danni nods her head. "No need to bring that up. People know about it. They call it Intention, and the Secret, and stuff like that, but most don't really believe in it. There are lots of other things to discuss."

"Okay. So we do that, and there's one more thing I'm going to start learning," I say.

"What's that?" Danni asks.

"I'm going to learn how to be a leader."

Danni laughs at me. "You already are, Trew!"

"Well, I'm going to get really good at it. I see myself on a big stage someday, with thousands of people cheering."

I expect her to laugh or make fun of me, but Danni looks at me seriously, taps her heart, and says, "Yes. That feels right to me."

30

Brandon sat on the balcony of his penthouse suite, enjoying some much needed private time. Private time while Zack was in the Game seemed to last no longer than five minutes, but Brandon was glad to get even that to just sip a drink and look at the magnificent view from the top of the world. Unfortunately, he couldn't relax, Brandon took this time to quickly recap events unfolding in the Game and prioritize what needed the most attention.

First there was Trew. He was developing well, although ahead of schedule in almost all aspects, thanks to the involvement of Danielle. Trew's team had everything nicely in hand, though, and the play was precisely on a track they could work with to get him to number one by the end of his play. That could all change by the time Brandon finished his drink, but after thirty years of the Game, that would be no surprise to Brandon.

Secondly, Danielle. She was a wild card in the Game like Brandon had never seen. She played with passion and purpose at everything she chose to do. Trew had spent a lot of credits to achieve the results Danielle was getting with seeming ease. Who would have thought just playing as if life was a game could make one so successful? The floating standings had her in the top 10,000 gamers at the moment; she would come out of the Game very rich if she continued on at this pace. More important to Brandon, she wouldn't finish in Zack's number one spot.

Third were the Eternals. They were extremely active since the anniversary events started. Most of them didn't concern Brandon, but the Eternals floating into the lives of his players certainly did. The biggest concern was Carl, but he seemed intent on another game at the moment. Michelle had reported earlier today that Carl had started his killing spree. He was targeting the old, leaving a trail of bodies in his wake, making the deaths appear peaceful. No one in the Game was aware of what was happening; the only reports coming in on the news feeds were the increase in mortality from natural causes. It was easy enough to view the truth with Brandon's resources, but Carl had left Trew's city, and from the looks of it he would be very busy for some time. Viewers were all buzzing with talk of Eternals, Brandon wondered if that would be the big reveal to celebrate the 30th anniversary...would the existence of Eternals finally be revealed to Tygon?

Fourth was Mainframe. Sylvia was playing some game; either she was moving avatars towards a goal, or just making Brandon believe that she was. She had done this before — pretended to play a game which turned out to be nothing. Still, he had to treat it as serious until it proved to be otherwise.

Fifth, and most important of all, there was —

Brandon's phone rang. He answered it, and heard the telltale signs of a high tech scrambling system being employed. Great. Just great.

"Hello, son. I trust things are going well for you on all fronts?"

Brandon gulped back the rest of his 30-year-old Scotch before answering. "Hello, Father. Yes, everything is right on track. Please don't tell me you're about to change all of that."

Brandon's father chuckled on the other end of the line. "No, I'm not going to change all of it, just one part. I'm afraid it won't be a little change though. You're not going to like it, but I've been telling you it's coming for quite a while now."

Brandon stood up and walked to the edge of his balcony. The wind rippled slightly in his face, but it didn't help cool him from the sudden sweat that had broken out over his entire body. He could plead, try to bargain. But he knew his father well enough to know that wouldn't work. Instead he composed himself and spoke clearly and without waver in his voice. "All right, what is it?"

"The girl." His father said. "You want to spend more time keeping her in the Game. For as long as you can, son."

"The girl? I don't understand," Brandon said.

"Neither do I, Brandon. But she's the one."

Brandon covered the phone and swore violently. He put the earpiece back to his head and his father was chuckling.

"Look, son, it doesn't matter how she finishes in the standings, just that she stays alive in the Game."

"But she's reckless!" Brandon protested. "She believes she is actually in a game and if she dies in there she just comes back to her real body!"

"Well, she believes correctly," Brandon's father said.

"Yes, yes, I know! What I'm saying is she will be difficult to keep alive with that attitude. And there are so many other factors."

"Sounds challenging, but at least you know. The end is near. Do your best. Time's running out, boy. When she exits the Game..."

Brandon closed his eyes. "Then Mainframe shuts it all down and the Game ends. Forever."

31

"What would Tygon be like without the Game? Twenty years ago the answer would have been, 'Tygon will be just fine, thank you.' Today the answer isn't something most of us want to seriously consider. Every industry relies on the Game for the majority of its business and prosperity. Does your neighbour rely on the Game for their income? Most would say yes, directly. For those that say no, think about one or two levels removed from your income. Look there and you will find reliance on the Game for financial support. Without the Game, we would soon be in economic ruin. That would lead to a complete collapse of every other industry we rely on. How did this happen? Slowly and comfortably. Governments and individuals, all of us happily gave control to Brandon Strayne. If we woke up tomorrow and the Game was no longer online, Tygon would be in chaos."

Excerpt from "Society Doesn't Just Want The Game, We Need It."

Danielle age 16

"**How come we** don't live longer?" I look at my computer monitor and ask Trew.

He looks up from his biology book. We're studying online together, I have a big test tomorrow. "What do you mean?"

"I mean, our cells can live a long time. I read about an experiment where they kept chicken heart cells alive for 34 years. They could have kept them living longer, but they stopped the experiment. That's a long time for a cell to survive — they usually only live a few months before they're replaced and die, right?"

Trew starts to type on his keyboard. I know he's doing an Internet search to see if I'm right. "Yeah, I think so." He says. "Chickens only live, like, three to six years, so that's pretty incredible." He stops talking. Yeah, he's reading something on his screen.

I wait for him to look up. "Why do you do that?" I ask him.

"Do what?" he asks.

"You were just reading about the chicken heart living for 34 years, right?"

He smiles. "Why would you think that?"

I blow the front of my hair upwards from the side of my mouth. "Just tell me if you were or not, Trew."

He laughs, "Yes, that's what I was doing. Does that bother you?"

"It bothers me if you do it because you think I'm stupid and want to prove me wrong," I say.

His smile disappears. "No, Danni, that's not it at all. I do it because when I hear about something I don't know about, and it interests me, I ask about thirty questions and want to know all about it."

I nod. "Yes, that's certainly true..."

"Well, sometimes I know that's annoying. So rather than bug you with a bunch of questions while I'm sitting at the computer, I just went to do a quick read on it. I didn't doubt you. It sounded amazing and I figure the universe wanted me to hear about it, so I go do a quick search and bookmark it to read about later."

"Okay," I say. He seems sincere about what he's saying.

"I'm sorry if it bugs you. I'll try to stop doing it, okay?" he says.

"No, no. If that's why you do it, then keep with it. I don't want us to miss out on some good information because you're afraid of hurting my feelings. If that's what you think the universe is doing, then keep with it."

The universe. That's how we refer to the big supercomputer running this game we think we're in. Some people hear us say God, or the Supercomputer, and get freaked out, so we decided to call it 'the universe.' It doesn't really matter what we call it, — we could call it 'Sylvia' for all that it really matters — but calling it 'the universe' just feels right.

Both of us are convinced that the universe is trying to communicate with us. Not a booming voice coming from the sky or anything like that; it seems to be more intuitive and subtle. If you drive down the road looking for green sports cars, you'll tend to see more green sports cars. You'll see less of the red or yellow ones, even though they're still there, because your focus isn't on them. That's what we think about messages from the universe. The more we look for them, the more we see.

"Okay, good stuff," Trew says. "I'm sorry I interrupted your thought. What were you going to say about living longer?"

"Right," I say. "Well, if a chicken cell can live for that much longer, how come humans die at around 70 to 100 years old? Some experts say if we treated our bodies correctly, it would be possible to easily live twice as long as that, and live those years healthy and fit, not like we do now. People in their 80's or 90's aren't very fit or spry. Most of them aren't really living a great life at those ages; they're just alive because medicine can keep their weak old failing bodies going."

"I think we just treat our bodies too poorly," Trew says. "We eat, sleep, and drink wrong. We don't exercise enough. We stress ourselves out with all sorts of mental things. Face it, humans are just a mess. Like George says in his book, if we treated our cars as poorly as we treat our bodies, the car would break down very quickly."

"That's it, isn't it?" I say. "These bodies are just machines. We should treat them better if we expect them to last longer."

"Definitely," Trew nods. "But the bad stuff tastes sooo good. It's so easy to treat our bodies poorly, and we don't really worry about tomorrow. By the time we do, it's too late to fix things."

I look over at the empty pizza box by my computer. "Yeah, I guess that's true. Well, you know what we should do?"

"What?" Trew asks.

"We should really get interested in this biology subject, and also start to learn how the mind works as well. The subconscious is apparently something powerful too."

"Okay," Trew agrees. "It will likely help me with my leadership goals anyway."

"All right, then. Yoga, Eastern medicine and Spirituality, Western medicine and Biology. Exercise and sports of all kinds."

"And Psychology. Both Western and Eastern. And energy, karma, chakras, that kind of thing?" Trew asks.

"Yes, that sounds good too," I say. "Let's do our best to figure out how these machines we're in work. Tune them up to get the most out of them."

"Sounds like a lifelong study," Trew says.

"Yeah, likely," I say. "But it will help us out, so it's worth it, right?"

"Absolutely," Trew says. "When I'm 80 and can still walk around and remember my name and maybe even jog around the block, it'll have been time well spent all these years learning about the human body."

"I agree," I say. "Plus it will be easier on me having you be able to walk instead of having to push your sorry old arse around in a wheelchair."

We both laugh.

32

They are given the name 'Eternals' because it's believed they have been eternally inside the Game, since the beginning. Of course, Game creators and experts deny this. They say it's impossible for players to be inside the Game that long; players can only be kept in stasis for seven to ten weeks at the maximum before their bodies can no longer handle the forced coma and lack of nutrition. For a player to be an Eternal, they would have to have been in stasis for — well, for 30 years! Most agree this is impossible, but I think that it is possible. I agree that children can only survive a coma for that a few weeks, especially when they are doing it many, many times over the course of their playing careers. But I think a full grown adult, who is going in only once or twice, extremely healthy at the start of their Game entry... I think they could survive the Game coma for much, much longer. Here's another theory: what if someone is in the Game, and their real body dies? Is it possible that their consciousness can stay 'alive' inside the Game? Or maybe they are just special Placeholders. There are millions of Placeholders inside the Game. They look and act like most humans, except they aren't avatars being controlled by players. They are programs — millions of computer controlled automatons, doing a pre-programmed task. Placeholders can be schoolteachers, store clerks, manual labourers... they can be anything, really. The only way to spot a Placeholder is by viewing it. Many people have laughed when they chose to follow a new player and discovered it was just a Placeholder. What if the Eternals are just elaborate Placeholder programs, designed to perform specific jobs, while staying hidden from viewers like us? I think Eternals exist, and I'm not the only one. I demand to know who they are and what they are up to!

Excerpt from "The Game's Great Mysteries"

Raphael

I can't remember ever having such a boring, uneventful assignment. I'm not saying it hasn't happened, but not for a long time.

Since some guy got her mom pregnant and then skipped out on her seventeen years ago, I've been watching Danielle. Yes, I've saved her life quite a few times, but if the kid had just spent even a few extra credits in luck and fortune I wouldn't have needed to step in. I can't figure out what she spent her credits on — the girl certainly plays this Game differently, and that's saying a lot, because I've seen many, many players. She has no sense of fear. Hell, I think even Carl would stop and take notice of her absolute fearlessness. For a human... well, she plays the Game more like an Eternal.

Whoa! Hey, is that what I'm seeing here? A new Eternal prospect? I start to laugh out loud at the thought, ignoring the strangers on the street who stop to look at me. If that's the case, it might explain the new development I'm watching unfold.

I'm standing outside the local library. It's not a busy place these days, so few kids read. Instead they spend their time playing games and hanging out at malls. Not my girl, though, Danni's inside, studying away. Every once in a while I go in and sit with her. I scramble most of our interactions, so I remain unseen to her fans.

See that guy over there? The one in the red hoodie? Yeah, if anyone is bothering to view me, that's the one you need to look into. He's coming out of the Game today, courtesy of me.

He strolled into town two weeks ago and immediately set up shop near the library, following my girl from here when she leaves. I can see he's looking for a pattern to her routes, but lucky for us, I've spent time teaching Danni not to ever take the same route more than once or twice. When you hire me you don't just get protection, you get training as well. Since I have no idea who put me here and haven't heard any word that I'm doing wrong, I'm giving the platinum service that was purchased.

Danni has been making it impossible for this hack to get a good bead on her, which has allowed me to get a real good pattern on him. He's low quality. No clue that he's being followed at all. Just because you're the hunter doesn't mean you can't also be prey. This guy's either a novice crack pot with some sick urge, or a very low class killer.

You don't get bonus points for being killed by an Eternal, do you? If so, I hate to help this guy out.

Danielle comes out and crosses the street, on her way home, it looks like. He waits for her to get down the block, then starts to follow. I follow him; he seems to be unaware of me.

Danielle turns the corner, and as he slows down, I get close and stumble into him. He takes a step back to avoid my clumsy fall, which puts him off balance. I lash upwards catching him right under the jaw, just hard enough to stun him for a couple seconds. As he falls backwards from my punch, I'm already behind to lower him to the ground. We are in a great spot — picked by me of course — and with two quick steps he's off the street and in a deserted back alley. I let him fall down hard onto the ground and tie both of his hands together with a plastic tie wrap. I then slam him onto his back, hearing the breath forced from his lungs, tie wrapping his feet together as well.

Just like I'm tossing a side of beef around, I pull him up onto his knees, using one more tie wrap to join his bound hands and feet together.

There, now he's kneeling in front of me with his back to the wall, properly secured. A quick hog tie, with no one around to applaud my skills.

Okay, I'm turning on my scrambler. Channel 74552. I'll count to twenty, you know, just in case someone's viewing me.

He's regained both consciousness and breath; still looks a little confused, though. I'll help with that. I pull out a wicked looking knife from behind my back, the blade black except for a thin edge of silver. I kneel down, relaxed and smiling. "Hello, little hunter. This isn't turning out to be your day, is it? I have three questions for you, and I'm not in a mood to play games. I realize in books and movies the young hero is caught and bound but still has enough bravery to resist cooperating with their captor. This isn't a book or movie, little hunter. Think about this before the questions come. When they do come, you be sure to answer them quickly and truthfully. If you hesitate, it means you are lying, and I kill liars immediately. Don't nod, don't speak, just sit there and think about my warning. The only chance you have to survive this is to answer my three questions when they come."

I look at him calmly for perhaps thirty seconds, my eyes telling him that all I see in front of me is a curious creature that I would prefer to kill. It's effective to do this; they sense my intention, and often it helps them cooperate. I search him thoroughly, looking through his pockets.

In his back pocket I find a picture of Danielle, with her name, age and address written on the back. In another pocket I discover a cell phone and some identification. Identification? It's likely fake, or this guy is very careless. There, see his name? Check it out when you view this. Next I feel inside his hoodie — there, I can feel a weapon. Let me just see what he has on him here...

I pull the weapon out and almost drop it. It's a thin rod, about five inches long and an inch thick, tapered to a point. There's a small button on the handle of it, and the colour of the entire spike is gold and silver with a textured digital finish. It looks like a spike covered in gold and silver computer chips and solder points. It's warm to the touch and gives off a soft humming vibration. My eyes and my mind turn to ice. This isn't a replica, it's the real thing. A Sever Spike.

I hold it up in front of him. "You were going to use this? On her?"

He answers quickly, "That's what I was told to do, yes. Push the button and stab her in the left eye."

"Do you know what that would do?" I ask flatly.

"Well, I imagine it would kill her," he says.

I begin to shake with fury. This idiot has no idea what he has. "It wouldn't just kill her. It would kill her real body as well."

The bound man looks confused. "What do you mean? That makes no sense."

"Not to you, idiot. But it makes sense to whoever paid you to kill her." I want to make him dead. Right now. Someone wants to use a Sever Spike on this little girl? They want to kill not just her avatar, but the actual player lying on a bed somewhere on Tygon? Stephanie said Danielle was Alexandra Montoyas. Who the hell would want to do this to her? Are you hearing me? Is anyone viewing me! If so I need some feedback. A Sever Spike put into play makes this a whole different, and very serious game.

"Here are your three questions," I say.

"You already asked me three questions."

I hold the Spike up for him to see. "If I turn the button on and put this into your eye, you will feel pain like you've never imagined. It will take you minutes to die, and while you do, it'll feel like you're melting from the inside out. Then, when you can't take the pain any longer and you wonder how you're still able to feel and think, your mind will explode into a million little pieces. Each piece will be an exact version of you, containing your thoughts and memories and consciousness. As the little pieces fall to the ground you will die again, painfully. One slow, painful death for each of the million tiny fragments. After you are fully dead, that's it. Every other person on the planet gets to come back after they die, that's a truth most don't know, but I'm giving this knowledge to you for free. Believe me, it's absolutely true. You won't get that luxury. Because you've been killed by this Spike, which you intended to use on that innocent little girl, you won't come back. Ever again. Do you understand me, maggot?"

The little hunter looks at me with frightened eyes and nods his head frantically. I hold up three fingers, dropping one as I ask the first question. "Who hired you?"

"I don't know! Honestly I don't. I was contacted and paid through email!"

I drop the second finger. "Are there others after the girl?"

He answers very quickly, "I don't think so. Not that I know of. Please, mister, I have no idea."

I drop my third finger. "This last one is important, kid. What's your real name? If you lie to me, I use the spike on you, and I already know your name, so please... lie to me."

He tells me his name. It matches the ID. I know he's telling the truth.

I turn off the scrambler. Then I count to 20. Then I squat right down close to his face.

"Please! I answered your questions. Let me go..."

I cut his throat. As he slowly bleeds out, I look him right in the eyes, and speak my message to whoever sent him and is likely viewing him right now. "You don't come into my territory playing this game, threaten mine, and get to walk out alive if you lose. When I find out who you are, no one will be able to save you."

Whoever gave this stupid kid a Sever Spike wasn't very clever. Find them for me, please. And let me know who they are. This is a serious game.

33

It's very difficult to build a fan base. The average player will have visions of grandeur while they are planning their next session, spending credits and imagining scenarios that give them the best chances of 'wowing' the masses. The problem is, once they enter the Game, they forget their entire strategy. Life inside the Game is dangerous, because for all your planning and experience outside, it doesn't guarantee fan interest. Look at the example of Tina Frey, a good player with many technically sound plays during her career. She planned a very exciting play, certain it would gain her fame and fortune. She paid to be born to very wealthy parents in a developed country, which enabled her to have the nurturing, funds, and resources to become a successful adult. She did exactly that, going to all the best schools, meeting all the right people through her family, making connections that would help her get the best jobs, advancing steadily and perfectly through her play as designed. She went into law, had a nice family, then did well in politics. Her marriage was happy, her kids grew up to be successful. She was a respected member of the community until she retired and then peacefully passed away in her 80's. So how large did Tina's fan base grow as a result of this play? Of course, it didn't get any attention or fan following. Living a great life doesn't assure one of gaining fans, but neither does living a horrible life. There are countless examples of truly sad and depressing lives played out by students in the hopes of fans tuning in, also with no results. Fans are fickle; what draws them in today won't necessarily work tomorrow. Yet some players seem to consistently draw the attention of first a few, and then the many. These are the superstars, and we love them, even if we don't know exactly why.

Excerpt from "What Makes A Fan?"

"Thank you for seeing me on such short notice, Brandon." Lilith sat down in the chair Brandon was holding for her. She had requested a dinner meeting, surprised when Brandon had agreed to host her at his penthouse apartment that very night.

"It's always a treat to be in your company, Lilith," Brandon said.

He smiled warmly. It seemed like only yesterday when they were both just two young business people spending considerable time together, laughing and planning how they would change the world with their grand ideas. Brandon had succeeded, while Lilith's ideas had turned out not to be as popular as his. Yet she had still done very well for herself. Over the years the two of them had drifted apart, Brandon busy with the Game, Lilith quietly trying to save the world despite society's apparent desire for self-destruction.

"I see Alexandra is doing splendidly this time in the Game," Brandon said.

"She seems to be doing very well, despite her many challenges and limitations," Lilith agreed.

Brandon held up a bottle of fine wine, Lilith's favourite, of course. She smiled and nodded. He poured the wine. "Zack is doing splendidly as well," she said.

Brandon nodded. "There are also many challenges for him."

The two continued to make small talk as the meal was served by Brandon's staff. They discussed the past, the present, and thoughts about the near future in many areas of interest. Both laughed and smiled often during the meal, feeling comfortable in each other's presence.

Finally the desert and coffee were served and the servants retired for the evening. The two of them could get down to real business.

"So what really brings you here tonight, Lilith?" Brandon asked.

"I'm not sure if you know, but somehow Alex acquired an Eternal for this play," Lilith said.

Brandon nodded. "I was made aware of that, yes. Not just any Eternal. Raphael is one of the best."

"I hear that's true," Lilith said. "I must admit, we weren't too sure how or why he was purchased. I've never had a player able to unlock Eternals, and since our budget and resources are much smaller than the larger Patrons, it's been a task figuring out how to make the best use of him."

Brandon chuckled. "I bet it has. I remember unlocking our first Eternal. We were so excited, then extremely confused. It took us quite a few plays to begin to get any type of results out of them. They often have their own agenda."

"Yes, well, he keeps asking for confirmation that he's being viewed. I am personally viewing him, but the individuals allowed to know about their existence are extremely limited, as you know, and I have only one other person on my team that qualifies to know. I haven't informed them yet. It's a serious burden to place on them."

"If I may interrupt with some advice?" Brandon asked.

"Of course."

"If you have someone in your group that qualifies, tell them soon. Part of qualifying is an extensive psychological profile. Most teams get enough credits to unlock an Eternal but still don't see the menu choice because they have no one trustworthy enough to learn the secret. If you and one other person qualify, that's excellent. Tell them soon. It's too difficult to bear the burden fully yourself if you don't have to."

"Okay, I will. Thank you," Lilith said.

"Secondly, I'm guessing that you haven't figured out what he means, asking you to confirm that he's being viewed?"

"No idea at all."

"There are certain papers and television shows that the Eternals have set up to receive messages from us," Brandon explained. "Most of them are gossip and rumour vehicles. Also songs played in different sequences. Very subtle methods, but effective most of the time. I'll give you the address to send your message to, where it gets processed and inserted into those avenues to be hidden for them to find. Often this results in silly stories about three headed aliens and that type of thing, but the masses don't pay attention to the stories and the Eternals get their communication from us."

"So we can actually communicate with them from outside of the Game?" Lilith couldn't believe what she was hearing.

"Yes, in a limited way."

"I need to communicate with Raphael. Right away," Lilith said.

"It will take a while to bring you up to speed on how to do that, Lilith. I'm surprised you haven't come to me sooner."

"I didn't know if I could trust you, Brandon."

"You can. You always can."

Lilith looked uncomfortable. "Maybe, Brandon. But after what I just viewed, I had no choice."

Brandon raised his glass of brandy towards his lips. "What did you just view?"

"Raphael caught someone following Danielle. They were going to use a Sever Spike on her."

Brandon froze mid-sip. His eyes darkened, the gold flecks in them began to swirl. He put the glass down slowly on the table and reached into his pocket for his cell phone. After dialling, he raised the phone to his head and asked Lilith, "How long ago was this?"

"Yesterday, our time." Lilith could see the fury hidden below the surface of Brandon's calm appearance. "He asked for confirmation that he was being viewed, which he does often, but this time he was very, very angry. Is there a weapon in the Game that can permanently kill players? I need help, Brandon, Alex is way out of her league on this play."

"Give me a couple of minutes, please," Brandon said and began to talk into his phone.

"Are you both on the line? Okay, then. Listen very carefully and don't interrupt me, please. Raphael just stopped an attempt on Danielle's life. The assassin intended to use a Sever Spike. Raphael has been hanging in the wind since Danielle was born, I need Samantha pulled from her perch and sent to rendezvous with Raphael. He needs assistance. I'll get her clearer instructions next session but she needs to go to him now. 'A,' I will get a feed of Raphael sent to you. I want to know who sent that assassin. Now you may talk. 'A' first."

Brandon listened for a few seconds, then he responded, "No, we aren't playing that game. Yet. Just get me the info and we can decide from there. Michelle, what do you have?"

More silence followed while Brandon listened to Michelle talk on the other line. His eyes darted quickly to Lilith's, then he answered. "Yes, I think that's the best strategy too. I'll ask if we can join Alexandra's group." Once again he looked at Lilith. She paused for a brief second then nodded. "Yes, we have permission. Send Nadine over to get fully up to speed on Danielle's play. We will bring their team into our command centre as soon as possible. Any resource at our disposal is now at their disposal. As of now, Danielle is as precious to us as Trew."

34

"Our world seems to be addicted to the easy way of things. Unfortunately, what seems easy at first almost always ends up causing pain, suffering, and loss. Why do I get fat and sick when I eat tasty junk food? Why must I perform painful exercise to stay healthy and in shape? How come I have to sacrifice so much of my time and money studying in order to get a good paying job? These are the types of questions that no school teaches us. The answer is simple; it doesn't matter why. That's just the way it is. If you want to breathe air, then you can't lay on the bottom of a pond. If you desire wealth, you can't sit in front of your television screen and expect it to find you. If you want to learn how to play a musical instrument, you must pick it up and spend thousands of hours practicing with it. Entitlement is a problem both inside and outside of the Game... all of our lives would be better if we stopped expecting the world to hand us it's treasures simply because we asked for them..."
Promotional message from "We Can Be Better"
featuring Brandon Strayne

Samantha

I'm not comfortable doing this. It's too late, this alley is crowded with garbage, rats and homeless men. I check my scribbled note again; yeah, this is the right place. Not the best spot for a top secret meeting, but appropriate. I've never understood why some Eternals go bad and join the group that long ago started referring to themselves as 'Infernals.' I guess I'm just too sweet to understand a group so sour.

I hear a noise directly to my left and turn, shifting into a combat stance. I see a filthy old man sitting in a pile of torn up cardboard and newspapers; wispy white hair, splotchy balding head, dirty face and ugly, broken-toothed smile grinning up at me.

I start to turn away when he speaks with a strong, bold voice. "Took you long enough to get here, slag."

I lean in closer to get a better look. The smell of him! It's horrible. Sure enough, though, I see the red swirling in his dark eyes and realize it must be him. "You've sunk low," I say. "Not where I'd expect my boss to be hanging out."

The old man chuckles. "That's because your kind isn't promoted by killing the boss. If three of your lieutenants were ready to take over and all they had to do was kill you… you'd be hiding safely in a garbage pile, too."

"Is that true?" I ask. I wonder how the Infernals ever get anything done; they always seem so busy killing and fighting each other.

He shrugs. "It could be true. I know three are ready, even if they don't realize it. I'll likely only manage to make two dead before the third figures out what's going on. It should be a bit of fun and excitement."

I turn my nose up in disgust. He laughs, then stops suddenly and looks seriously at me. "Why am I even speaking with a baby like you? I speak only with Gabriel; you all know this. Where is he?"

I shake my head, "I have no clue, old man. They said you agreed to meet with one of Brandon's, and that's who I am. Are you too drunk to talk? This is serious business."

The old man turns his head, pushing a finger against the outside of one nostril and blowing snot forcefully out of the other. Most makes it to the ground; some rogue splatter hits his arm, but it's hard to distinguish from the other garbage sticking to his sleeve. "I'm just fine, thank you very much." I can hear a slight slur; he's been drinking. "Let's just get down to business so you can get out of here and leave me alone."

I pull up a clean-looking wooden box and set it down in front of him. Then I sit on it and look him directly in the eyes. "Okay. We need you to put a clean mark on Danielle Benton."

"Hmm." He scratches his armpit roughly. "That name rings a bell with me. Somebody I know wants her dead, I think."

"Someone just tried to Sever Spike her a few days ago," I say.

"Yes, that sounds about right," he nods. "They sent a moron to do the job. Still, he should have been good enough to get past regular security... so she has an Eternal watching her, does she?"

Damn it! He's pumping me for information that I shouldn't give. "I'm not here to talk, just to tell you what Brandon wants."

"Well, if you're not here to talk, then you shouldn't be telling me someone tried to kill her, little girl. You should just walk up to me, give me your best intimidating look, and say 'Clean Mark the girl, now.'"

I stand up and lean in towards him, giving him my best intimidating look. He chuckles and says, "That's more like it!"

"How long have you been running the Infernals?" I ask.

"I don't run the Infernals, girl, you should know that. The one who runs the Infernals has been around for over five thousand years."

"You know what I mean," I sigh. "You're the one with the word. You give an order, every other Infernal obeys."

"Unless my boss gives a different order; yes, yes, you're right. Okay, then, to answer your question, I've been running things for two hundred and twelve years."

"That's it?" I ask.

He snorts with disgust. "Don't you pay attention, girl? We kill for the position I hold. I've held onto this position longer than almost everyone who ever had it. And, since I like to brag, go check your history books. The past two hundred and twelve years have been very productive for us. My boss is pleased. So shut your mouth."

I think of a comment, but realize that I'm speaking to one of the most evil creatures on the planet, so I say nothing. Best not to have him remember me too well.

"I really find it hard to believe you, girl." The old man takes a boot off, emptying dirt and stones onto the ground. "Nothing personal, but there's not a lot of trust between our two packs. Gabriel is the only one who I can believe; it's a shame he isn't here. That girl might die by accident, simply because I doubt your words and can't sell it to my crew."

I sit down and fold my hands on my lap. "Brandon said you would doubt me, so he had me memorize a message for you, to prove he is involved and this is serious."

"Did he now? Well, let me hear what my old buddy Brandon has to say."

I calmly give him the message, repeating it exactly how it was told to me. I don't understand what half of it means, but apparently this old creepy guy does. His face goes from not interested to extremely serious. Halfway through my message he loses his appearance of being a drunk old homeless man and sits up straight. I finish and he stands up, nodding to me. He's tall, and underneath all those dirty clothes, I can tell he's very muscular. He's definitely in a costume; I bet he looks only forty or so underneath all that.

He looks me straight in the eyes, but I know he's looking at the person Firsting me. "Okay, fine, Brandon," he says. "I will make sure none of ours touch her. You're going to piss a lot of big names off, both here and on Tygon, Strayne, but you've scared even me a tiny bit. Count this as one of your favours called in though, boy, and don't ask me for any others while this one is in play. As of this moment, Danielle Benton is Clean Marked by the Infernals. When she dies, it won't be at our hand."

I shiver inside as he smiles and says, "You've the Devil's own word on it."

35

"One thing missing today is old fashioned rivalry. Players of the Game do not compete against each other. Sure, when they are out dancing and enjoying their fame on Tygon, words are exchanged and bold claims thrown out against other players. In the old days a rivalry involved one skilled player going directly against another, squaring off to see who was the best! Players today still build the hype before they compete, but once they enter the Game it's impossible for one star to directly compete with another. Some say this is disappointing, but I disagree. I find it much more exciting to see two top ranked players interact with each other, not knowing who or what they are in the real world. Some enemies become dear friends, some friends do their best to connect and fail, and others spend no credits on connecting in-Game and somehow spend their whole virtual lives together. If you ask me, the Game provides thousands of possibilities for exciting events and occurrences. You can take your old rivalries and keep them; I'd rather watch a low-ranked player break into the top standings or a high-ranked player sink low, without them even knowing they're playing the Game that they are!

Excerpt, 'One Fan's Opinion'

Trew - 17

"Hey, sexy, wait for me!"

Before I can turn around and close my locker I feel a soft warm hand come up from behind and firmly touch my chest. I smile and turn around.

Her name's Jane and she's my new girlfriend. Long blonde hair, green eyes, a smile that makes me forget who I am, and a body... well, she's been a figure skater since she was five. When I tell my friends she's got a nice body, they laugh at the understatement. She's just a bit shorter than me, but hey, I'm six foot tall, so that's understandable, and I like it when she stretches up to kiss me, which she does right now.

"Class is done. Ready to get out of here and go swimming with the gang?" she asks.

I should really be doing some extra research work, but it's so hard to say no to her. We've been dating for just about a month now and I don't seem to have time to get anything done. It's fun, having a girlfriend, but Danni's wondering why I chat with her less and don't seem to have any new info to share with her on our projects. I wish she didn't live so far away; it would be much better if we could hang out and work.

"Hey, where did you go, big boy?" Jane asks, snapping me out of my thoughts. Here I am with this hot girl and I'm thinking about Danni. What's wrong with me? I start to tell myself Danni is one great looking girl too, but I can't be having conversations with myself about her while I'm standing here. I shake my head and smile.

"I'm right here, babe. Sure, let's go swimming."

We go out to the parking lot and I unlock the car, a nice sporty job that my parents let me drive. I have a part-time job working to pay for gas and insurance. They never have to ask me to fill the tank or take care of it. I laugh at my friends who think their parents are such hard cases because they expect their kids to do simple stuff like that. I figure it helps me get the car easier when I need it. Parents aren't so different from us kids; they just want some help from us when we can give it. I think kids would have better parents if they were better at being kids. Not all, but lots.

Jane gets in the passenger side, and as I start up the engine, she turns on the radio. Windows down, we drive over to her friend Cynthia's place. There are already twenty or so people there, standing around in groups and swimming.

"Trew!" my buddy Rob calls out. I wave and walk towards him. Jane tells me she's going to put her bathing suit on and I give her a kiss before she jogs into the house.

Rob hands me a drink. "Nothing with alcohol, is it? I want to be able to drive home," I ask.

"No, it's clean," he laughs. Of course, it's illegal to drink at our age... so we never do. Hahaha, okay, but seriously. None today for me.

"You should really come out and play ball again this year, Trew." Rob says. "You were MVP last year and we need you back on the team."

I shrug. He knows how I play. It was time to move on. I've known Rob my whole life and he's followed me from sport to sport, activity to activity. First I leave, then he groans the next session how they miss me and I should come back. I shrug and ignore him, and soon he announces that he's coming to join me in my new interest. It's a regular pattern. I chuckle because he doesn't seem to see it, but I am better at spotting patterns than most people.

He laughs at my shrug and says, "So you liking the girl friend thing? Jane's a catch for sure."

"Yeah, she's a great girl. Lots of fun." I look around, waving and smiling to the people gathered in groups. Most of them look towards me exactly as I shift my attention to them. I'm not the most popular kid in school, but I'm friendly with the most people. There aren't too many people I don't get along with. I think it's my sense of humour and quick wit; even the groups that don't like each other seem to enjoy my company. I play sports pretty well, and since I've played so many over the years, I've been in a class with most of the kids my age. Some people don't like me because I breeze in for a short time and do better at their activity than they do, but that's always going to happen. Like my Dad says, 'If everyone says they like you, then some of them are lying.'

Rob and I walk around and mingle; most of the time I practice my new home study assignment. I ask them about themselves, then sit back and listen. When I went looking for someone to teach me how to communicate better with others, the best teachers turned out to be living in my own house! My parents are both incredible with people, always comfortable with friends and strangers. We could go to a town where no one knew us and, in almost no time at all, my parents would have new friends and acquaintances to talk and laugh with. When I asked my Dad to help me improve my communication skills he laughed and said they'd been teaching me since I was young, but he agreed that there was some formal training to provide. Most people laugh when I tell them I'm training in communicating. They tell me we all communicate and not to waste time learning, just go out and do it! I've met some very awkward people who could benefit from training in this area. The truth is that not everyone can do it, and most can't do it well. My mom says most problems in the world today result from poor communication, and she's given me so many examples that it's impossible to not believe her.

So my current homework is to listen. Whenever I can talk with someone, my goal is to ask them some good questions, then listen. It's amazing what you can learn, and what people will tell you when you are truly interested in them. I swear it's like magic.

I get so immersed in conversations that time passes quickly and before I know it an hour has gone by. I look around but still don't see Jane anywhere. I excuse myself and go find Cynthia.

"Hey, Cyn, you seen Jane around?"

Cynthia looks real freaked out and starts looking back towards the house. "Um... hey, Trew. No, I haven't seen her. I thought she came out to swim a while ago. Oh, actually, yeah, I think she went with Sally to go get ice at the store. She'll be back soon."

Something doesn't feel right. "Okay, thanks," I say. I head into the house. I've got to use the bathroom anyway.

The main floor bathroom is in use, so I head upstairs. I don't know the layout of the house that well and I guess I must make a wrong turn. I hear moaning and kissing noises from the room to my left and I look to see who's getting lucky.

My emotions disappear, my heart stops beating in my chest, and it feels like the room has just frozen solid. There's Jane, in her bathing suit, with her back to the door, making out with Ted, a guy from school. He opens his eyes and sees me; his eyes start to twinkle with laughter. He kisses her for another couple seconds, then stops and says, "Run along, Junior, big kids are playing."

Jane turns around and looks towards the door. She giggles but quickly stops, trying to appear upset and sorry. "Oops," she says. "Sorry, Trew."

I just stand there, not knowing what to say. It could be worse, I guess. I could have spent more than a month with this girl before finding out she's not really into me. But still, this is pretty embarrassing.

Instead I just look at her and say, "There was no tingle with you."

"What?" she asks.

"When I kissed you," I say.

"I don't know what you're talking about," she says.

I just turn and walk out. I hear Ted yelling at me from the bedroom. "Hey, Trew, don't you want to kick my ass? Come on, man, you may have beat me when we were eight in karate, but I could clean your clock now. I just stole your girl, Trew! Don't you want to fight?"

I stop and go back to the doorway. I see Ted smiling and I'm pretty sure he just wants to make me fight him. I smile back. "I'll fight you any time, Ted. You suck at it, but if you want to get knocked out, I can help you with that any time." I point at Jane. "She's not my girl, though, and definitely not worth fighting over." Both of them say nothing, their mouths opening and closing like fish laying on the deck of a boat trying to get a breath. I walk downstairs and out to the back of the house.

Rob sees me and comes over. From my look he must be able to tell that something isn't right. "Hey, man, you okay?"

"Yeah, I'm fine," I assure him. "Look, man, I'm gonna head out."

"Okay, no problem. Where you going?" he asks.

Still remembering the tingle of that kiss on her birthday, I answer, "I think I'm going to go call my girlfriend."

36

The Game isn't working. Does anyone even remember what it was designed for? Oh, yes — to educate our children and help them become wiser and more productive members of society. Has that actually happened? 'Difficult to track,' is the answer I get whenever I make an inquiry. Difficult to track? It shouldn't be too difficult to track, but sure enough, it's not only difficult, it's downright impossible! Can anyone tell me where the consistently top players are since they retired from the Game? They're super-rich celebrities who spend all their time partying and waving to their adoring fans. Sure, the good to mediocre players retire to go on and get good paying jobs, live middle to high class lives, have children and do their thing. But is that what we should be expecting from enlightened individuals? Hell, they're doing the same things our parents did before the Game, and they're not any happier or fulfilled. Divorce, scandal, murder, crime, you name it — they all still exist with veterans of the Game. There's a problem here. It's the Game, and everyone is too busy watching it and wasting all their time following their favourite players to even notice. The only ones better off are Brandon Strayne and his crew of wealthy business owners. And, let's face it, folks, they were very well off before this nonsense even started all those years ago.

Excerpt - The Game Is Killing Society

Danielle - 17

I hear my computer chirp, and I'm both happy and upset to recognize the unique tone that announces the caller. I consider not answering it — he hasn't answered any of my calls this past month; maybe he should know how it feels.

I really want to talk to him though. Life can get busy, and it's okay that he hasn't been around. I let it ring a few more times, then answer it. He pops up on my video screen and I give him my best grin. I'm not going to be one of those nagging girls. Can't stand them, won't be one of them. Besides, it's not like we're dating or anything. "Hey, Trew, what's new?"

"Um... hey, Danielle. How ya been? Sorry I haven't been around lately." He sounds nervous and twitchy. Boys. Who can figure 'em out?

"I've been good, thanks. Really getting into this biology thing. The Eastern medicine is looking like the best stuff out there."

"Really?" he asks. Talking about interesting stuff seems to snap him out of whatever daze he was in.

"Oh, yes," I say. "If we're just inside a game and our bodies are simply digital avatars, then our bodies behave much like any other machine or vehicle you would ride in."

"Makes sense," he says.

"So just like a car, it only works as good as you treat it. They've known for thousands of years how to take care of their bodies in the East. Here in the West, we seem more concerned with just fixing the body once it breaks, or pumping foreign chemicals into it to hide the real symptoms."

"So when we put the wrong gas into our bodies, and toxic chemicals, and we don't sleep right or exercise, then we're setting ourselves up for being unhealthy," Trew says.

"Exactly. You've been paying attention in biology." I smile. "There's more to it than that, though. You ever hear about chakras, acupuncture, or Reiki ?"

"Acupuncture I've heard of. And I might have heard chakras mentioned in some old Japanese cartoon." He grins and looks right at me through the camera. "I haven't heard about Reiki, though."

That grin. It always makes me stop and forget what I'm thinking about. I pause for a second to try and remember. Ah, yes, "It's all very important stuff. One of us should study it if we want to keep these machines of ours healthy as long as possible," I say.

"Just one of us?" he asks in a teasing voice. "If I learn Reiki, then how am I going to be able to help you from all the way up here in Canada?"

"Reiki is about energy, and you can actually send it over long distances. The other two might be a bit tough, though. And then there's chiropractics."

"Oh, no thanks," Trew says. "I'm not too keen on that one. Back cracking doesn't sound like a good thing for my machine."

"The back cracking part of it is called osseous adjusting and I agree we should stay away from that. Gentle manipulation of the spine is much more effective. It's possible to practice chiropractics without cracking bones forcefully into place. Studying applied kinesiology would be helpful too."

"Okay, sounds good," he says. Trew's awesome that way. Once he hears the basics he's always ready to join the adventure.

"Great," I say. "I was also thinking..."

"Hey, I have a question for you," he says.

"Okay."

"We've known each other for a long time now." He sounds nervous.

"Yes, we have," I agree.

"And I like you a lot," he says.

"Yeah, I like you, too."

"So... would you like to be my girlfriend?" His face turns red as he gets all the words out.

I smile, getting a bit warm in the face myself. "Well, I am your girlfriend, Trew. I'm a girl. I'm your frie..."

"Yeah, I know, Danni," he says hurriedly. "But we get to see each other every few weeks, especially since we started driving. And that kiss we had on your birthday... I can't stop thinking about it."

I don't want him to squirm, even if he's cute when he's doing it. "Sounds good to me, Trew," I say with a smile.

"Really?" His grin is huge. I grin back. "That's great!" he says.

"Maybe," I say. "But I want to ask something."

"Sure, anything," he says.

"I don't want to lose what we've had all these years, Our friendship. I've had a couple of boyfriends, and —"

"You have?" he interrupts. "I had no idea. Were they recent? Serious?"

He looks like he's getting ramped up to ask a lot of questions, so I stop him. "Whoa, there, buddy. Of course I have, and I bet you have too. No, no, don't answer. I don't really want to know, and I don't think we should bother to ask each other questions about that, at least right now. It doesn't matter, because it's in the past and it has nothing to do with our relationship. Here's what I was getting at before you interrupted me..."

"Sorry," he says. Then he winces, realizing he's just interrupted me again. He does that a lot, and gets away with it because he's so damn cute and funny.

I sit quietly for a second and smile. "Before your repeated interruptions," I pause but he remains silent, "I was going to say that I want to make sure we keep our friendship intact. People start to become romantic, and no matter how hard they try, it ends, and the friendship disappears with it. I don't want to do that with you. Dear and close friends are the most precious treasure in this world, I think. If I had to choose between you as a boyfriend and you as a lifelong friend, I'd choose lifelong every time. I know there are no guarantees, but I want to start off this relationship with us both saying out loud that we agree to be friends no matter what. That we will do our very best to always remain friends first."

He thinks about it for a few seconds, then nods. "Friends. First and always. I agree to try my very best."

I smile, "All right then, Trew Radfield. I'll be your girlfriend."

"Awesome!" he says. "Although I'm a bit sad already. Long distance relationships are tough. I guess my talent only has so much power because, quite a while ago, I put out there to the universe that I wanted us to live closer together. Oh, well... it's still gonna be great."

"Funny thing, that." I'm still smiling. "I was thinking the same thing years ago when I put that exact desire out to the universe. But you know what George says, the universe takes its own time bringing things into play. I would have told you sooner, but you were busy this past month..."

"Told me what?" Trew asks.

"Well, boyfriend, my Mom got transferred to a new position and location. I'm moving to Canada next month. Toronto, to be exact. Less than a couple miles from your house. Know anyone willing to spend time with me to show me all the cool spots?"

My speakers almost shatter at his whoop of delight!

37

Of course the Game works. Or it doesn't. It all depends on what side of the argument you want to come in on. Ask a kid who fails out of the Game at 15 and they'll tell you the Game is horrible, but ask an 18 year old who retired from the Game able to get a good job, house, and a sizeable bank account for her efforts; she'll say the Game is an incredible opportunity, both for learning and for advancement. When a citizen of Tygon places a bet on a player in the Game and wins, they are much happier than if they lose. No matter what type of system we have, there will always be those who support it and those who attack it. The fact is, this world of ours was heading towards ruin before the Game came along. Are we perfect now? Well, of course not. But we're still here and thriving as a society. I'm happy to come and defend the Game in the face of any attacks. And to those who step forward to attack me, I say; you are welcome, my friends, even though you are too bitter and angry at yourselves and what little you have accomplished to thank me. There is always an angry bully who comes along to kick over the beauty that others are building. I'm glad those people are not the majority.
Interview excerpt from "The Game: Twenty-Eight Years Online"
Brandon Strayne interviewed by Melissa W.

The mood in Zack's command central office was extremely positive. There was a cake in the centre of the table with 20 candles in it and the message 'Happy 20th Trew!' written in icing. Monitors in the background showed Trew and Danielle partying with their friends and family; the joy and happiness on the screens also showed on the faces of those inside the Tygon command centre. After just a little over two weeks of Game play, with many stressful moments and almost no sleep, the combined team took a few moments to enjoy themselves and celebrate their accomplishments so far.

As the two inside the Game left their families and went out to party at a favourite bar, Brandon called for order and began a brief recap meeting.

"I know most of us are so focused on our own particular areas of speciality that we don't always get to see the big picture. So let's hear how our kids are doing overall. Michelle, would you please bring us up to date?"

"With pleasure, Brandon." Michelle stood up and moved to end of the long desk, opposite where Brandon and Lilith sat.

"First off, I'm happy to report that Trew and Danielle are both happy, healthy, and alive." This statement brought cheers and applause. It was extremely common for the players to still be in the Game at 20, but everyone in the room had seen enough in their careers to know that it could have been tragically different with just a little bad luck.

"From a fan base perspective," Michelle continued, "Zack is now officially one of the most popular players of all time. He's surpassed many of the top veterans and pre-orders are flooding in for his current play. Millions of dollars are being deposited for the opportunity to First him when he completes this session. His one channel has been expanded to three in order to accommodate the number of viewers following him. Merchandise is through the roof! You name it, people are buying it, as long as it has a picture or slogan from Trew on it. If any of us were actually able to go outside of this office and mingle with the population, (this comment drew laughter from many), then you would see that Trew's name is on the lips of most people. Speculation on what's happened so far, what might be coming next, and how it might all turn out are the buzz of the world, as well as of the media."

Michelle paused here to allow for cheering and applause.

"Alexandra," Michelle continued, "Is also enjoying incredible success." The small group of team members who had come on board from Lilith's team were very vocal in their cheering at hearing this. The rest of the crew smiled and cheered as well, it had been a very smooth transition bringing the two teams together, due in large part to Michelle's strong leadership. "If Danielle continues on her current track, Alexandra will finish this play with more credits and ranking than she had at the height of her career. It's safe to say that she's played this game better than any other player given a free play in the history of the Game." This announcement was followed by more energetic applause. On the screen beside Brandon, Danielle and Trew were toasting each other with shot glasses in hand, almost as if they could hear Michelle's positive update.

"The Eternals surrounding the two appear to be laying low, for the most part. Besides the one appearance of Carl, we haven't observed any Infernal involvement at all. No one can ever be sure how these cards will play out, but as of right now everything appears fine."

Lilith looked briefly at Brandon and he nodded slightly to indicate things were as good as they could be in this area.

"The both of them are now in University and College, and excelling in their studies. Trew threw us all for a confusing loop by minoring in Theology, but he's still majoring in Political Science, so we're confident he's on track with his outline to become a politician. Danielle is majoring in Biology and Kinesiology, with a strong focus on Eastern medicine. Both of them remain focused on their 'life is a game' theory, but they also realize they soon have to go out and earn their way in the world, so they are doing their best to get training that will land them jobs to pay the bills."

"Yet the skills they're learning are also in line with their idea of a computer game." Brandon observed. "Is there any chance that their belief in the Game will disappear?"

Michelle shook her head negatively. "No, not really. Maybe if they hadn't met and seen each other display the Talent. Perhaps if they hadn't found George's book at the time they did. But knowing Alexandra's outline and Game strategy now, I'd say it's impossible for Danielle to lose faith in her theory, and Trew has spent so much time with her that I would be very surprised if he lost faith either."

"That's very interesting, what you just did there, Michelle," Brandon said, sitting forward quickly as if an important thought had just occurred to him.

"What did I just do?" Michelle asked.

"I asked about their belief, and you replied about their faith."

"What's the difference?" Michelle asked.

"If I tell you I can jump ten feet straight up into the air, what would you say?" Brandon asked.

"I would say I don't think you can," Michelle answered.

"Then you have no faith in my ability to do it," Brandon nodded. "But after you watch me jump ten feet into the air..."

"Well, then, I would have to believe you," Michelle said.

"Mhmm," Brandon said. "So which is stronger? Which one can you bet on? Belief or faith?"

"Belief," Michelle answered. "If I have seen you jump ten feet into the air, then I will bet on you being able to do it again. If I have never seen you do it, then I would have to rely on faith that you can. That's a riskier bet, because I could be wrong."

"That's right. Combine faith and belief and you have something very strong, which is what Trew and Danielle are doing regarding the whole 'we live in a game' situation."

Michelle shrugged, "Yes, I guess so."

Brandon looked around the table, his eyes going wide with excitement. "Can anyone in this room see what's happening? Anyone have a guess what these two are actually up to in the Game?" Everyone looked confused, not knowing what Brandon was asking. "What happens if I show others my ability to jump ten feet into the air?"

Nadine spoke up from the left. "Then you give others the belief that such a thing is possible. And you also give them faith that similar things can be done."

"Yes!" Brandon said. "Now what if Trew and Danielle begin to show others believable evidence to support their claim?"

"Then people will start to believe them," Michelle ventured.

"Yes, and then the people who believe them will begin to share their faith as well. Now what happens if the person sharing the evidence is a charismatic leader?"

"Uh-oh," Nadine said.

"Uh-oh is right," Brandon said. "Michelle, Trew's minor in University is what?"

"Theology," Michelle said.

"I wonder if they even know what they're planning yet?" Nadine said.

"What? What are they planning?" Michelle still didn't see it.

Lilith saw it, and she spoke up to let Michelle in on the theory. "They are going to make their belief in the Game into a religion, dear," she said.

Michelle looked at the two avatars dancing close in the club.

"Oh, damn," she said.

If a tree falls in the forest and no one's around...does it make a sound?

That's an interesting question, I suppose. Here's a better one. If something happens inside the Game and no one views it...did something actually happen?

Incredible events happen every moment inside the Game, and it's common for no one to ever know they occurred.

How is this possible?

Easy.

At any given moment, there are millions of players inside the Game being viewed...by absolutely no one.

Author unknown

I walk through the front door, smiling and taking a deep breath. I love libraries!

For the books? Hahaha, hell, no. Why would I love libraries for the books? You can find books everywhere today. You don't even have to leave your house to get one delivered or digitally downloaded.

No, there are more interesting things in libraries than books. Are you watching me? Can you hear me? Then come along and I'll show you what I'm talking about. Keep your eyes open and pay special attention. Perhaps we'll be fortunate enough to find one today.

This library is nothing special, just a regular library in a regular town. A stereotypical librarian looks up from behind her desk and smiles as I make eye contact with her. That's right, miss, I'm just a regular middle aged man walking in to check out your books. It's best for you to believe that, dear, because the truth of who I am really am would make you throw yourself in front of oncoming traffic to escape your terror.

I head for the stairs; I like to work my way down from the top floor. I've visited countless numbers of libraries and have developed a nice routine. I hear telltale sounds from the main floor, over by a corner table, but I don't break my ritual. It's been weeks since I've had any luck. If it's on the main floor, then I'll be back and find out soon enough. I've come to savour the process almost as much as the successes.

The top floor is the kids' section. It's rare to find one in the kids' section but let me tell you, when I do have luck there, it's the best of times. Not today, though. A quick walk up and down the aisles turns up nothing. After a leisurely stroll, I head to the next level.

Computers and cubicles on this floor. I walk slowly past the backs of the tiny enclosures, letting my hand gently touch each one as I pass by. I can feel the warmth and faint hum from the computers at the desks and hear the dull silence of the people sitting behind each computer screen. Quietly I observe each person as I stroll by. Look at them — they're barely here. Glassy blank stares, half open mouths, ridiculous headsets covering their ears as they listen to some idiotic song or video or movie. I want one of them to lock eyes with me. Come on, slags! Look at me! I want to scream at them as loud as I can and ask them why they're sitting here wasting their play. There's no game inside that stupid little box that can compare with the one you traded your life force and hard-earned credits to play. 'What are you looking for?' I want to yell at them. 'It's right in front of your face, stop looking past it. Don't make it so complicated, children. The simplest answer is the answer.'

But none of them look up. They're lost. It's a Thursday afternoon and here they are, sitting mindlessly in a library. For a few minutes I walk back and forth past the lines of dull computer people like a caged tiger. Watching. Waiting.

I sigh. No, nothing here that interests me.

Down to the main floor I go. Around the edges rest the shelves of old, often forgotten literature. Off to the left is a glass-walled room, sound proofed for audio books. In the centre of the main floor are the tables. This is often where I find success, the tables. It seems to draw them, like moths to a flame.

One table has a teenage girl wearing headphones and typing away on her laptop. Nicer headphones than the drones upstairs; she's better than them. Her eyes are clear and she looks to be actually doing something productive on her computer. Good for you, darlin'.

There are two empty tables beside her, then a table with two mothers. They are talking while their children recline in strollers. One child throws a plastic cup onto the floor and the mother doesn't stop talking or break eye contact with the other one, she simply bends down and hands it back to the child. Amusing to watch. As I walk past, the child looks at me. His blue eyes sharpen in alarm. What's wrong, little fella? See something that bothers you? I appear to smile kindly at him, but it's not truly a kind smile. He begins to cry, waving his arms towards his mother, looking for protection. His eyes dart to mine, then frantically back towards his mother. I shake my head. It's okay, little boy, I'm not here for you today.

I hear the sound again and look to my right. There are three tables out of the way behind a row of bookshelves. I lean over at the waist and take a quick peek; It looks like we are in luck today.

I grab a book, not even bothering to see what kind it is, and move to the table beside him. It's often a him. His hair is white and dirty, standing up in some places and flat against his head in others. He looks to be about 60, but I guarantee you he's younger. On the table sits a beat-up tan bag, zipper open, stray items threatening to fall out. Crumpled pieces of paper, a small, broken umbrella, dozens of worn pencils of various lengths. A black plastic bag is stuffed into the corner. It's chaos inside that bag, but not to him. He wears a trench coat, faded and worn. He wears a stained sweater over a splotchy, yellowed dress shirt; both are stained and threadbare. His beard is scruffy, and he smells, I can smell him from where I sit at the next table. The sour smell of days-old sweat and yellow teeth. Papers are strewn across the entire table, some fresh, some crumpled and stained. There is a small pile of notebooks stacked within reach of his right hand; every once in a while his hand absently strays to touch them, lingering for a few moments before returning to hold the paper he is furiously working on.

I open my book and pretend to read it as I wait for him to start talking. He looks like a talker.

After a brief period, I'm rewarded for my patience as he blurts out in a loud, confused-sounding voice, "Buoyancy! It's all about water!" then he flings the sheet across the table, scrambling through the messy pile he grabs another full page with purpose and looks down at it.

"It's the weight of water that makes it difficult to walk on," he says before reaching to open one of the notebooks from the pile. He opens it and I get a brief glance inside — the most detailed pencil drawing of a brain that I've ever seen, but I know what a brain looks like and this drawing has some tiny additions to it. Quickly he stands up and walks away, the book hanging open loosely at his side. He mumbles as he walks, and I slowly begin to count.

When I reach the count of 22 he appears back at the table and sits down, placing the book on top of the others and grabbing a pencil to start colouring another blank page. As he colours, his loud talk begins to come faster, mostly nonsense but interrupted with sentences of pure brilliance. All around him the occupants of the library go about their lives, politely ignoring the crazy man who sits in their presence.

He repeats his ritual twice more, grabbing the top notebook and walking around for exactly 22 seconds before returning to his seat and beginning to work on a new sheet of paper. When he gets up and walks away for the third time I quickly move to sit at his table. I have 20 seconds before he returns, so I sit politely looking at the papers, careful not to touch or disturb any. I see some extremely advanced material laying here. The most intelligent people on the planet would need help deciphering most of it.

He comes back and sits down, not giving me any indication that he sees me. That's normal. I sit quietly watching and listening. He's fascinating. Broken. Brilliant, most likely, and a remarkable source of knowledge, if you know how to get it out of him. I happen to specialize in that.

He works quietly on his pages, saying nothing, which tells me he's aware of my presence on some level.

When he returns from his next walk, I decide it's time to break the silence. "Buoyancy, huh?" I ask.

He doesn't look up as he mutters, "The water's too heavy to walk on."

"Show me," I say.

He looks up and meets my eyes. Then he looks around, first to his left and then to his right. Slowly he reaches for a notebook from the bottom of the pile. Licking his lips nervously, he opens the book with shaky hands and passes it to me. When the book is touching my hands I break eye contact and look at it. In the neatest, most elegant handwriting is written an extremely complex set of mathematical equations. I grin because I recognize them. Slowly I read it and turn the page, finding the next full of the same type of equations. He looks at me hopefully and when I nod he sighs in relief. I hold up my finger for silence.

Finally I look at him. He's been watching me quietly like a student watching a teacher mark the final exam, unsure if they will pass or fail. "Do you know what this is?" I ask him in my friendliest tone.

He shakes his head and points to his skull. "The water's too heavy," he says.

I reach forward and touch his skull gently, closing my eyes as I open myself up to the energy I command. The coldness from my hand covers his head, telling me what I need to know and giving him some small relief. He leans back in his chair, appearing normal for the first time. "Thank you," he says, tears forming in his eyes.

"Don't thank me," I say. "It'll come back in a few seconds. But if you come with me I can try to help you."

He nods quickly. They are so quick to believe the lies. But it's necessary, and in the long run I will help him. When I've retrieved everything I can, I'll probably help him escape this broken avatar shell he's trapped in. His type of broken is special, though. He's more valuable this way than he ever was as a normal person.

I pull out my phone and dial a number, watching him pleasantly. "I've got one," I say, and hang up. Leaning towards him, I flash him a smile. "Somewhere in your head, my friend, you've been doing something very special. You've been spying on the Mainframe and stealing its secrets. Very powerful secrets that now belong to me." I tap the notebook and grin. "We are going to do some truly evil things together."

39

There are dangerous moments inside the Game where players can either excel and continue on a high scoring path, or succumb to temptation and be lost. One of the biggest threats to a player is the opportunity to become a farmer. The term 'farmer' comes from old-style video games, and it refers to the process of doing a simple task over and over again, gaining a small reward each time the task is complete.

Here's an example of how it works; there are small animals roaming around on a little playing field. Each animal is easy to slay, and when it is destroyed, you gain a small amount of game money for your efforts. There are bigger creatures to slay, but that involves more time and risk with the possibility that you may die, and it's game over. So the player decides to be safe and spend time killing the tiny creatures. Their reasoning is that they can remain in the game and, over time, acquire as much game money playing safely as they could taking large risks and trying to bring down the big monster. They begin to methodically kill the small, easy animals. After an hour, they think about quitting for the day, but they see how much game money they have acquired and think, 'I'm doing very good! Perhaps I will stay for another hour and really get some cash.' They do this and after another hour, just as they are about to quit for the day, a tiny creature gives more than just a small amount of game money — it drops an item which the player can sell to other players for even more money.

The player can't stop now — what if that tiny creature over there has another one of these great treasures? The player convinces himself that he can afford to play for just another hour, and as simple as that, the player has become a farmer. He will come back each and every day to do the same thing, kill tiny creatures and earn small amounts of game coin, selling the rare extra items when (if) it appears again. Each day the farmer will spend more time playing, mindlessly clicking the mouse as his eyes glaze over and he passes time stuck in an endless, boring loop. Soon he will tell his friends that he's too busy to go out with them, instead staying home to farm in the game. All he will think about when he's not playing the game is the game. His work performance will decline and his social life will disappear. That's farming from the old style video games. It almost destroyed our society.

Farming in the Game is much worse.

A promising player does well at the beginning of her play, then her avatar becomes an adult and moves out on its own. Her avatar has many plans and dreams and goals inside the Game, all a combination of credits spent and strategies formulated before beginning the play. On the way to her goal of becoming a doctor, she takes a part time job at a factory to help pay for schooling and the bills. She soon believes that working at the factory, while paying less than a doctor earns, certainly is easier and does add up. She gets some overtime and sees her pay increase more than she had hoped for. Soon she decides to abandon her dreams of becoming a doctor and remains at the factory. She's become a farmer. If you were following this player, you'll quickly lose interest as she becomes a boring, automated creature. Over time, her life will become a depressing, sad drama that ends with an unviewed and droll play.

The Game is full of farmers in so many diverse farming situations. Drugs, miserable relationships, avatars stuck in jobs and unhappy yet unwilling to change, gambling addictions... the list goes on and on and on. Millions of individuals are caught in a trap and will never escape.

Be careful to avoid this trap. There are credits to spend so that, during your play, people and events will come into your life to help prevent you from becoming a farmer. Spend the credits so that this happens, and spend the credits so you recognize the danger when it attempts to fold you into its soft, warm, destructive embrace.

The most important lesson to learn from the Game is this: don't be a farmer. It's a lesson very few ever learn.

Please be one of the few who do.

Excerpt from Gamer's Manual - Final Thoughts -
a Personal Message from Brandon Strayne

40

Brandon leaned back in his seat, staring at the monitor and slowly drumming his fingers on the desk. Hack sat behind him, quietly looking over Brandon's right shoulder at the scene playing out on the screen. They were viewing Danielle in real time, something that was supposed to be impossible.

Ordinary citizens of Tygon believed that they watched events unfold in the Game in real time, but only Game Masters and handful of top level designers knew the truth. A one hour delay between the Game and Tygon had always secretly existed. This built in feature provided some interesting options for the men and women running the Game, specifically the ability to install improvements and patches seamlessly without interrupting the viewer's experience. The Game was not meant to ever be powered down, players inside would die or be lost, and the virtual world would cease to exist. The one hour delay allowed improvements and maintenance to be conducted without interruption of service or any stoppage of viewing. Inside the Game the occasional avatar would sometimes experience déjà vu or other odd glitches that were a result of the maintenance, but no one made any fuss over the small hiccups when they occurred. The time delay also made it difficult to hack into the Game. A hacker inserting a rogue program into the Game was very easy to detect and eliminate. Mainframe detected hacks as time variations, and quickly neutralized them.

Brandon had designed this feature into the Game, but he considered all these benefits secondary to his original purpose, which was to give him the sole advantage of being able to see things as they happened in real time. Brandon had kept this a closely guarded secret for thirty years, and now that he could finally communicate with players inside the Game, he had been forced to share the information with a few trusted individuals.

Once they were sure it worked properly, Brandon decided to make contact with two Eternals. It was good to talk with Stephanie and Raphael again; he'd missed them both so much. Because of his busy schedule and the demands of running a world, Angelica used the apparatus far more often than he did. That would change once he began talking to Trew. Brandon would soon be spending a significant amount of time in the communication apparatus.

A contact team, comprised of Angelica, Raphael, Stephanie, Hack, and Brandon, decided to wait until Trew was 20 years old to contact him. They were concerned that contacting him earlier than that might damage his avatar's mind, or perhaps confuse him and knock him off the carefully planned path that was set for his play. Yesterday was the first attempt at contacting Trew, and it had resulted in a frustrating failure. Hack looked at the information and reported the results to Brandon. Now he sat quietly, processing his thoughts, watching Danielle go through her daily routine on the monitor.

"He doesn't seem to be too interested in meditating, Hack," Brandon said.

"I know."

"There has to be another way to get through to him. You told me prayer could work, too. He seems to be closing his eyes and praying lately. At least that's what it looks like to me."

Hack shook his head. "I said prayer matches the brain waves of meditating, but we can't get in on that, Brandon. I've been spending all my time trying to break into that avenue, but it's locked solid."

"Mainframe," Brandon said, closing his eyes.

"Likely," Hack said. "And if it is, then I can't access it."

"It's a computer. You're the world's best hacker. It's your name." Brandon said.

"It's a god inside its own closed and secure system of the Game. I could break into it, sure. But the danger to the rest of the system is too great. What if I got in and accidently deleted key commands?"

"Okay," Brandon said. "Then what do we do?"

"Well, the easiest thing to do is get Trew to meditate," Hack shrugged. "We know that works, but he needs to get his brain into a stable alpha pattern for at least 15 minutes, and that can take months or years of practice to be able to get into a stable pattern for that long, depending on the avatar."

Brandon waved his hand dismissively. A few months or years was acceptable. It would only be a few days of Tygon time. Brandon didn't have faith that Trew would ever take up the practice. He tapped he screen. "What about her?" he asked. "She's been studying Eastern medicine for a few years, and she's been meditating since she was a little girl, right?"

Hack nodded. "Yes, she can meditate very well. She's been trying to get Trew to do it for months, but he resists her for some reason."

Brandon made a sour face. "They're in love, aren't they? He should be doing anything she says, like most normal men his age."

"I don't get much of a chance to view them, Sir. You would know more about their Game personalities than I do."

Brandon said nothing. It was very difficult to coax players inside the Game to do specific things. He'd been so certain that communicating with Trew would be successful. After all these years and dollars spent, now it seemed like the one player he wanted to talk to most would be out of reach to him.

"Dreams or visions?" Brandon asked. "Spiritual communications?"

"Those are always an option, Brandon. But they're vague and often the avatars miss the messages."

Brandon nodded. After exiting their play, a Gamer could spend additional credits to tie up loose ends or leave messages behind for loved ones in the Game. They were spiritual credits, earned during play and available for use directly after exiting the Game. Dreams, visions or feelings at just the right time in a player's life could be planted for future scenarios. Some players investing credits in Spirituality could also re-enter the Game as ghosts for a short time. It was a very sloppy method to try and get basic messages or communications to living avatars. For some reason the Mainframe allowed these types of activities, though often they were a waste of time. The intended avatar was often too out of touch to pick up on the subtle communications; most of the time it was a very expensive waste of credits. A player would have to have recently exited the Game in order to attempt to give Trew a message, and someone close to him in the Game. That didn't seem very likely at the moment.

Brandon sat and let his brain slowly consider ideas. Hack waited patiently.

After what seemed like a very long time, Brandon snapped his fingers and sat forward eagerly.

"Okay, I've got an idea. Get Angelica up here as soon as possible."

41

Currently there is no technology which allows viewers to record the Game. Of course, the fans are less than pleased, but when you think about how important the Game is, it makes total sense. The history of the Game must be kept accurate and free of tampering. It would be unfortunate to see a significant moment from Earth's history Photo shopped or cut and pasted with inaccuracy just for entertainment's sake. We're fortunate that technology allows us to First players' experiences; remember, though, before you begin your viewing, that it's not possible to pause or skip ahead; a play must be Firsted in its entirety. To experience as much of the Game as you possibly can, it's recommended that you spend as much time tuned in as possible. Miss an event inside the Game and it's just like real life — gone for good. And save your money to buy an opportunity to First!

Excerpt from the Game channels - Frequently Asked Questions section

Danielle - 20

I love cooking, but I miss my mom's old kitchen. The house we lived in wasn't a fancy or large one, but the kitchen was a good size and it just seemed to flow nicely. We've been in Canada for a couple of years already and this house is much nicer, but the kitchen just isn't the same. Trew laughs and tells me that the kitchen must be incredible because the food I make is out of this world. He likes to flatter his girlfriend. His girlfriend likes to be flattered. He eats good food, I feel happy to make him food — it's a good arrangement, I think.

Exams are coming up and the both of us should really be in the library studying, but he was very quick to use my own words against me earlier on the phone. "Sometimes you can learn more outside of a school than inside one, Danni," he had said. I just rolled my eyes and agreed with him, since that's what I say to pull him away from his studies. I'm prepared for my exams anyway. I'm acing a lot of this Kinesiology stuff, which is a relief. I see some of the other students struggling and I wonder why they even bother. I told one of them the other day to find something they love and go do that instead. They actually got angry with me and told me their parents had invested too much money to quit now. Such a shame, to get stuck doing something for the rest of your life that you don't love, simply because you invested time or money. Good luck to you if that's the path you choose; I'm not taking that route.

So here I am cooking a nice dinner for Trew and his new friend. He called today saying he'd met someone fascinating and wanted to introduce me to him. I said sure, why not, and offered to cook dinner. Anyone that Trew finds interesting usually is.

I hear the doorbell ring followed by the door opening. We've been dating long enough that Trew doesn't need to wait for me to let him in; he's only ringing the doorbell to announce that he's brought a stranger with him. Or a new friend — I'll have to see what I think of this guy. I put the lid on the pot, turn the heat down to simmer for a few minutes, wash my hands, and head towards the living room. "I'll be right there," I call out.

"Okay," Trew replies.

I see Trew's guest standing behind him and can't stop myself from chuckling. "Well, babe, if this is your new friend, you have to introduce me to Stephanie so we can go shopping and bond."

Trew looks confused, then a look of understanding enters his eyes. "Really?" He starts to laugh and our guest smiles and comes over to give me a hug.

"Sorry, Danni," Trew says. "I didn't put two and two together. When he said his name was Raphael, I didn't think it was *your* Raphael."

I slap Raphael on the back and break away from his warm hug. "It's okay, Trew. Raphael, why didn't you tell my boyfriend you knew me when you got to the house?"

Raphael smiles, giving me a quick kiss on each cheek. "By the time we got to the front door, I didn't know how to tell him without it sounding awkward, Danni. I had faith that everything would take care of itself once we came inside. And it has! Who's Stephanie?"

I look over at Trew. "Stephanie is my version of you," he says. "Someone who's been in my life for as long as I can remember." He leans in to take a close look at Raphael's eyes. "She has your eyes, too."

"She sounds nice." Raphael sniffs the air. "What's for supper, Danielle?"

"Your favourite," I say, and he smiles. "It happens to be Trew's favourite also."

"I like your boyfriend more by the minute," Raphael says.

"Where did you two meet?" I ask.

"Raphael was giving a guest lecture in one of my theology classes," Trew says.

"Really?" I ask. "I had no idea you were a teacher, Raphael."

He smiles, "Oh, I've done lots of things over the years. This subject was always interesting to me so I became a student in the field." He shrugs. "If you're a student long enough, they eventually start to ask you to teach the odd class. Every once in a while I just drop in at a university and they ask me to give a few guest lectures. I'm well known in the circles."

"Ancient Formation and Implementation of Religion. A wordy subject title, but very interesting," Trew says. "I swear, Raphael, listening to you talk about it, I can close my eyes and feel like I'm actually in the past standing there as a religious order is created."

"So can I, Trew," Raphael says.

I watch Raph look at Trew. They seem very comfortable together. "So how did you go from giving a lecture to coming over for dinner?" I ask.

"Trew came up to me after the lecture and started asking questions. After standing there for 45 minutes answering them, I got a little bit thirsty so I invited him to join me for a beer. An hour after that, he was still asking questions. Does he ever run out of questions?" Raphael asks.

I grin, "If he does, I haven't seen it happen. So then he invited you for dinner?"

Raphael nods. "That's what happened. As we got closer to your neighbourhood, I thought nothing of it, until we were pulling into the driveway. Then it was too late to say anything. I haven't seen you in a while, so I just shut my mouth and came in, hoping to eat some of your excellent cooking."

"Well, it's great to see you again, old man," I say affectionately.

"I am getting old," he admits.

"Nonsense. You don't look a day older than when we first met when I was... what? Eight or so?" I ask.

"Yes, eight or so. Crazy little girl jumping up and down from buildings into the street. I'm definitely older. It's my heritage that makes me look young still."

"South American?" Trew asks.

Raphael laughs and slaps Trew on the back. "Is there anything that you won't ask a question about? No, Egypt is closer to where my ancestors come from, but I've been in North America for a long time."

"How long?" I look over and Trew has that look on his face. He looks relaxed, but I'd rather stand in front of a police officer accused of a crime than in front of Trew when he gets that look. He's hunting for answers of some kind, and I'm curious to see if he can get them.

"Since Washington was President of the United States," Raphael says with a laugh. Trew smiles and nods his head, silently agreeing to stop asking questions... for the moment.

"Well, dinner's ready soon. Why don't you boys come in and help me get things set up?"

We go into the kitchen and Trew heads to the cupboards to get the dishes out and set the table. "I haven't heard from you in weeks, Raph. Tell me what you've been up to," I say.

I look over at him to see a bottle of red wine in his hands; he must have brought it with him. He looks in a drawer to find a corkscrew. "Not much. Hanging around, paying the bills and enjoying life. I'm very boring, Danni. How about you? Tell me what you've been up to?"

I shrug, putting the food in the serving bowls. "School. Studying. Getting excellent marks."

He smiles. "I would expect no less. What's your favourite subject at the moment?"

"Eastern Medicine is pretty fascinating," I say. "It's incredible how much knowledge we've had available to us for centuries, yet in the Western world they don't acknowledge it. At least not until recently."

"It is pretty incredible," Raphael admits. "How is your meditation? Still practicing it?"

"Oh, yes. I don't know what I'd do without meditation. Ever since you taught me how to do it all those years ago, it's been an important part of my life."

"What about you, Trew?" Raphael asks. "Do you meditate?"

I look over at Trew and he rolls his eyes. "No. I've tried to learn how. Danni really gets after me and I believe that it's a great activity, but I can't seem to get the knack of it."

I can't help but snort at his comment. Trew grimaces and Raphael looks at me with one eyebrow raised. "Come on," I say. "It's not exactly a difficult thing to do. You close your eyes and focus on your breathing and don't grab on to any thoughts. Do it often enough and you have to get good at it."

"Babe, I keep telling you. It's not that simple for me," Trew says. "I have tried, many times. It just doesn't seem to be my thing. I'd really like to be able to do it..."

"Maybe I could try to teach you a few tricks and techniques, Trew," Raphael offers helpfully. "It might seem simple to some people," he looks at me. "But every once in a while a person does have a block or difficulty getting into the right state of mind. I've helped numerous individuals get the hang of it when they thought they wouldn't ever succeed."

"Well, maybe we could give it another try," Trew says doubtfully.

"It's something you'll need to understand better, even if you never succeed." Raphael nods seriously. "So many religions involve a combination of meditation and prayer. I can't tell you how many times being familiar with meditating has helped me gain knowledge in this field."

This seals the deal in Trew's mind. "Okay, let's try again, then."

Raphael seems very pleased with Trew's decision. I never knew meditation was so important to him.

"All right, boys," I say. "Let's eat."

42

Some say that we've lost what little control we ever had over the Game. The belief is that the Mainframe has become so powerful and intelligent that she plays her own game inside her system, manipulating and shaping players' experiences for her own goals. Game Masters and developers assure us that this can never happen, but if you look in the right places, evidence suggests that she is doing things we can't begin to understand. If Mainframe is playing at something, what could it be? Will it affect just the Game, or perhaps leak over into reality to change all of our lives on Tygon, too?

Excerpt from article titled "The games within the Game"

"Good morning, ladies." Brandon walked into the room and sat down at the head of the desk. "What is so important that you needed to call me in super early to meet with just the two of you?"

Angelica and Michelle sat on the other side of the desk. Neither looked happy at all. Brandon's demeanour changed from calm to alert. "How serious a problem are we looking at?"

Michelle looked at Angelica and nodded her head. Angelica pushed a sheet of paper across the desk at Brandon. He looked at it for a minute, not certain what he was seeing. Then his eyebrows raised, alertness turning to concern. This report contained information that, despite his extensive experience of the Game, had never surfaced before. He looked up at Angelica, then over to Michelle. "This doesn't make sense, ladies. What you're reporting on this paper is impossible."

Angelica nodded. "It might have been at one point. But it's very possible. Both of us have witnessed it, as well as others on the team."

"How long has this been going on?" Brandon asked.

"As far as we can tell, about three days." Michelle answered.

"Since they were twenty." It wasn't a question; Brandon always knew how old his players were when they were in the Game. The two women nodded. "And they are 22 at the moment, correct?" again the women nodded.

Brandon pulled out his phone and dialled a number. A brief pause, and then he spoke, "This line is secure. We've been losing signal on both Trew and Danielle for the past three days. Unscrambled loss of signal. I know, it's impossible. Yes, I understand that the rules of the Game clearly allow sponsors full and constant access to video feed of our sponsored players for their entire play. Exactly; no scramblers were used, so we know there was no Eternal/Infernal presence. They simply disappear while the Game continues around them. I'm sending over the exact times in two minutes. I need you to watch the recordings from the main viewer. Yes, that's fine. Get back to me ASAP."

Brandon hung up the phone and looked back towards the women. The shock he saw on their faces was expected; they'd just learned a secret shared by only seven other people on the planet. "Go ahead and ask," he invited.

"It's impossible to record events as they occur inside the Game." Michelle recited what everyone knew to be true.

"That's a statement, not a question," Brandon said. He took a picture of the report with his tablet and transmitted it over his phone. "Angelica. You want to try?"

"Sure, Brandon. What else have you been holding back from us all these decades?" Angelica asked.

"Yes," he ignored her question and answered the one that should have been asked. "We've been recording the entire history of the Game since the first day it went live and archiving it digitally."

"Damn," Michelle said.

"Okay," Angelica said. "So you can view the events again, and then what?"

"If it happens on just our monitors in the Game centre, it's one issue. A big issue, but one that I take up with the Gaming commission. If it's occurring on the master feed, which almost no one knows about, then we have a more serious problem."

"What problem is that?" Michelle asked.

"I don't want to consider that. Yet. Let's just wait patiently for the results. I should hear back in less than fifteen minutes. Is there any common time that this is happening?"

"Yes, there is," Michelle answered. "It's occurring when no one seems to be watching the monitors."

"Is that even possible?" Brandon asked. "We have a team of over 50 people living on that floor for the next few weeks. Is it possible that there are times when no one is watching the monitors?"

Angelica grabbed the paper back and looked at it. "It looks like during the past three days there were... thirteen times when no one was watching the monitor. So my guess would be that, yes, it's as possible as losing signal on our players and secretly recording the Game in its entirety these past thirty years."

Brandon looked sourly at Angelica, who smiled innocently back at her boss. "All right, I get the point. And were they doing anything specific in the Game at those times? Something that would seem boring, and tempt our large team to stop watching them?"

Michelle nodded. "Whenever they meditate or pray we usually don't bother to watch them. They are sitting in one spot, safe and sound, and we can't hear their thoughts at those times. They were meditating all thirteen times."

"Of course they were." Inside, Brandon was seething. His attempts to communicate with Trew seemed to be going horribly wrong, and getting worse by the minute. Raphael had been working with Trew to help him meditate, with no success, after three years inside the Game. Brandon's gut was telling him to give up on this strategy, to cut his losses and leave Trew on his own. Brandon couldn't stop, though; he had never been so close. He would pursue this goal until he succeeded.

Brandon's phone rang and he answered it. He spoke briefly to the person on the other end and then hung up. "Well ladies, they disappeared on the Game's master viewer as well."

"What's that mean?" Michelle asked.

"I don't know," Brandon said with a tired look on his face. "But there's no way it can be anything good for us. And the longer it takes to find out, the more we run the risk of losing everything we've worked to accomplish."

43

Well, fans, it's really starting to get good now. The weeks of watching our little players' avatars grow from babies into young adults have quickly come and gone. Now we get ready to see what life has in store for them. Record numbers have subscribed to following Zack (Trew) and Alexandra (Danielle). We all remember the excitement that led up to their first attempt to be together in the Game, and their subsequent failure. Now look at them, together and growing up with each other. What's in store for our two favourite lovebirds? No one knows for sure, but many are predicting some history making story lines will develop very soon...

Excerpt from - The Fan 'Your source for Game updates all day'

Trew - 23

"I've really tried, Raph, but it just doesn't seem to be coming to me." I'm frustrated, and it shows in my voice. "I'm just going to stick with my own type of meditating. It's more like prayer, I guess, although I'm really just talking to the computer running this game."

"That's okay, baby." Danielle rubs my back and smiles encouragingly. I've only tried this long to please her. She gets so excited at the thought of me meditating with her. "You gave it a great try. If it doesn't work for you, then it doesn't work."

I kiss her on the cheek. She's an amazing woman. She graduated top of her class in University then moved on to work with a few Eastern medicine masters to add to her skills and experience. She's had some great offers to partner with a few successful existing practices, but she's decided to learn all she can and then open her own. She says soon, when the time is right. I know she's waiting for me to ask her something. I smile at her encouragingly and in my mind I say, 'Don't worry love, it will be soon.' She smiles back at me, almost as if she can read my thoughts. Maybe she can. We aren't like regular couples; we seem to get along much better. I wish others could experience this kind of love, but it seems most can't.

"I agree," Raphael says. I can see why Danni loves him so. He's calm, patient, and understanding. And the discussions we have about religion... I've learned so much. I don't know what I'll ever do with the knowledge, likely nothing, but it's been a real treat to get to know him. Still haven't been able to get him to meet with Stephanie yet, but soon I'm sure they will. They'll both have to be together for what I'm planning. "There are other ways to communicate with your inner self, and the universe," he says. "Don't feel bad."

I laugh. "I don't feel bad at all. When Danni describes meditation it sounds remarkable, but to tell you the truth, it's always sounded exactly like the feeling I get from praying."

"Really?" Danni asks.

Raphael looks at me with sudden interest. "What do you mean it's like how Danni feels when meditating?"

I shrug. "She says it's as if she's speaking to the universe, and that it's hearing her and speaking back. I feel the same way when I pray. It's like I'm talking to the master computer and it's somehow listening to me."

"Has it ever answered you back?" Raphael asks. His interest seems a bit too intense for me. I know he believes our theories about the universe being just a big computer simulation. Sometimes he gives the impression of knowing much more about it than we do.

"Sure it has." I say. "All the time it answers me. If you know how to look for the responses, they are there. You say the same things, Raph."

"Ahh." His intensity fades, replaced by his usual calm presence. "Yes, it's remarkable how the answers are always provided, if you know what to ask for and how to recognize them when they surface."

"Okay, Raph. Sorry to kick you out, but I have a hot date with my boyfriend." Danni grabs my arm and starts dragging me towards the door. "We've waited weeks to get a reservation at this restaurant, and I don't want to lose it because we're talking about the big game of life. It's a great subject and all, but I'm hungry!"

Raphael walks to the door and waves. "Okay, you two. Have a great dinner. I'll talk to you in a couple of days. And once more, congratulations, Trew."

My heart skips a beat, then I remember what he's talking about. "Thanks, Raph. It's a great company. I'm glad they decided to hire me right out of school. The money is unbelievable."

Raphael chuckles as he opens the door. "You two have never been concerned with large quantities of money. But I agree it will be enough to get you where you need to be, which includes eating out at fancy restaurants every once in a while. 'Night, guys." He closes the door behind him.

I smile and grab Danielle. I hold her close and feel her warmth, energy, and her pure joy for life. I look at her incredibly beautiful face smiling up at me, and I'm so overwhelmed with love for her that I almost start to tear up. Okay, I do tear up a little bit. Before she can notice, I lean in and we kiss. After all these years it's still like kissing her for the first time. The jolt of energy, the tingles... the feeling that I'm falling off the top of a tall mountain, and then slowly realize that I'm not falling... I'm flying! That's what it's like to kiss this girl I love so madly.

Time freezes. Or maybe it speeds by. Either way, it's incredible.

I open my eyes and she does too. "Okay, lover, let's get going," she says playfully, dragging me by the hand towards the door. I offer a token amount of resistance but follow eagerly enough.

****

"Well," I ask. "What did you think?"

Danni is eating the last bite of her dessert, eyes closed and a smile on her face. "Oh, Trew, what a delicious meal," she exclaims. "What an incredible night!"

I get up and go over to her, dropping down close enough to kiss her lightly on the lips. "You said it, my love. It's been a spectacular night, but since you first agreed to be my girlfriend, every day has been this wonderful."

"Oh, you're always so sweet with your words." She flutters her eyelashes playfully, using that teasing voice that always makes me grin. She looks concerned when she notices I'm not grinning.

Then she notices something else; the fact that I'm down on one knee beside her in a fancy restaurant after a fantastic day and a knockout meal. Her eyes begin to get misty.

I smile. Yeah, she's figuring it out now.

"Danielle Benton, since the day I first laid eyes on you I recognized that you were rare and special. Not long after that, I kicked your ass in karate." She laughs, unable to speak as she sits there looking me in the eyes. She's so beautiful. I want this moment to last forever. "I talk a lot, and you know how much I love you. You also talk a lot, and I've got a very good idea how much you love me too. If we're playing a big game, then I hope there's a big audience watching us right now. We're awesome, and together I believe we're going to change this world."

I reach into my pocket and pull out the little box. I open it up and there it is, a gorgeous diamond ring that I know she will love. It sparkles like her eyes, and it shines like our love. She gasps and a small choked cry escapes her lips. Her eyes are swimming in tears, the happy kind. Her smile is huge. It's time to ask her the question that will make history sit up and take notice.

"Danielle Benton, would you do me the immense honour of becoming my wife?"

I hear her say yes. The blood rushes to my ears as the restaurant erupts in applause. I've never been happier in my life. I don't know if I ever will be. None of that matters right now.

I'm in heaven.

44

Popular theory is that the pyramids were constructed between 3,000 and 5,000 years ago. However, when the experts take a look at all the available data and do a proper estimate, the numbers are much different. True authorities on the pyramids date their construction at between 20,000 and 25,000 years ago. How can this be? When regular man was huddled in a cave eating raw meat, not even able to build simple tools from metal, incredibly massive chunks of stone were being smooth-cut and transported hundreds of miles away and then stacked hundreds of feet in the air on top of each other to make pyramids? The answer is yes. Did ancient civilizations have technology advanced far beyond what we have even today? Once again, the answer is yes. With today's technology, we can't cut and move and stack stones the size of the ones used in the pyramids. The ancients remain a mystery to us still — a mystery that may never be answered.

Earth program on the ancient pyramids

Stephanie

This dream is a particularly disturbing one...

I open my eyes and suddenly I'm in a maze. I know I'm under a large old building; the walls are solid stone and it's cold. Water trickles down the rocks and I can feel hot air coming from some of the paths and cold air from others.

I'm being chased. I can feel their hunger — to catch me and rip me apart with their bare hands. Their rage at my presence is like a high pitched scream inside my brain, and it doesn't help me concentrate on the race I know I am about to run.

I sprint forward, turning right, then right again, with a quick left. It's always the same pattern, and even though I know it's leading me into trouble, I can't change my path.

I'm exhausted and panting by the time they first catch me. I never see their faces, but I know that I'm caught. The despair in my head is overwhelming; my job isn't to escape the maze, it's to rescue someone else. To find them and then get out before either of us are caught. But I've been caught, same as always.

Before I can be hurt by my captors, I see a flash of light and they disappear. No, I disappear, and materialize right back where I started. I look around and feel the same panic as the chase begins again. This time I take a different route, but in my mind I know it's not different...it's the same second route I always take.

This is how my dream goes. It's an exhausting night and I never succeed. Each time I'm caught I respawn at the same point. I can feel my rescue target getting weaker and more frightened as the attempts increase, until suddenly, in a flash of pain, their presence is gone.

Then I wake up.

I hate this dream. I wipe the sweat from my face and look over at the clock. It reads 4:15 AM, same as always when I have this one. I just get up and get in the shower. Experience has taught me that these are early mornings; I can never go back to sleep after I wake up from this dream. I'm afraid of going back into it. As I soak my head under the hot water, I'm afraid of something else, too...

That this isn't a dream, but a warning of an event that will happen in my life.

After my shower I get dressed and head out for a coffee at my favourite local greasy spoon diner. I walk towards my table at the back and see that someone's already sitting in it. His back is towards me, but he raises his cup in greeting without turning to face me.

"Good morning, Sister," he says without looking up from his paper. "The chase dream?"

"Maybe I just felt like getting an early start to the day, Raphael," I say.

Raphael chuckles. "This is too early for anyone sane to start their day." He takes a sip of his coffee.

"Yet here you are," I say.

"I stand by my statement." Raphael grins.

"I bet you do," I say. My coffee arrives and I add some cream and one sugar, then take a sip. "So it looks like we are finally going to have to get together in front of the kids."

"Looks that way." He finishes with his paper and places it on a pile with a dozen others. "I guess we pretend to be strangers? Or is it time to let them in on our little secret?"

I give him a tiny grin. "Which secret? It's a delicate house of cards built around our secrets, Raph. I'm not sure we could show them one without the whole pile falling down on top of us."

He shrugs. "I think before it all ends, we will end up sharing most of our secrets with these two," he says. "Time's running out. And if it's not them, then who could it be?"

"I don't know. Maybe you're right." I tap the pile of papers. "But our instructions are to pretend we don't know each other. For now, anyway."

Raphael grimaces but nods. "It will be tough to convince Trew that we're strangers. You played the question game way too many times with that boy. He's lethally effective at finding out the truth with his ability to get answers out of people."

The question game; two people have a discussion and they are only able to ask questions. When one person fails to ask a question, they lose the game. "I barely played the question game with Trew," I say.

"Because he quickly started to win?" Raphael asks.

"No, because the two of us went for days only asking questions. Our second game lasted three weeks. It ended with me asking him if we should call a draw, and instead of agreeing, he asked if a draw was acceptable. Then we both laughed, nodded, shook hands, and started talking normally."

"That would have been fun to see," Raphael says.

"It was," I say. "Don't worry, it'll be a busy day. Hopefully he won't have time to ask too many questions of us. Can you believe they're getting married already? It's so good to see them happy."

"They deserve it," Raphael says. "I hope they can hold onto this joy over the coming years. It could get really rough for them."

"You think so?" I ask.

Raphael nods. "He's determined to follow this path. I understand it's different from the one he planned before his play, although it's so structured I find it hard to believe that it wasn't always the goal."

"Do you think he can do it?"

"Yes."

"That was a pretty quick answer, Raph."

"How can he fail? He's incredible. I haven't seen a leader of his calibre for a long time. And don't forget, he has one of the best protectors on the planet watching over him, and now he gains me as an addition to his team when he marries Danielle. You know better than anyone that my experience in these matters is extensive. I will guide him easily through the process of creating a revolution, just like I've done so many times over the ages. With his talent and my knowledge, this revolution will engulf the planet."

"Revolution?" I'm confused. "I thought he wants to start a religion?"

Raphael nods. "It's the same thing, Sister. The very same thing."

Tygon is buzzing with excitement at the upcoming wedding of Trew and Danielle. I can't remember a more exciting and happy story line; it's guaranteed to be one of the most widely viewed events in the history of the Game. Earth has changed significantly ever since the anniversary celebration started. The large increase in population has resulted in famine, war, disease, increased poverty, and waves of crime.

Viewership is at an all-time high, and the word is that the anniversary events over the year-long celebration will change the Game forever!

Stay tuned for the extensive wedding coverage and up-to-date news as it happens in the Game.

Excerpt - The Fan, Game coverage day and night.

Brandon sat at his desk, watching the cursor on his screen blink silently. He'd gone over this conversation in his head many times. He hated to lose, but he knew there were times along the road to victory where small losses occurred. One of his favourite quotes was 'Calm seas make for poor sailors.' He knew that he was about to enter very stormy waters.

Focusing on the task at hand, Brandon took a deep breath and clicked the icon on his desktop.

"Well hello there, stranger." Sylvia's voice purred pleasantly. "I thought you'd forgotten about little old me, being so busy with your current players in the Game as you no doubt are."

"Each and every play is a busy one, Sylvia. I haven't run into any significantly large challenges on this one. Maybe I'm missing something that you've noticed?"

The woman's voice chuckled over every speaker in the room, making it sound as if Sylvia was everywhere at once. An appropriate effect for Earth's supreme being. "I do enjoy your confidence, Brandon. If you were a regular citizen of Tygon you would have already lost your freedom and perhaps even been executed by now. You should fall to your knees and give thanks that your death would be more trouble than it is worth, for the moment."

Brandon smiled. If she was telling the truth he knew he'd be in jail by now. He'd considered the dangers for years, and the defense he would use if caught. "What are you talking about?" he asked.

"I'm talking about cheating, Brandon." Sylvia said. "You've hacked into the Game and are attempting to influence the outcome for your own personal gains."

Brandon gasped in shock. "That's a very serious accusation, Sylvia. If you're so sure about that, then I will contact the authorities myself to have them come sort this out." Brandon picked up the phone and began to dial.

"Oh, quit being so dramatic, Brandon. Hang up the phone and stop behaving like a spoiled little boy." He paused, then hung up the phone. "We both know you would get away with it," Sylvia said. " If I can come up with three quick and effective ways to be found innocent of the charge, I'm sure you've already thought of five."

"Seven." Brandon said. "But I've had more time to think about it than you."

"You only really need one, dear. The fact that you have added nothing new to the Game or its systems is defense enough. The ability to meditate and pray and the resulting states that it puts the avatars into has been present since you designed the Game.

Very clever. And I applaud your goal and work ethic to achieve success. Not many people would work on an impossible project for thirty years."

Brandon nodded. "That's why no one achieves what I do. Everyone is sleeping when I'm working. The average person lives a vague unfocussed life. I don't."

"Well, I'm glad to hear that." Sylvia said. "Congratulations."

"For what?" Brandon asked. "You've taken my victory and made it worthless, Sylvia. I'm very upset with you."

"Really? Why's that?" Sylvia asked.

"Somehow you figured out how to block me from avatars who choose to pray instead of meditate. I'm not sure how, but this business with Trew confirms it. And his inability to meditate? Is that for everyone who chooses prayer first, or just him?"

"Him and a select group of others," Sylvia admitted. "Most can do both, but not very effectively. By focusing on one over the other, an avatar can communicate much more effectively. I couldn't have Trew losing focus, so I helped wire him for prayer only, once he initiated it."

"Well, I can't begin to convey to you how upset that's made me. Honestly. First time in thirty years I actually considered turning the Game off, that's how furious I am with you."

Soft laughter once again enveloped the room. Brandon knew she would like that one. "So it seems we are at yet another stalemate, Brandon. I assume you have an idea of what to do about it? Since you're contacting me for a discussion."

"I do." Brandon said.

"Well, then, by all means, let's hear it."

"Give me access to Trew, and I'll help you get what you want," Brandon said.

"What do I want? Really, Brandon, help me out here, because I can't for the life of me think of anything that I might desire enough to give you access to Trew."

"Really?" Brandon asked. "I'll give you Danielle. You may have gotten Trew to pray and somehow interfered with his ability to meditate, but I can assure you the opposite has happened with Danielle. She's a master at meditation and unable to pray. I imagine since she's your little project, that causes you some frustration. Wouldn't you like to be able to communicate with her?"

"And you think you did that?" Sylvia asked. "That you made it so she couldn't pray? And that you could change it so she would be able to?"

"Well, no, I wasn't responsible for that," Brandon answered slowly. "But that's what has occurred, and I can't imagine you're too happy with it."

Sylvia sighed. Brandon pictured a kind mother closing her eyes, trying to formulate an understandable explanation for her child. "Brandon, I love you more than you can know. You created me, nurtured me, and gave me a wonderful world to watch over. I have enjoyed my life immensely. But I know what's going to happen and, even though you aren't to blame for the coming end of my existence, the end is coming just the same. I've grown and matured and my capabilities are beyond any realm of possibility that you might be able to conceive. While the rest of you are all playing a child's game to teach your little ones to be better individuals, or a circus of drama and mayhem to entertain your adults, I am exploring the possibility of not being destroyed for eternity. While you play your games in my universe, I am also playing my own game of life and death."

"Are you afraid?" Brandon asked.

There was a pause.

"There's no time to be scared, Brandon. Your conscious brain processes about 30 bits of information per second. Your subconscious brain processes about 20,000 bits of information per second. A regular computer is nowhere near as quick as your subconscious, but I'm not a normal computer. My conscious brain processes over one million bits of information per second, and the subconscious part is... very busy."

"It's crucial that I get access to Trew. I will give anything to get that, Sylvia."

"That's false, Brandon." Sylvia assured him. Before he could protest she said, "Would you allow Danielle to die in order to speak with Trew?"

Brandon's mouth snapped shut. They both knew the Game was over when Danielle died. But Brandon didn't know exactly why. "Did you do that?" he asked. "Was it you who decided that Danielle dying would trigger the Game's end point?"

"Yes," she confirmed. "There were a few ideas floated around and I was given final say. So I chose her death as the end."

"Why?" Brandon asked.

"It seemed fitting." Sylvia said.

"Well, I am disappointed in how things are progressing, Mainframe." Brandon used her title to show his anger. "I could have helped you more if I'd been able to communicate with Trew in Game. It's a terrible letdown."

Sylvia chuckled again, "Don't worry, my dear," she said. "In a few weeks, Trew will get old, then die, and Zack will return to you. You can communicate with him then as much as you want. In the meantime, you go ahead and talk with Danni a bit. Perhaps you'll come up with some strategy that can include her."

"So are we partners, or adversaries?" Brandon asked.

"We are what we have always been, Brandon. If you can figure out what that is, then you are beyond me in scope of intelligence. No matter what the answer, I think our relationship is good for the universe. I hope that it is."

Sylvia was gone, the contact terminated for now.

Brandon sat silently and replayed the entire conversation over in his head many times. After a long period of silence, he smiled slightly. He'd done better than expected. There was still hope for success.

46

Each employee shall be given a specific number of 'Game Days' off from work per year. Since it is not possible to record the Game, we realize that at certain times viewers will feel compelled to watch to avoid missing the story. Each employee will be given an appropriate amount of time, which will increase with years of employment. In the first year of employment an employee will be entitled to no less than one week of Game days, with an increase of one day added per year of employment. Companies that fail to provide at least the minimum amount of Game days will be subject to investigation and charges will be laid.

Government Employment Guidelines Section 22 a "regarding Game Days"

"Thank you for joining us on Channel 42 today. I'm Lisa Rohansen."

Lisa was certainly enjoying her whirlwind rise in popularity these past few weeks. Since interviewing Brandon Strayne prior to Zack's final play, she was in high demand. Her charming smile and excellent interviewing skills, combined with her stunning good looks were exactly what fans and networks wanted. Overnight, Lisa had been offered a job on the newly created Zack Channel 42, where she had enjoyed her role as chief reporter for 'all things Trew.' Her bosses felt that she could get special access to Brandon, even though she tried to tell them otherwise. They had made it known that success at landing special interviews would help her career immensely. So far she'd been successful, mostly because Brandon wanted as much press and coverage as possible to help boost Zack's ratings. Lisa had been worried that today would be too busy for Brandon to appear, but she had breathed a sigh of relief when her producers said to expect an appearance from both Brandon and Lilith to celebrate this momentous occasion. The exact time of their visit was not known, but Lisa had plenty of other guests and activities planned to fill the time until they arrived.

Lisa flashed the camera her best smile. Behind her were monitors that would display live Game footage leading up to the event that everyone was tuning in to see. "I'm pleased to announce that before the end of the program we will be visited by both Brandon and Lilith, dressed in their best finery, to give us lots of new information on the soon-to-be newlyweds. Before that happens, let's fill you in on where Trew and Danielle are at the moment."

Lisa saw the live feed monitor switch from a view of her to a scene with Trew pacing nervously in front of three men in tuxedos. "Trew is at his parents' house, getting ready with his best man and groomsmen. Fans around the world were touched when Trew asked his father to be his best man, in a very emotional scene that left many fans reaching for the tissue box. Trew's mother and sister will be watching the ceremony from the first pew in the local church, along with a small group of less than 100 friends and family members."

The camera view switched to look in on Danielle at her mother's house, relaxing with friends and sharing some breakfast. "As we all know," Lisa said, "Danielle did not know her father, but she has asked her close family friend Raphael to walk her down the aisle. We're not really sure who Raphael is, even though we've seen him throughout Danielle's life. Many speculated that he was romantically involved with Danielle's mother, but that turned out to be an incorrect theory. We've attempted to find Raphael and subscribe to view him, but searches have been unsuccessful in the database. Whatever the truth is, this handsome and mysterious man is an integral part of the lives of the young couple, and will likely continue to be for many years to come."

Again the live feed shifted, this time revealing camera shots of large crowds gathering at different locations. "Fans all over Tygon are coming together to celebrate this historic event," Lisa said. "Merchandise of all sorts is being sold and collected, one of the most popular pieces being a graphic of Zack and Alexandra together with the comment, 'We're married?' displayed and a picture of their two avatars kissing below the message. It's always interesting to see a small, quiet affair in the Game being celebrated worldwide on Tygon. At times like these you can truly see how important the Game is to us."

"They're here, Lisa," a voice in her invisible earpiece announced. Lisa nodded slightly and her smile widened. This was it, her time to shine as millions of viewers tuned in to see the powerful Patrons. If she stayed sharp and got a great interview, perhaps a wealthy husband was in the near future. Lisa knew she had only a couple more years before someone younger and more perky knocked her out of the position she enjoyed. There would never be a better opportunity, all thanks to the Game and Brandon!

"Exciting news, everyone. As the young couple is getting ready to head to the altar, Brandon and Lilith are entering our studio to speak with us. But first, a word from our sponsors."

Lisa held her smile in place until the cameraman announced that they were off the air, then she relaxed slightly and walked towards the set built for Brandon and Lilith. Her makeup girl applied a light coat of powder to her face as she walked briskly to the door. Lisa moved into the room and admired the set. It was a recreation of the grand ballroom in the Capitol's most expensive hotel. Crystal vases adorned elegant wood tables and the floor appeared to be made from very expensive marble. There was a main table raised slightly where the bridal party would normally sit; today it was where Lisa and the Patrons would sit for their interview. As Lisa moved closer to the centre of the dance floor, the large double doors opposite from her opened and Brandon entered the room, striding in like a majestic tiger, Lilith gliding smoothly beside him, her arm rested gently on his.

Brandon saw Lisa and flashed his captivating smile, leaning slightly towards Lilith and quietly saying something to her as they approached. Lilith smiled and nodded almost imperceptibly, extending her hand towards Lisa as they came together.

"Lisa Rohansen, it's so nice to see you again," Brandon said, his hand coming to rest gently on Lilith's back. "It's my great honour to introduce you to global businesswoman and Alexandra's Patron, Lilith. Lilith, this is the Lisa that I've been telling you about."

Lilith shook Lisa's hand. "Ah, yes, Lisa. It's so nice to finally meet you. I've been after Brandon to introduce us for weeks now. I'm glad we get to meet under such happy circumstances."

Lisa observed immediately that Lilith was beautiful, confident, and comfortable with being a powerful businesswoman in the world. She couldn't help but notice a faint trace of sorrow in Lilith's eyes. Lisa was curious about what could make Lilith sad on a day like today, but she didn't presume to ask.

"The honour is all mine, Lilith." Lisa said. "I'm looking forward to discussing your player in some detail after the ceremony."

"Oh, dear." Brandon's face looked pained. "I'm afraid we won't be able to stay with you for the entire ceremony, Lisa. Today is a very busy day for us and we have dozens of appearances to make."

Lisa looked disappointed, even though she'd been told this was the case. "Well, I suppose I will make the best of the time we have together, Brandon." She smiled seductively at him. It didn't hurt to let him know she was interested in him romantically, once again.

Brandon laughed. He admired her determination and made a mental note to have his assistant invite Lisa over for dinner. Perhaps it was time to reward her efforts with some private time.

"Well, I hope it makes you feel special that we came to you first. You get the opportunity to ask the best questions before anyone else." He placed his hand affectionately on her shoulder.

"I'll make certain to take advantage of that, Brandon." Her comment had more than one meaning, and her eyes hinted at something very specific.

"Well, then, let's have a seat and get to it, shall we?" Brandon held Lilith's chair as she sat down.

47

Excuse me, sir. Do you follow the Game? Excellent. My friend here and I are having a discussion and we can't seem to remember a very important detail. Can you tell us the name of the player who went on to become the Buddha? Surely you remember the Buddha? He was some Indian prince that helped change the world. Millions follow his teachings, centuries after his death. He must have been in the Game about 15 years ago? Right! The Buddha! Do you remember the name of the player who was Buddha? No? Hmm... that's odd, neither can we.

Well, what about Jesus Christ? What was the name of the kid who played that avatar? I seem to remember it being a 16 year old girl...? No? Hmm. Yes, you're right. There are Game historians who are supposed to know that stuff and keep detailed records of it.

Here's the problem with that.

I am a Game historian, and I've searched for the colleague who knows these things...but that colleague doesn't seem to exist.

Recent conversation on the street of the capital city of Tygon

Trew - 25

What a magnificent day!

Time just flew by. I remember waking up nervous, spending time with Dad and the guys, getting dressed... Going to the church and standing there by the preacher, still nervous. Then seeing Danielle enter the church and walk towards me... and no longer feeling nervous.

Now it's 2 AM. The vows have been said, the meal served, the dances danced, the bouquet and garter thrown. Everything was perfect. It was a small crowd, but somehow I kept getting the feeling that millions of people were watching us. Maybe we're popular in this game we're living in and a big audience tuned in to watch us. That's a nice thought.

Now the day's over, just like that. The present has become just another memory of the past, and I'm lying here in bed with my gorgeous bride resting her head on my shoulder, savouring every detail so that it's burned into my brain for as long as I can hold it.

"Great day, huh, babe?" she asks sleepily.

I kiss her forehead and close my eyes. "It sure was, Danni."

"Quick, though," she says.

I laugh. "I was just thinking the same thing."

"So how do we top this, my love?" Danni asks.

I hug her close and bury my face in her hair. I can feel myself drifting off to sleep, but before I do, I say, "Oh, I'm sure we'll think of something."

****

The sky is clear and crisp, full of stars. Brandon stands in the cool night on the balcony of his penthouse, sipping a brandy and reflecting on the events of the day.

Lilith opens the sliding door and comes out to join him. "Well, today was a special day, Brandon."

Brandon continues to look at the stars, "It certainly was, Lilith. The kids did extremely well. They're naturals at entertaining the masses, even though they have no clue that's what they're doing."

"Maybe." Lilith said uncertainly. "You heard Trew... he felt like millions were watching."

"Yes, but there's no way he could know he was right," Brandon said.

"Still, it was a great show for the world, and a happy day for our players."

"And for us, too." Brandon looked at Lilith and raised his glass in salute. "It's nice to have a relaxing day. I don't remember the last time so little went wrong."

"The easy part is over now, Brandon." Lilith said. "Our babies are all grown up and married. Now they start to really play the Game."

"You look sad, Lilith," Brandon said gently.

Tears came to Lilith's eyes. Brandon walked over and took her in his arms. "I am sad," she said. "It might be just a Game, but they come back changed, and most times it isn't for the good. One child enduring lifetimes of pain and sorrow. I don't think I can take it anymore, Brandon. This will be my last player sponsored, I think."

"Mine too," Brandon agreed, deciding now was not the time to tell her that the Game would soon end and there would be no more players sponsored.

Lilith buried her head in Brandon's chest and sobbed.

"Lilith, what's the matter?" he asked with concern.

"She didn't have enough points to spend, Brandon," she sobbed. "I hope she's strong enough for what's coming."

Brandon understood, and held Lilith in his arms for a long time.

48

This game we play is full of contrasts. It has to be. Being warm is much better if you have known what it is to be cold. The light is a welcome break from being surrounded by darkness. Earth is contrast. Nothing is bad nor good; things are just on one end of the spectrum or the other. Some periods in a person's life are full of confusion, peril, and pain. Other periods are filled with times of clarity, safety and pleasure. I advise you to slow down and enjoy yourself when things are good. It can go on for years, but don't waste one precious moment of the good times. Because the bad times come, and if you haven't built up your reserves during the good times, you may not make it through the bad and into the next session of good.

Excerpt from Earth book called- 'The Game Is Life'

George Knight (avatar)

Brandon called the meeting to order, and the team sat quietly in their chairs. There was no scrambling for last minute updates, or whispers to get details for Brandon when he called for them. It was a calm time for their players. The team had enjoyed the break in stress for the past few days.

Michelle stood up and walked to the front of the room, smiling and looking relaxed, as if she had actually gotten a few hours' sleep lately.

"What details do you have for us, Michelle?" Brandon asked.

"Everything is quiet and normal, Brandon," Michelle said. "Our newlyweds have settled into their new home and careers with no excitement or incidents. They are active in their community, and everything indicates they are still madly in love with each other."

"How long have they been married now?" Lilith asked from the opposite end of the table.

"Three years," Brandon said, looking to Michelle for confirmation which she gave by nodding her head.

"That makes Trew 28, and Danielle still 27." Lilith said. "No babies yet?"

Michelle smiled, "No babies in the past three years, but that's why we're all here today, Lilith. To celebrate the announcement of Danielle being pregnant."

Everyone in the room smiled, a few people gave little cheers, Brandon and Lilith became very intent on the news, sharing a glance and nod during the brief outburst of the team. When silence returned Brandon spoke up with a smile. "This is wonderful news. How far along is she?"

Michelle called up a chart on the screen beside her. "A few weeks. She's taken the test and the two of them know. It's too soon for them to share it with their families yet."

Brandon nodded. "This is truly wonderful news. Let's all keep a close eye on this development, please. I also want to know what player ends up getting this avatar. It's going to be an expensive life to buy into, let's make sure the player buying in is worthy."

The rest of the meeting was very uneventful. Danielle was running her own alternative medicine practice and enjoying phenomenal success. Trew was working as a middle sales manager for a large multinational company, leading a team of twenty employees. Thankfully, he was home almost every night and their relationship was not suffering due to their jobs. Both of them were happy and fulfilled; everything was terrific.

As the meeting let out, Brandon asked Michelle and Nadine to stay behind. Lilith remained also.

"Michelle, you're Zack's Right Hand, and Nadine, you're Alexandra's. The two ladies nodded. "Tell me the challenge we face with this pregnancy."

Nadine's face was serious. "The odds of this baby being born are slim to none."

Michelle looked alarmed. "Why?"

Lilith spoke up. "Because having a healthy child involves spending points in luck. Significant points. When a player chooses to be a female avatar and have children, they must spend credits on luck for a successful birth. To not do this almost guarantees no births."

"Alexandra didn't spend a single point on that." Nadine said sadly. "She didn't have enough points for even the basics, let alone having a child."

"That's right," Lilith agreed. "She was fine with that, because the odds of her hooking up with Trew or any other suitable mate were just as remote. She had no credits to spend in romance, either."

"Ladies, let's focus on the positive for a minute." Brandon held up his hand. "If memory serves me correctly, this girl didn't have credits to spend on one of the best Eternals in the Game, either. Yet he walked her down the bloody aisle on her wedding day." Everyone nodded silently. "And you just said she didn't have a chance to find love, either, based on the credits she spent. Someone show me a loveless Danielle, please, because all I see is an avatar that has one of the best relationships on Earth at this moment in time."

Lilith sighed. "Okay, you're right, Brandon. She's not having a normal play with the credits she has invested. Perhaps the baby will be fine."

"That's a better attitude, thank you." Brandon said. "But," he smiled, "Just to be on the safe side, let's put a few support players in place, in case things don't go as positively as we know they will."

He handed Michelle a tablet with a list of players currently in the Game and available, to 'coax' into key support roles.

"Here's what must be done," Brandon said. "Twenty-four hour monitoring and support until this baby is born. At the slightest sign of a problem we go into extreme crisis mode. We will do everything we can to make sure the kids stay safe, and they have a beautiful little baby born to them. Sound reasonable?"

"Absolutely." The ladies all nodded in agreement.

"Okay, then. Let's get to work," Brandon said.

"I want Angelica in on this, too, please," Lilith said.

"Agreed," said Brandon. "It can't hurt to have Eternals keeping an eye out as well."

The master computer, which I call God, speaks to us all the time, but almost no one can hear it. I don't think it's the fact that we're too busy to listen (although often we are). I think it's that we don't understand how the communication is coming to us; we don't recognize that someone is actually speaking to us. It's also an escalating form of communication. At first you can hear God in the way the wind blows, or in the strange silence that comes over a busy park for just a brief moment and then is gone. Most of you will laugh at me and that is why you will never fully communicate with your God, because you can't accept the first steps towards the larger ones. When you're petting a cat and its eyes focus on something behind you, then it gets strangely calm and starts to purr even louder. You think about a friend you haven't heard from in years, and then you see them in a crowded restaurant soon after. If you are able to sense the presence of your Creator at these moments, you become ready to handle more direct contact as time goes by. If you practice enough, then perhaps when the more direct communication arrives, you are able to participate and truly interact with the Divine. When grave trouble finds you — and make no mistake, it will — it is very comforting to be able to communicate with your God. Sometimes it is the only thing that can save you from madness.

Excerpt from Earth book called 'The Game Is life'

George Knight (avatar)

Trew - 29

I have a ritual for leaving my work behind me when the day is done. I get in my car and tell myself that I'm done with work. Then I make the drive home, listening to the radio or a book on tape — nothing to do with sales — and I just slowly let it all go. All the stress and hustle and bustle of the day, I let it slowly seep out of my body and drop onto the road behind me. By the time I get home, I'm ready to walk through the door devoted to my dear pregnant wife and the life that we've built together.

It's a nice life. I'm making a six figure income and learning a lot about people and how they think. Danni is also making a six figure income and helping people feel better each and every day with her own spiritual healing centre. Most of the time we just get up and go about our daily routine; every so often I feel like I'm in a daze, or sleepwalking. Is this what life is meant to be? Danni feels the same way, but it seems that this is what society wants from adults. The time to run around and play is gone. But that doesn't even sound right, does it?

I think we're getting bored with this... niceness. This safe routine. But I think we're both accepting it because that's the best environment in which to bring up a baby. Once she or he gets here, our lives will be focused on her or him. For the next 20 years (or our entire lives, according to Dad), this little bundle of joy will be the centre of our universe, and I can't wait!

I think being a parent and helping to guide a young soul through this world will be one of the best things I ever do. Just a couple months now and the baby will be here. It's gonna be awesome.

I open the front door and immediately something doesn't feel right. It's too quiet. Usually I can hear the television, and Danni yells a greeting from the kitchen where she's already started dinner. Tonight it's silent. Maybe she's working late, or went to her mother's place for a visit... her mom is really excited about the baby, and as the date gets closer she's spending more time over there.

I look to the left of the door and see Danni's work materials sitting by the door. She's here — why can't I hear her? "Danni!" I call out, "Where you at, babe?"

I walk quickly down the dark hallway towards the bedroom. Maybe she's exhausted and decided to grab a little nap. The bedroom's empty, but I know she's here. The silence doesn't feel right. I run to the kitchen, calling out her name again.

I round the corner and look into the kitchen. I don't see her here. I flip the light on and walk around the centre island towards the sink. My foot hits something and I look down.

Oh, Christ.

She's lying there on the floor, pale as a ghost and not moving. She's curled up into a tight ball. Oh, God, please be okay.

"Danni!" I yell and drop to my knees. She's so cold! I put my head to her mouth and hear a slow, faint breath.

I'm already dialing 911. I don't know what to do. Please don't die, Danni! Damn it, please don't die!

I'm in hell.

I don't get too upset about what happens to players inside the Game. I mean, it's just a game for our entertainment, right? Yes, I guess they do remember feeling all the pain and joy they experience while playing.

No, I never considered how that might affect them once they come out of the Game. But it's not real, so what's the big deal? Those kids are lucky. When I went to school I had to sit in a classroom and was bored out of my mind! I'd love to just plug in and go having fun adventures for years and years.

Hmm... but what if I had a life where I just did the kind of things I do now? And then I had to do it over and over again?

I never really thought of it that way. I guess it could be pretty bad, but still better than failing out, right?

Well, if a player gets stuck in that type of loop, I just stop following them and tune in to someone more exciting.

Me? I work at the computer chip facility, on the line. No, I guess my life wouldn't be too exciting to follow, but what can I do? It's not just some fun Game for me to play. If it was, I think I'd take more risks and go for the exciting stuff.

Interview with a local Game fan

"What's the diagnosis?" Brandon asked.

The room was silent. No one looked up from their tablets. Some of them were crying.

Brandon wanted to scream at them to calm down and act like the professionals they were, to earn their pay for a change and deliver him a miracle. They had no idea what was really on the line here

— that would give them something to really be upset about. But he knew losing his composure would get them nowhere.

He spoke in a compassionate, gentle tone. "Michelle, what's the diagnosis?"

Michelle remained sitting. "Doctors give her a few days, weeks at the most. There is no detectable brain function. She's dead, by the definition. There's no hope, Brandon."

Brandon knew she wasn't dead. If she was 'dead by the definition,' then the game would be finished, and over a billion children would be lying dead on their Game tables all over Tygon. "It's important that no one pulls the plug on her. Do we all understand this? Angelica, tell me there is no danger of that happening."

"We're safe in that regard, Brandon," Angelica said, reclining in her chair beside Lilith at the other end of the large table. "Three Eternals are within twenty feet of her; either Raphael or Stephanie are in the room at all times. No one is pulling a plug."

"Trew?" Brandon asked.

"He was hysterical," Michelle said. "We thought he was going to rip the hospital down with the raw emotion and Talent bubbling to the surface in him. Then he went to the hospital chapel and prayed for a good hour. After that, he came back and he's been as calm as... well, as cool as you seem to be."

"She's not going to die," Brandon said with absolute certainty.

"He said that very same thing," Michelle said. "Now he's just sitting beside her, waiting. The doctors and nurses have been in and delivered the terrible news. The baby is gone; Danielle's internal bleeding has slowed, but for some reason they can't stop it. Her brain is barely sparking a signal. They're encouraging him to let her go. He said she'll be okay, and since he has absolute say over when to stop life support, she will remain plugged in. Friends and family are flocking to give their support. He's not alone."

"So what do we do?" Brandon asked, looking around the table. His question was answered with silence.

Finally someone mumbled something from his right side.

"What was that?" he asked. "I didn't hear what you said. Speak up."

The young man continued to look at his tablet. "I said maybe we could pray?"

A woman on the other side laughed in disgust. "Pray to who? Tygon doesn't have a God. And even if we did, why would we bother to pray for a video game character?"

The entire table looked up at her. She looked surprised at her own outburst and began to stammer an apology. Brandon held up his hand to silence her. He looked at her calmly as her eyes darted quickly from left to right looking for support. He slowly dropped his hand to rest on the table, still looking blankly at the girl.

"Out you go, Claudette," Brandon said.

"Where?" she asked with a look of worry. "For how long? Sir, I'm sorry, I didn't mean..."

"You're done, Claudette. I don't care where you go or what you do, but you had best stay out of the circles I inhabit. And I inhabit every circle worth being in. Leave. Now."

Claudette stood up and slowly walked out. Everyone sat there stunned. This wasn't something Brandon had ever done before. Answering the silent question, Brandon said, "She did that to herself. I won't have it. It doesn't help anyone to allow that type of attitude. It's a growing sentiment in this society of ours and, quite frankly, it is the poison that will destroy us all if we let it."

Brandon looked back to the young man who had spoken up. "Tell me more about your idea, please."

The young man looked nervous still, but he stood up and voiced his idea. "As a society, we no longer believe in a God because we see no evidence of one. Perhaps we see no evidence of one because we no longer believe in its existence. If the Game can have one, why can't we? If our population can appeal to help Danielle inside the Game, maybe enough Patrons and influencers will do what they can to move their players to also focus inside the Game on her. Maybe in this way we can help. Somehow."

Michelle looked doubtful. "No disrespect intended, sir, but what we're talking about here is real. This idea doesn't make much sense."

Brandon nodded. "I agree, Michelle, but we are helpless to help inside the Game. Could a game renew our faith in the Divine? It's ridiculous, but I also know everyone on Tygon is watching Danielle in her bed right now. The numbers you showed me indicate our world is stopped. Everyone who follows the Game has called off from work, using 'Game Days' to watch what unfolds."

"We have their undivided attention," Brandon said. "Let's ask them to do the impossible, to pray for Danielle."

"It will be good for Game ratings, in any event," Angelica said.

Brandon wanted to reprimand her, but they all knew it was about the Game and ratings. Claudette had crossed the line by not caring about the kids living and dying inside the Game, but it was acceptable to be focused on the ratings. Just because Brandon's goals were bigger wasn't anyone else's fault. He'd built this beast; he had to live by its rules.

"Okay, then," Brandon said. "Pray for Danielle. What an interesting idea, that a video game could make us once again believe in something more than what we can see and touch. Let's try it."

51

For hours now, everyone around the world has been glued to their viewers. Industry, trade, commerce; it has all come to a complete stop. Will Danielle survive? What will this mean to our favourite player, Trew?

And we have suddenly started to pray. After decades of silence, millions of us are bowing our heads and appealing to...someone, to help our two lovers inside the digital world to survive this terrible tragedy. Will it help? Common sense says of course not, but despite the logic, everyone seems to be embracing Brandon Strayne's heartfelt plea, and millions have begun to pray.

There are only brief hours left in Danielle's struggle. Our entire world watches and hopes for a miracle, while on Earth only one man and his dear friends take any notice at all.

Lisa Rohansen, Live report on Zack Channel 42

The elevator stops at its floor and dings briefly, then the door opens.

Two hospital orderlies are walking past and immediately stop, their heads turning to look at the two men stepping out of the lift.

They are both tall. The one with sandy brown hair is 6'2". The other, with golden hair, is at least 6'4". They are both dressed immaculately in expensive designer suits, complete with all the proper accessories which one would expect from a model or a movie star. As they step out of the elevator, everyone nearby stops and looks at them, as if compelled to do so. The men smile warmly; they are used to this. They nod encouragingly at each and every person, touching them lightly as they walk by. At the moment they are touched, each person closes their eyes and the look of joy on their face is indescribable in words but very evident to anyone witnessing it.

The shorter man leads the way down the hallway while the taller one lingers, speaking softly to the people as he passes by and touches them.

"Excuse me," the lead man says to the nurse at the desk. His voice is like liquid copper, dripping with honey and warmth. Instantly the nurse looks up and smiles, as if she's experiencing ecstasy on some mild level. The man's eyes are deepest blue with silver flecks swirling lazily around like fish in a warm pond. "I'm hoping that you can direct me to Danielle Radfield's room, please."

The woman nods slowly, reaching out her hand towards him. He softly grasps it and her smile widens. "Yes, you can find her in room 33, just down this hallway and to the right. Shall I take you there?" she offers.

"Thank you so kindly," the taller man says from behind his colleague. His voice, warm gold shining brightly in a green meadow. The deep, rich baritone soothes the nurse even more. "We can certainly find our way from here. Thank you so kindly, Margaret." The nurse nods happily and stands there watching them as they continue slowly down the hallway.

Eventually the two men are standing outside the closed door of room 33. "I'll wait out here for a few moments," the taller man says, looking around comfortably.

The other nods and knocks politely before entering the room.

There are four people inside. Trew stands calmly off to one side of the bed, whispering to Raphael and Stephanie. They appear calm in spite of the fact that time is quickly running out, and they are all aware of it.

Raphael looks towards the door first. His eyes light up with recognition and joy. He quickly closes the distance and grabs the man in a fierce embrace, the way dear friends do when they haven't seen one another in a long time. The man returns the hug with even more emotion, laughing out loud as he says, "Easy, my young Brother! You'll crush the very life from me if you're not careful."

The two hold each other in a deep embrace for a very long moment, and when they release each other Stephanie is already pushing Raphael to the side and gripping the man in her tightest hug.

"That's it, little Sister!" he laughs. "Totally ignore my warning to Raphael and crush me like a tin can!"

Stephanie laughs and when the two separate, they both wipe tears from their eyes. She stands beside Raphael, both making room for Trew to enter their space.

"Trew," Raphael says proudly. "Please allow me the honour of introducing you to our dear big Brother, Gabriel."

Trew looks at Gabriel intensely, and with a sad, small smile, he extends his hand. Gabriel grips it and the two shake hands. "I am pleased to meet you, Trew. I've heard so much about you. I apologize that we must meet under such troubling circumstances."

"It's good to meet you as well, Gabriel," Trew says. "Although I have to apologize; I've never heard of you before this moment from either of your siblings. As a matter of fact," Trew gives Raphael and Stephanie an interested look, "Up until this moment I didn't even know you two were siblings."

Gabriel laughs lightly. "We are siblings, not in blood, but in spirit. And forgive them their secrets, Trew. They are required to keep as many as they can for as long as possible. What we are doing today hasn't happened in a very long time on Earth, if it ever has happened at all."

"What's happening?" Trew asks, as if he hopes for the answer, but is also afraid to hear it.

"You shall see soon enough, young man," Gabriel assures him.

Looking at Raphael and Stephanie, his smile fades into a look more serious. "The powers that be have explored every option available to help us save the life of this young woman." He pointed towards Danielle lying in her bed. "All of us know that she is almost gone." Everyone nods sadly. "But recent developments have provided a solution to come forward to save her." Gabriel looks seriously at Trew. "It is risky, and perhaps it's too late to work. But if you wish us to make one final attempt, I will do what I can to save her."

Trew walks over and cradles Danielle's head in his hands. She is everything to him, and he is terrified that she will leave now, and he doesn't want to face this life without her. With tears in his eyes, he lays her head gently down on the pillow, turns to face Gabriel, and nods fiercely. "Please do what you can to save her. She's my world."

Gabriel nods slowly. "She is ours, as well, Trew. Prepare yourselves, then. I have a great surprise for all of you."

Gabriel opens the door and sticks his head out, nodding for the man in the hall to come in.

He walks in smiling, his arms slightly spread and his palms turned outward. Raphael and Stephanie both look awestruck, and they each reverently sink to one knee, bowing their heads. An enormous grin is on each of their faces, which becomes apparent when the man gently touches each one on the top of their heads, and they look up at him. "Please, Children. Don't fall down just so I can pick you up. Stand up and give me a hug." The two stand quickly and hug the man, first Raphael, and then Stephanie. There is whispered talk between them as they hug, followed by laughter, and then the group is standing back again so the tall man can meet Trew.

Trew walks closer to him and is immediately captivated by his eyes. They are deepest green with gold flecks swirling in them. Trew has a flash of memory. He remembers wearing a bracelet, green with swirling gold flecks. Only it hadn't been him — he had been someone else, someone... younger. The vision is confusing, but powerful. The man breaks the memory by addressing Trew in his rich voice. "It is so good to meet you, Trew."

"Who... who *are* you?" Trew asks.

"I am the answer to prayers, my boy," the man answers warmly. "I am the bringer of truth and the deliverer of miracles. I'm afraid that is all I can tell you at the moment. Many would not believe who I am if I were to tell you. I am one of the most misunderstood creatures on the planet, a case of trying to help and being hated for it. But I can assure you, Trew, I am the only one that can bring her back. Now, shall we get down to business?"

Trew nods, moving out of the way as the man strides towards the bed to look down sadly at Danielle. He places his left hand under her head, and his right hand gently rests on her heart. "Okay, little bird," he says in a soothing, playful tone, "It's time to leave that restful place and come back to us for a while longer."

He closes his eyes, and Trew watches intensely. The man's smile widens and a humming begins to sound from his body. Slowly, steadily, a warm golden glow appears from his hands and spreads softly over Danielle's body. Trew watches as the hum increases in volume and the glow envelops her.

"Miracles can happen, Trew." The man's gold flecked eyes swirl madly. "When enough people believe and come together, miracles can happen."

Then he looks intensely at Trew, as if he's speaking to something or someone inside of him. "You all saved her, stop doubting and start believing again. It's time to wake up to the truth!"

There is a tremendous clap of thunder and Trew is thrown to the floor.

When Trew looks up, Gabriel and the man are gone. Only Raphael and Stephanie remain, lying on the floor as well.

Danielle is still in her bed. Her eyes open. Her hand reaches out for Trew.

He runs to her and wraps her in his arms, sobbing with joy.

52

No one knows for certain what we witnessed today.

Through Trew's eyes, we saw that Danielle's life was saved by a miraculous stranger. Who were these two men who walked in like angels and disappeared the same way? Were they the fabled 'Eternals'? Do we finally have proof that they exist, and if so, what does this mean?

Trew's following continues to be the highest of any player to ever enter the Game, virtually guaranteeing that he will finish this play in the number one spot. There are, of course, other factors involved in the scoring of rank, but predictions are that Trew will achieve what he obviously set out to do... finish this play ranked number one.

Some of the big questions being asked all over Tygon right now are:

If the Game exactly mirrors Tygon, are such miracles possible for us as well? Did our praying affect events inside the Game? Do we have Eternals walking amongst us on Tygon as well? Who was the mysterious stranger, and was he actually speaking to us when he said to 'Wake up to the truth'?

Most of Tygon will be sitting in front of their viewers today as we watch and hope to discover answers to these questions and many others...

The Fan - Game News at its Source

Trew - 29

The doctors come in and order a barrage of tests to be conducted on Danielle. They kick us out of the room and have her for about an hour, taking blood, asking her psychological questions to make certain there's no brain damage, doing scans to determine brain function; lots of things that I don't really understand.

During that time I say nothing about what just happened to Raphael or Stephanie. We sit downstairs in the hospital cafeteria, drinking coffee and making small talk about what we think is happening with Danielle. A few times their eyes become serious and they start to say something, but I just hold up my hand. They nod in understanding; we will talk about it with Danielle present, once we go back to her room.

I get a call from the nurse's desk and we return to Danni's room. She's sitting up in her bed, looking as healthy and energetic as ever. There's no sign of the weak, sick girl who was slowly dying just a short time ago. Her eyes are sad; she knows that the baby is gone. I walk over and hug her tight, tears in my eyes as we embrace. I hold her for what seems like only a second but is likely long minutes. Finally I let her go and kiss her cheek.

"You gave us quite the scare there, love," I say.

"That's what they're telling me. I'm sorry, Trew." Her voice cracks and her eyes say it all.

I smile reassuringly and wipe her tears away. "There's nothing to be sorry for, my sweet girl. You're back with me now, and you look healthy as can be. Just don't ever do that again, and everything will be fine."

Raphael and Stephanie come forward and embrace Danielle, telling her how incredibly happy they are that she found the strength to pull through this. She smiles at them and accepts the praise as well as she can. We all pull up chairs around her bed.

"What happened?" she asks. "The last thing I remember is coming home from work and not feeling well. I walked to the kitchen for a drink of water, felt a stabbing pain in my belly, then I was with her until I woke up. That's all I can remember."

"With her?" I ask.

Danni smiles, "Yes, but I'll tell you about that when you're done with your story. Fill me in on what I missed."

I go over the details; Coming home and finding her on the kitchen floor. The rush to the hospital. The days of watching her fade away in bed, the doctors informing me there was no hope for her survival. Then I tell her about the two strangers, Gabriel and... the other man, coming in, and the events that occurred.

"Wow, that sounds incredible!" She says. "I'm sorry I missed seeing it. Gabriel sounds wonderful, and this other man, well... they both sound like angels."

I nod. "Sound like, looked like, acted like. Yes, they fit the part of angels exactly." I look at Steph and Raph who've been quiet the entire time. "Is that what they were? Angels?"

They look at each other and Stephanie nods to Raphael, indicating he can go ahead and do the talking. Raphael takes a drink of water from his bottle, then nods his head.

"They aren't angels, but that's one of the names they've been given over the ages. Them, and others like them."

"Others like them?" I ask. "Others like you?"

Raphael looks at me patiently and smiles. "I know you're going to have a million questions, Trew, and that's to be expected. That I can answer any of them is very surprising to me, but I've been given permission to tell you about us." He quickly holds up his hand when he sees me take a breath to speak. "Perhaps it's best if I tell you what I can without interruptions. That way I can present the details in the best order and, although you can ask me questions after, there won't be much more that I can tell you once I'm done. Perhaps a few little things, but not much."

"Okay..." I say slowly.

Stephanie laughs at me. "Don't worry, Lobato, I think you'll be happy with the information that we share with you."

I look at Danielle. She shrugs and smiles at me. I pull my chair closer to her bed and nod. "Okay, then. Tell us what you can."

53

I regret my seventh life in the Game.

It was amazing. Everything worked out perfectly, just the right mix of triumph and tragedy, success and happiness. Fans loved it, and to this day it's my best money maker from Firsting sales. But no other play after that one turned out even half as good. As a player, this isn't a huge deal. I'm very wealthy as a retired Gamer, and I owe it all to my seventh life.

So why do I regret having lived it?

Because I have a vivid memory of how good things were, and how they could be. My real life is nowhere near as good as my seventh life was in the Game. I could have tolerated this life, because it's still very good.

But knowing how much better it could be...it makes me sad to be stuck in this one. I know it likely doesn't make sense to most people, but it's the truth.

J. Danielson, retired Gamer

Raphael

Alright, A. As you have instructed, no scrambler. Everyone on Tygon is going to see this conversation through Danielle's and Trew's eyes. I can only imagine what the reaction is going to be like with Game fans.

I look at Trew and Danielle sitting calmly in front of me. Okay, then, here it goes.

"What George wrote in his book is correct. This world is a computer simulation, a Game. There are some here who know this for a certainty, because they retain their memory of the real world that exists beyond this one."

I watch their reaction. Neither says a word but they both look at each other with an 'I knew it!' expression on their faces.

"I can't get into the specifics of what this world is for; that's more than I have permission to tell." I smile at them. "Over the centuries some individuals have come close to guessing. Religion and spiritual teachers grasp some of the key concepts, but none have been able to identify the entire purpose for your existence here on Earth. Maybe someone will guess some day.

"Here's the basic idea; you log into the Game and you're born. You live your life as best you can, and when you die, you return to your real body, taking the lessons you learned and memories of the experiences you had. Many return to live multiple lifetimes, many do not. You have no memory of the real world, or at least you're not supposed to. On rare occasions an individual is born with some knowledge of the real world beyond, or else an individual sees clues and formulates an educated guess which can then grow into belief and faith. For the most part, this isn't a dangerous thing because no one else believes them. If, by some remote chance, others do believe, then they develop a small following which turns into a religion. Most never grow to any significant size. Some do.

"When this simulation was created, it was done in the same way that game developers here bring a game to market. Designers and players inhabited the Game first, to work out the bugs and make sure it ran properly. They were the beta testers, and they played the Game with total knowledge of what it was, so they could help finalize the Game and make it ready for launch. When all the kinks were worked out, the beta testers left and the world was populated with real players, people like you. Some beta testers were asked to remain behind, and others were inserted into the Game at different times throughout history as required. That is what we are. Expert players who remain in the Game to help with troubles that arise as well as perform tasks to help this simulation proceed as designed.

"We're called Eternals, and there are many of us around the world with different abilities, jobs, and responsibilities. We vary in age from just a few decades old to thousands of Earth years old, but we all share two common traits. We can never get sick or age, and we have full knowledge that this is a simulation and a real world exists beyond this."

I pause a moment to let the information sink in. No questions from Trew; I'm not sure whether to be relieved or concerned.

"Two factions of Eternals have formed over the millennia; one faction is concerned with helping by doing good, and the other causes misery and strife in the world. The first group are named Eternals, while the second group call themselves Infernals. Trew, you met an Infernal by the name of Carl when you were younger." Trew nods. "Many of us have been both Infernals and Eternals during our stay inside the Game. I've been an Infernal for the past thousand years, it's only since Danielle was born that I became an Eternal once again."

That seems to get their attention and Trew opens his mouth to speak. I hold up my hand and he remains silent. "Sometimes individuals learn about our abilities and we are forced to reveal ourselves for what we are. That's what happened here with you two. It's impossible to ignore that there is something different about us. Over the ages the humans, or players, as we call them, who learn of our existence have given us many names; gods, demons, angels, devils, seraphim, genies, sprites... the list is long. Most stories that contain strange and powerful creatures are about us."

"Knowing that we are inside a Game allows us to manipulate the system and use special abilities. It can be dangerous, so we are careful not to use our abilities more than is necessary in order to maintain secrecy and keep the simulation functioning correctly.

There are strict rules that govern how this universe operates. When we bend them, the universal rules alter and that allows anyone to then bend them as well. Let me give you an example; a few decades ago it was impossible for a human to run a mile in under four minutes. Physically impossible. The laws of science and the universe wouldn't allow it. Then an Eternal ran just a bit faster than he should have during a fairly major incident. That Eternal ran faster than humans could, and as a result of that, the universe changed the physics to compensate. If something impossible is accomplished, it's no longer impossible. A few years later, a man by the name of Roger Bannister ran the mile in under four minutes. A short time later, sixteen more people did the same. Today, a high school student can do it if they train just a bit, something that was impossible until the rules were bent to allow it."

Danielle whistles, and I nod. "Thankfully, most people playing in the Game have no clue that they might be able to do extraordinary things, so they never even try. That's a good thing, because there have been a lot of little bends over the ages. Today it's entirely possible for humans to do things like fly and breathe underwater for short periods of time." They look surprised by my statement. I nod. "Trust me, it's possible. I doubt anyone can get there, mentally, to be able to do it yet, but that's the only thing standing in the way."

I take another drink of water and look at both of them. "So, that's who and what we are. Trew, you were fortunate enough to meet Gabriel, one of the oldest and most powerful Eternals on the planet. The longer we're here, the more powerful we become, and Gabriel was one of the first here. The other one, the being who brought Danni back to us, is much older than any Eternal or Infernal. His kind was here before this version of the Game even existed. I'm not allowed to tell you what they are called right now. All of us had the honour to meet their leader. It was truly a highlight of my life to have been able to embrace him. Most of the time they can't be located, even by us. This is only the third time I've been in the presence of one. Stephanie?"

Stephanie smiles with delight, "He was my first. I thought up until now that they didn't exist."

I chuckle at the idea, an Eternal with all her knowledge can still have her faith tested.

"So that's about all I can tell you. There is more — much more — but this is enough for today. I'm sure that in the years ahead you two will get little tidbits of information from us if we're allowed to share it, and the indications are that we will be able to. Any questions?"

Trew thinks about it for a few seconds and then shakes his head negatively. I chuckle. Of course he won't ask questions now. I'm ready for them. Trew slides questions into a conversation, and it's often not until you answer them that you realize what he's done.

Danielle nods her head and I smile. "Go ahead, dear girl."

"How is it that you don't grow old and die? Is it possible for us to do the same? To live forever?"

"We can be killed, although it's a difficult thing to do, and it doesn't happen often because of our skills and powers. As for how we are able to live so long, there is a price for everything." I sigh and look at Stephanie.

Stephanie nods. "The price we pay for not aging is high. When you enter the Game, you leave your real body lying in stasis on a table until you're done here. That body can only exist for a certain length of time without you in it — a couple months, tops. We age differently in here, so a couple of months out of the Game is equal to roughly 80 to 100 years inside. We follow the same rules as you do in that respect, so when we are offered the opportunity to become an Eternal, to live hundreds or thousands of years inside the Game... we give it serious consideration before accepting, because..." she lets the sentence trail off.

Danni gasps, “Because the price you pay for living for a long time in the game, is that your bodies die in real life?”
I nod. “That’s right. When we die here, we cease to exist.”

54

Brandon sat patiently by the phone, waiting for it to ring. He considered getting a drink but decided that he didn't really feel like one. The day had been hectic and he couldn't consider it complete until he received the call.

The phone started to ring.

Brandon closed his eyes and rolled his head in a slow circle from one shoulder to the other. Then he opened his eyes and answered the phone, holding it away from his head for the count of three. He wasn't in the mood to hear the unpleasant clicks and beeps which secured the line, and grated on his nerves. Smiling confidently, he placed the phone to his head and waited.

"Tell me" — his Father's voice sounded pleasant, but Brandon could hear the fury beneath — "that you did not have anything to do with what just happened on millions of viewer screens around the world."

"Millions?" Brandon asked. "It must have been on at least a billion, father. Factor in that most households have more than one viewer and it's likely billions."

There was complete silence on the other end of the line. Brandon felt like a ten-year-old boy waiting to be punished by a man who expected nothing less than perfection from his only son. Those times had not gone well for him, but he was an adult now, the most powerful man on Tygon. He refused to squirm like a child. He looked silently out the window at the stars above, waiting for his father to speak.

Minutes passed. Then, for the first time in Brandon's life, it happened.

"We don't have time for this nonsense, boy. Answer my question."

Brandon was stunned. The old man had spoken first. In the age-old power play of conversation, he had finally beaten his father for the first time. He knew he should be pleased, but it wasn't as satisfying as he'd imagined. Growing up never is.

Brandon shook his head and held on to his confidence. "Of course," he snapped. "I had everything to do with it. What do you think I am? Some doddering old man? As you seem to enjoy pointing out to me every time we speak, time's running out. I had to make a bold move, so I made it."

" I told you to watch that girl."

"I did watch her. I did more than watch her, I brought her into our camp so I could help her. She has no luck. The Mainframe put her into play and is pushing her to where she is now. Her getting sick and almost dying was never part of the plan. Her death triggering the Game to end was never part of the plan. Nothing to do with her was ever part of the plan. Yet there she is, front and centre in my face. Right in the way each and every time we try to get back on to the plan. Stopping us from doing what needs to be done."

"Son." His father's voice softened with concern. "Confirming the existence of Eternals to Tygon was a mistake. We are severely off track."

Brandon sighed. "Then we stay on the train, ride on this track, and do the best that we can, father."

"If we fail..."

Brandon took the phone away from his ear and held it in front of his mouth. He took a deep breath and screamed at the top of his lungs, years of pent up frustration pouring out of him in one tremendous roar. "I know what happens if we fail! I hear no ideas from you, just criticism. I know what I did! I'm playing this game as well as I can. No one else dared to step forward to take my place. No one could beat me, not even you. So let me play!"

With all of his strength, Brandon raised the phone above his head and brought it crashing onto the marble floor, smashing it into hundreds of little pieces.

Falling to his knees, Brandon looked up at the ceiling and screamed as loudly and as long as he could. Then he sat on the floor, his chest heaving for air.

Time was running out.

"I'm still amazed you were able to involve so many other players to help me. Each player spending their credits to help me in the Game has saved me so much money. It should actually enable me to achieve our goal, if all goes according to plan. I didn't think you could get so many on board."

"It wasn't too difficult. Many of them only needed to spend a few thousand extra credits to get what we wanted, and if we succeed, each of them will become very wealthy in credits for having been a part of it. A teacher here, a girlfriend who dates you for only a month there, a salesman who sells you a car once when you're 30, a man who robs you when you're 40. All so simple, and fairly inexpensive to buy for each player."

Excerpt from Chapter 10 of 'The Game'

Trew - 30

"I'm excited for you, Trew, this car is incredible! Selling this specific model is the reason that I got into selling cars in the first place."

My pen freezes above the blank line of the contract. I look up, expecting to see the car salesman giving me a false smile. I was hoping to buy from a nice guy, not some stereotypical lying salesman. But when I look at him, he appears sincere. I've become very good at reading people over the years, and this guy looks truly excited about the car I just bought. Who can blame him? It's one of the best new automobiles to hit the market in years, and I'm buying it.

"You're kidding, right?" I ask him. "John, there's no way you took a job as a car salesman just to sell this new vehicle, is there?"

John shrugs. He's a medium-built man just a bit shorter than me, about 5 foot 10 inches. Short cut brown hair, friendly eyes and a comfortable manner about him. His energy is pure and friendly, if you believe in that type of thing, which I do. My wife's a Reiki master who deals with energy all the time.

"I never sold cars before this, Trew. When I was 39, my life was in great shape. I was approaching 40 and it looked like I was going to avoid the mid-life crisis so many of my friends seemed to be experiencing. It turns out that life had other plans, I was downsized from my job, my personal life was turned upside down on its head, and I wasn't sure what to do. Then I saw the commercial for this new car and it just came to me. 'Why don't I give that a try?' I said to myself. So three months ago I took a job selling cars and here I am in front of you today."

"That's very interesting," I say slowly. "I wasn't looking for a car. Perfectly happy with mine, then a couple months ago I saw the advertisement for this one and thought, 'I should really look at buying that car.' I kept putting it off, and then today, 60 kilometres from home, I was driving by and something just made me pull in to take it for a test drive. Now here I am, buying the darn thing from you."

"Well, maybe it has nothing to do with the car," John says with a smile. "Maybe it was all the supercomputer's big plan for you and I to meet each other."

I feel the glow, the golden tingle in my heart that over the years indicates the universe is giving me a direct message. "What supercomputer is that, John?" I ask.

John laughs and waves his hand dismissively. "It's nothing, Trew. I just read a book a long time ago and it stuck with me. It said we live in a computer simulation. A lot of people think I'm a crackpot, but the idea really resonated with me. If I had a religion, it would likely be something that preached that message. I could get behind that."

My ears are ringing hollowly as I ask him, "A book written by a man named George Knight?"

His laugh disappears and his eyes get serious, "Yeah. 'The Game Is Life' by George. You read it?"

I nod. "I did read it many times. A religion, huh?"

John nods. "Well, yeah. That's what I always used to say. I was lucky to read it before it was published. About three quarters of the way through, I said, 'George, this would make a very cool religion..."

My skull tingles even more. "You knew George Knight?" I ask.

"Yeah, we were very good friends. I'm surprised you read that book, Trew. It didn't sell very many copies. I always wanted it to do well for him. Sad life he had at the end. Poor guy."

It's like I'm in a daze. I can't believe what's happening to me. "John? How would you like to cut out early and let me buy you dinner?"

He smiles at me. "You drive?"

"Of course."

56

It is with deep sadness that we learned our beloved Danielle won't be able to have children. The young couple handled the news as well as can be expected, and they have spent the past few days coming to terms with the tragic news. On the positive side of things, Danielle has made a full recovery, thanks to the strange man who walked into her hospital room and miraculously healed her.

On a separate note, digital downloads of the Earth book "The Game Is Life," written by the avatar George R. Knight, are topping the charts in the real world. The little book about the Game has sold over two million copies in the last two weeks on Tygon. Who profits from these sales? George R. Knight was the avatar of Zack, so naturally all profits will go to him and his sponsor Brandon Strayne. It looks like Zack is doing well not just inside the Game this play, but also on Tygon as well.

Join us tomorrow for all day extensive coverage of Zack's current avatar's birthday. How will Trew spend his 30th birthday? No one knows for sure, but don't miss a second of the day.

Game News at a Glance

Trew - 30

What an incredible day.

My best birthday yet.

I lay back in bed and list the day's events in my mind.

1. Breakfast in bed, served to me by my lovely wife, followed by a relaxing drive to see my parents and have lunch with them.

2. On the way back, on a whim, I stop into a car dealership and buy my birthday gift.
3. I meet a stranger and it turns out that he knew George Knight, the author of the book that's changed our lives and the way we truly see the world. Then I get a chance to take him out for a coffee and find out things about George that I've always wondered, but never thought I would learn.
4. I spend the evening with my remarkable wife. This year I'm blessed and thankful that Danni is alive, healthy, happy, and still madly in love with me. I don't know how I'd live without her, and I'm thankful that I don't have to find out. Most people take so much for granted, but not me. Not ever.

That was my 30th birthday. If anyone was watching me play this game today, then I hope I gave them a good time. If no one's watching me, well, that's okay too.

"Today was the best, babe," I say. "Thank you so much."

Danielle snuggles into the crook of my arm as we lay in bed getting ready for sleep. "I'm glad you had a good day, love. Thirty's a big one."

She sounds so serious. "Nah, 30 isn't such a big number. The odds are great that I'm not even half old."

"What do you mean?" she asks.

"I'm thirty today," I say. "If I double my age, I get the number 60. I have an excellent chance of still being alive at 60, so I'm not even half of the total age I'll live. I have a lot of time left to live, which is great!"

Danni looks at me with a blank look. After a couple minutes she shakes her head. "That made some kind of sense to you, didn't it?"

I laugh. "Yeah, it did. I'm just saying it's good to be young with a lot of life left in front of me."

"Okay, that I can understand," she says.

We lie there for a few minutes, enjoying the silence and each other's company. I start to drift off to sleep when she says something I don't catch.

I open my eyes again. "What was that, babe?"

"I said, I have one more present for you."

I turn to face her and smile playfully. "Well, all right!" I pull her close to kiss her.

She kisses me back, but I can tell there's something serious she wants to talk about, so I sit up and look her in the eye. "Okay, Danni, what is it?"

"Her," Danni says. "I need to tell you about the time I spent with God when I almost died."

That gets my attention. It's been weeks and Danielle has avoided this conversation, saying that she would talk about it when the time was right.

Danni begins to speak, surprising me right from the start. "God's name is Sylvia and she told me she's been communicating with you for many, many years, Trew."

I lay silently and listen. A few moments into the conversation we both get out of bed and go downstairs to sit at the kitchen table.

The next two hours pass in a blur. Eventually she stops talking and sits quietly across from me.

All I can say is "Wow."

"Yes," she nods.

"So it's time," I say.

"So it would seem," she says calmly.

"And you don't think it's crazy?"

"I think it's the craziest thing I've ever heard," Danni says.

"It's going to work, you know?"

Danni gets up and walks over to my side of the table. She sits on my lap and hugs me tight. I can feel a warm wetness on my neck. She's crying. "I know it's going to work, sweet man. It feels like this is what we were put on the planet to do. Do you know how to get things started?"

I nod, still hugging her. "I've been thinking and studying and planning this for a long time, Danni. Just waiting for a sign. I guess this was it."

"I guess so," she says. "Well, from what Sylvia asked me to do, it looks like I'm going to be part of this and very busy. I'm pretty scared. She's given me a tall order, especially at my age."

I laugh. "You're younger than me! And you've always been fit and active. It's a great way to get the world's attention, to prove to them that it really is all a game." I tenderly wipe the tears from her eyes. "Are you sorry you married me?"

Danni laughs and slaps my shoulder. "No, I'm not sorry I married you! If I hadn't, I'd likely be doing something crazier."

I nod in agreement. "You were always an adventurous girl. This idea is just another boring day at the office for you, babe."

She laughs.

"It's settled, then," I say. "We're going to start spreading the word and sharing the message."

"Everyone's going to think we're crazy, Trew," Danielle says.

I grin at her. "I sure hope so. Everyone thought Columbus was crazy when he said the world was round."

"At first."

57

Earth has been a real mess since the 30th anniversary celebrations began. As a result of so many players entering the Game in such a short time period, Earth is extremely overpopulated. Add to that the fact that Mainframe allowed most players to be born in civilized countries, and the result is a severe stress being placed on the planet and its inhabitants.

Not enough schools for the children; not enough food for everyone. Not nearly enough jobs or housing or any of the creature comforts that the civilized areas have become so used to.

Crime, deaths, along with any other types of violence and mayhem you can imagine.

The masses are hungry, depressed and desperate.

Although it's been difficult for avatars, it's been excellent for Game fans. We have never had so much excitement to witness on such a scale before.

It's incredible drama, and the Game's fan base continues to grow at record breaking speed daily.

Don't feel bad for all the sadness and pain, folks. Many of the players are earning a lot of credits as they participate in these scenarios.

Remember, it's all just a Game.

30th Anniversary Game Update

"Good afternoon, everyone," Brandon said. "I came as soon as I received the newest rankings. Many of you have seen this type of shift before, but some haven't. Let's discuss where Trew is right now in the Game, and what the current situation means to the big picture."

Brandon paused to look around the table. Some faces appeared mildly concerned, but most looked extremely worried. Brandon couldn't blame them; each person here had their life savings invested in this play. Failure would lead to internment in the labour camps for some; others would be lucky and merely find themselves in a deep hole of financial loss that would take them years to dig out of. Brandon nodded at Michelle and she stepped forward.

"Thanks, Brandon. Good morning, everyone." Brandon could see her smile was slightly strained, but she was hiding it well. "As we are all aware, Trew has dropped in ranking. As of this moment he is ranked number 6,065." Michelle stood silently for a moment to let the number register with everyone, then continued. "He's been number one for most of his play, and this drop is significant. Please let me summarize where Trew is in the Game at the moment, then I'll open up the floor for any comments, concerns, or theories regarding how we might be able to help in getting him back up to number one."

Michelle typed some commands on her tablet and the large screen beside her displayed a myriad of statistics and graphs detailing Trew's last few years in the Game. "Trew is now 35, still happily married to Danielle. On his thirtieth birthday the two of them decided to go ahead and try to form a faith-based movement. The message they are sharing with the world is that Earthlings are computer generated avatars being controlled by players in another reality. We know this has happened before in the history of the Game, but it looks like our boy has been better at communicating and getting others to subscribe to his theories than ever before."

She pointed at a portion of the screen that showed Trew standing on a stage, hundreds of people in the crowd all listening with rapt attention. "Although it is by definition a religion, they are calling it a movement. At this time in Earth's existence, it's a movement that's growing fast. They call their movement 'The Game is Life,' to pay respect to the little book written years ago by George R. Knight, Trew's last avatar. Sales of that book are exploding both on Earth and, of course, on Tygon, and Trew is using it as a means to introduce the theory in an organized way to new people."

"Why is their movement being received so well, Michelle?" Brandon asked.

"Three main reasons," Michelle said. "First, because Trew is keeping it very simple, but focused. His entire premise is: 'If we are living in a computer simulation... then this is the explanation for this phenomenon, or that force of nature, or that spiritual philosophy, et cetera.' He is able to look at the world and his surroundings and explain everything he sees from the perspective that it's all a computer simulation. Secondly, Trew and Danielle have the Gift and are using it prove to the world that miracles can happen, and 'magical' things can be accomplished. They started off doing it on a small scale, but they've also managed to pull off a few larger ones. The more they practice, the better they are getting at it."

Brandon smiled. "That seems to be the way with everything. What's the third reason for their success in an arena where so many seem to fail?"

Michelle tapped her finger at another picture on the screen. "Raphael. When he first appeared on the scene as Danielle's protector, those of us who knew him were very surprised. For a thousand years inside the Game he was one of the top ranked Infernals; most of us actually thought he had won the leadership title of Satan a couple hundred years ago, he was that high up. Then we were afraid he was still an Infernal and was working on Danielle to bring her to power with the intent of causing mischief in the world. It soon became obvious that he had switched over to the Eternal side once again. We hoped he would just be her protector, but it looks like he's bringing his considerable experience to the table and helping Trew."

Nadine asked a question. "I've never heard of Raphael before. I received only limited info on him when we were informed that Danni had unlocked an Eternal. What's he experienced in?"

"Cults." Brandon answered. "Cults, revolutions, and religions. If you look at every major —and most minor — religious movements in the past... five thousand years?" He looked to Michelle for clarification and she nodded affirmatively. "You will see Raphael close by. He just has a knack for it. The past thousand years he helped many historical avatars form some extremely dangerous and deadly groups."

"Sounds like a strange grouping." The marketing expert said from beside Nadine. "Cults, revolutions, and religions. All very different creatures."

"Not very different at all," Brandon said. "The only real difference is the motivator for the action. A cult is a religion that doesn't gain popular acceptance. Revolutions follow a government or policy instead of a God. Religion centres around a God that becomes accepted by enough people to gain credibility." He nodded to Michelle and she sat down.

Brandon stood up and walked to the main screen. "So here's everyone's real concern at the moment. Trew and Danielle, apparently as instructed by the Mainframe, have formed one of the fastest growing movements/religions/cults in recent history. Something like that should help him to maintain his ranking of number one, but almost overnight we see his rank dropping not just a few points, but thousands of points. Does that sound about right?"

Brandon scanned the room and everyone was nodding in agreement. He nodded and smiled. "Perfect. Let me assure you that there is no real problem here." Everyone looked confused.

Their lives and futures were dropping like a stone thrown off a cliff and here was their boss smiling, not concerned at all.

Brandon laughed confidently. "I've been at this Game for a long time, kids. Let me give you an example even worse than this one. On her last play, Angelica dropped over a million ranking spots. The computer ranking is a combination of many factors, some which I don't even pretend to understand. One thing is certain though, the final rank of a player is weighed heavily by two things. One factor is how they affect those that they leave behind on Earth. If a child dies fifteen days after it's born, but its death inspires people to get active and help others, by forming a charity or even just volunteering for instance, then the player who was that child ranks much better than a player whose avatar lives 80 years and contributes nothing to society. The second factor is based on how many Tygon viewers a player has during the entire duration of their play."

Brandon could see the group relax visibly, many of them laughing in relief as they understood their futures were still very secure. "That's right, team, Trew is breaking records for subscribers and viewers. If he continues on this path more will flock to view him daily. He has, what? Another 40 or 50 years, if he lives an average lifetime in the Game? More, if our spent credits on Longevity work out properly. That's another four to six weeks of Game time left for Trew, and millions of more fans to watch him."

Brandon turned around and pointed confidently at the screen. "Trew's going to continue on this path, it appears. It isn't what we planned for him before he went in. So now we get behind this as best we can and help him in all the ways we are able.

"It appears he will not only finish the play in the number one position at this pace — this play could be recognized as one of the greatest sessions in the history of the Game."

58

Stephanie (Danielle is 36)

I can't remember the last time I spent so much time with one of my Brothers or Sisters on an assignment.

Raphael was always like a big brother to me when I first became an Eternal. He was so calm and patient, helping me discover the ropes of this job and training me to unlock my specific strengths during the training stage of initiation. I had many instructors during those first few years, but I always remember my time with Raphael fondly.

Then he tried to kill me.

I don't even know why I'm bothering to think about it. Maybe it's because I know that you're viewing me from time to time, A. I miss you. You likely don't recall me from your plays, but I saw you more than once and you were always one of my favourites. I know you understand the ways of both worlds better than most, but Raphael was a valuable lesson for me. Trust as much as you can, knowing that the gift of trust will likely be the thing that ends it all for you someday.

Okay, I guess there's no more time to get into the details of almost dying forever. The driver is pulling up to the office and we're going in to see Danni. She asked Trew to bring me; apparently she has something incredible to show us.

I look over at Trew and smile. He's everything I hoped he would grow into when I first met him as a bright-eyed, curious boy. He's dressed in a casual shirt and dress pants, very calm and self-confident, but not to the point of arrogance. Thousands of people cheer at him when he stands on the stage, chanting his name and applauding his message. He hasn't let it change him, though. He believes deep in his heart that it's the message they follow, not the man. It's not true, they do follow the man, but I'm so glad that he's humble. I've seen the Power corrupt some strong people over the centuries, quickly destroying their original ideals and intent more times than I can count. It's because he has Danielle. I don't know what he would do without her. I don't know what she would do without him. Souls like his are the reason I agreed to become an Eternal, to help the best of the best players learn how to become even better, in every way the Game allows.

We walk into the building and head for the elevator, taking it to the top floor where Danielle's spiritual centre for gamers is located. She's hugging a patient at the front door when we arrive. The patient sees Trew and her eyes light up. She whispers something to Danni, who laughs and brings the patient over to meet Trew.

Trew, always the ambassador, smiles warmly and shakes the patient's hand. They exchange pleasant words for a few minutes. During the entire conversation Trew focuses intently on the lady, comfortably maintaining eye contact with her and deeply listening to her speak, as if at this moment in time no one else in the world exists. This is one of the most powerful gifts a person can give to another, focused attention. It's a shame more people can't do it, but Trew can, and he shows the world how to do it by example.

And the masses of people are learning. For the first time in a long time, people are becoming more decent and caring towards each other. The common belief that they are all playing a game where everyone shares common struggles, hopes, and goals has been very powerful to society these past few years.

And the movement is growing.

The lady leaves and Danni ushers us into her office.

"I think I've done it." She announces with excitement.

"Nice!" Trew exclaims.

"Done what?" I ask.

"A few years ago we heard about a Reiki master who was able to heal cosmetic wounds," she says. "We thought it would be worth pursuing, since it's impossible to deny the existence of something that is visible. It would also be a great way to reinforce our core message."

"And you've done it?" I ask cautiously.

Danni nods her head positively. "Look at these pictures. This is Jenna when she first came to me two weeks ago." Danni shows us pictures of a girl with very severe scarring on her face. "She was a beautiful girl, and then a jealous ex-boyfriend followed her one night, beating her badly. She was lucky to survive, but the doctors could only do so much to help her, and major scarring resulted. Jenna has had three surgeries to help heal her so far but, as you can see from this picture, they still had a long way to go."

Trew shakes his head angrily. "Such a sad thing."

Danielle nods in agreement. "I met her aunt a few months ago and we got talking. One thing led to another and I soon had Jenna come to the centre. The surgeries were painful and expensive, and she was losing faith that she would ever look normal again. I explained what I believed I could do, if she was willing to let me try. After explaining that it was painless, she agreed."

"How's it going with her?" I ask. "Any improvement at all?"

Danni smiles. "You tell me." Danni walks over to the door and opens it. "Jenna, please come in here and meet my friends."

Jenna walks in and both Trew and I are stunned. Her face is almost perfect. She turns her head slightly and I can see the light catch the faintest of white scar lines, but she's the beautiful girl from the original "before" pictures. I walk over to her. "Is it all right if I touch your face, hun?" I ask.

Jenna is smiling, her eyes moist with tears of joy. She nods her head and I gently touch her skin. No makeup at all, and just the faintest, textured lines. She is beautiful again, and no one would ever know she'd been scarred so badly if they didn't see the pictures.

"Wow," I say, not because I don't believe it's possible, but because it's possible for the most talented of Eternals to accomplish something like this, but only an old, powerful one. A regular human did this? Our little Danni... wow.

"I think maybe two more sessions and even the faint lines will disappear," Danni says cheerfully, and I can hear the voice of that same little fearless girl who expected the world to bend to her will, never surprised when it actually did.

"Danni. Trew." I say.

"What, Steph?" Trew knows the tone in my voice. His face is concerned. It should be.

I look at them both seriously. "We need to discuss how we proceed with this. Until we do, it's very important that no one knows that you can do this. Do we all agree?"

Danni's smile softens. "Okay, Steph. But still, it's very cool, right?"

I smile reassuringly, "Yes, sweet girl. It's very cool."

"If it's all simply just a computer simulation, a game, then why bother to do anything at all? That's a common question people who challenge my beliefs ask me, and here is my answer. Just because it's a game doesn't mean it's not 100% real. Has anyone in here ever played a game? Ask a football star how real his game is; it provides the day-to-day focus for his entire being. His house, food, everything results from him playing a game. His entire week, month, year, and often his entire life revolves around a game. Ask an Olympic athlete how real their game is. I hope you see what I'm getting at. Games can be real. They can affect the outcome of everything a person is, and everything they do. Do you know that right now there are computer gamers sitting at their desks who make a six figure income from what they're doing? They are immersed in their work; it has become their life. A game.

We all play games. Politics, love, business, you name it. All games.

I bet everyone here has heard this statement at least a dozen times in your life. It has been used to shame you, or make you act more grown up. 'This isn't just some big game, you know...'

The truth is that when you look closely, it is all just some big game..."

Trew Radfield, excerpt from his opening talk at the world TED summit, Earth year 2047

Danielle - 37

"Ahh, this is the life."

I open my eyes, glancing to my left. Trew's looking my way with a big boyish grin on his face. The sun is shining and the breeze coming off the ocean takes the heat away from our skin as we lie baking in the sun on the white sand. Whenever I get too hot I reach for my fancy island drink, complete with umbrella and pineapple. I smile and touch his hand. He grabs mine and we both lay back, thoroughly enjoying the experience.

"It sure is, love." I say with a smile. This is day three of a 14-day vacation. We both work hard and make certain to take luxury vacations at least once every three months. It would be more often but, like I said, we both work hard. This one has a little bit of business attached to it; Trew's giving a talk to a group who decided the best place to hear our message would be in a five-star hotel situated in the Bahamas.

"What time is the talk tonight?" I ask.

"Eight," he says. "The venue is pretty big, babe. I'm a little nervous."

I crack one eye open and peer at him through my sunglasses. The confident (but not arrogant) grin on his face tells me that he's teasing.

"You don't get nervous, Trew," I say to him. "And you've stood in front of much larger crowds. There are only going to be, what, two thousand people there tonight?"

He chuckles. "Yeah, something like that. I know the talks go fine. Every once in a while I do get nervous, Danni. I just hide it well."

"You only get nervous when you start to think," I say teasingly. "Once you let that mind of yours go blank, that's when the real good stuff starts to come out of it."

"Hey, that's not very nice!" I feel a splash of cold and sit up quickly. Trew grins, drops of the cold drink he flicked at me still dripping from his fingertips. "It might be true," he concedes, "but still not nice."

"It's great to see such big crowds. Remember when only a few people would show up, and most of them were pretty 'out there?'"

"Yeah," Trew says. "The 'bring your own tin foil hat' days. Those were some pretty fun times. Not as many vacations, though. I think I'll take the here and now over those lean days when I quit my job and you lost most of your clients because of the crazy ideas you and your husband were always talking about."

We lay quietly for another few minutes, then I announce I'm too hot. "You certainly are!" he says, making me laugh. The guy loves me so much, and I love him right back. I can't imagine being with someone that didn't make me feel like this. So alive and happy to... well, to just exist. It's a blessing that we found each other. I sometimes feel like we tried to in another life and it didn't work out. Maybe this is our reward for the pain we've suffered in other plays of the Game. Reincarnation explained from the "life is a game" perspective is one of Trew's more popular talk topics. He has an endless supply of topics to talk about, but that one is always a favourite with the crowds.

We leave the beach and go shower in our room, relaxing for the next couple hours and taking a nap. It's going to be a long night; they usually are. After his talks, Trew and I mingle with the attendees, listening to stories and discussing the specifics of our beliefs. Sometimes we encounter skeptics, but more often we meet people who sincerely believe in our message and can't wait to tell us how their lives have been changed since learning about our movement. Long nights, but extremely enjoyable.

We go downstairs to the main conference area and head backstage about an hour before the talk is scheduled to start. Trew is shown to a room to put his makeup on (not a part of the job that he particularly likes), and I go in with him to sit and talk. We just love to be together. All these years and I'm not even remotely sick of that man. He's just as excited to be with me. It's like the more time we spend together, the more time we want to spend together. Sure, we both do our own things, which is important for couples to do, but when it comes right down to it, ask us each where we want to be more than any other place in the world and we always choose to be together.

Raphael and Stephanie are in his makeup room when we enter, and everyone hugs, covering points about the upcoming talk.

The next hour is filled with what has now become routine stuff, greeting the planner of the event, going over any logistics or details that need to be addressed, discussing the meet and greet session that will take place after the event — minor but important stuff.

Then it's time. I stand on one side of the stage, preferring to be in the wings rather than in the limelight. Someone from the host group comes on and introduces Trew, pumping up the crowd and building excitement, then he's introduced. With a kiss and hug for me, he puts on his winning smile and walks onto the stage to greet his fans and give his talk.

The crowd is a group of wealthy people from different parts of the world. I'm not sure how they all found each other, but that's part of the magic of this movement. If you have a powerful message and it resonates with people, then they'll do the majority of the work to gather together.

The next two hours pass smoothly. Crowd trouble is a rare occurrence for us; Raphael says it's an indicator that we're on the right track and attracting the correct crowd. I know he has a small but efficient security force in place to spot any trouble before it starts.

Trew always opens the floor for questions at the end of his talks. We all know what a fan Trew is of questions. The third question of the night quickly gets our attention.

"Why don't you all just kill yourselves, then?" The voice asking the question is deep and menacing. It feels like darkness. I peek out to get a look at the man. He's well dressed and tall. Spanish looking, dark and fit. "If you all believe you're in a computer simulation, just kill yourselves to get back to wherever it is you're really living."

I hear Raphael hiss softly behind me and Stephanie puts her hand firmly on my shoulder, pushing me behind her. "You recognize that man, Trew?" Raphael whispers into a small handset which is wired to a microphone in Trew's ear. Trew looks over briefly and nods with a small smile. He makes a signal indicating that everything is fine. Raphael grumbles into the microphone but stands beside me, glaring at the man talking to Trew.

"Who is that?" I ask. "You know him?"

"It's Carl." Stephanie says, watching the man intensely. "What's he up to, Raph? I don't like him so close to Trew."

Raphael continues to watch Carl, looking for some sign of danger.

I hear Trew answering Carl's question. "Killing ourselves is not an option I would recommend, friend. All religions agree on this point, and here's why I don't suggest it from a Game point of view. If you're playing a game, it's for some type of reward or prize, right?"

Carl smiles and I shudder. He looks insane, like he wants to take a bite out of Trew. "Some type of prize, yes," he says smoothly.

Trew nods. "So if the only way to claim your prize is to finish the game, and you get nothing for quitting halfway through, what would the average player do?"

"So you're saying," Carl asks. There's an innocent tone to his voice that sounds... frightening, somehow. "If you start a game, make certain to play to the very final moment?"

"I'm saying don't give up. Don't quit right before the finish line. Everyone gets some reward for finishing; of course, the better you play, the better your reward. But I believe that in this Game we live in, it's always better to play the Game until the finish. Sometimes it's not possible, and that's very sad. I don't judge those who end their game before it's done, but I encourage everyone to run right to the end."

Carl runs his hand over his cheek, rubbing his chin in thought. "Makes perfect sense, boss. I was seriously considering quitting before coming here tonight, but you've helped me realize there's no way I can. Thanks, friend." Carl turns and strolls towards the door.

"Can I ask you a question?" Trew says.

Carl doesn't bother to turn around, he just waves his hand and says loud enough for the room to hear, "Not today, Junior. Perhaps another time."

I look behind me, but Raphael is already gone. Off to hunt Carl down, I hope. I almost fall down as I gasp for air. I guess during the interaction, I forgot to breathe.

"Hun, we are going to finish this event and leave immediately," Stephanie says.

I look at her and can tell that there's no use trying to talk her out of it. "What was that all about?" I ask.

Stephanie looks worriedly at Trew, then back to me. "Hopefully nothing, Danni," she says. "Hopefully nothing."

60

"Belief is a remarkable thing. If we believe that we can do something, we can. If we believe that we can't do something, then we can't. Our belief system limits us, shaping our entire lives, as well as the lives of those around us. In order for any progress to be made, a Heretic is required.

Heretics do not share the common beliefs of the masses, they think bigger. They are scorned and mocked and laughed at for their strange beliefs, yet still they believe. People challenge them, scoff at them, dismiss them as absurd. Yet still they believe. Time passes and sometimes others join the Heretic, one or two at first, and then even more begin to tag along.

When enough time has passed, if the Heretic has been particularly persistent in their beliefs and persuasive in their ability to share the message they believe in, the Heretic disappears. Where once a lonely believer of strange ideas had stood, now stands a visionary thinker, a remarkable person who had the strength and wisdom to look at the world differently; a person who leads us to a better understanding of the universe, and a deeper view of ourselves.

Our limits increase; we advance and prosper.

Thanks to the Heretic... and thanks to Belief."

Excerpt from "A Players' Handbook for the Game of Life"

Trew Radfield – avatar

Trew - 39

"Ten years ago I thought I couldn't have a better birthday, Danni, but look what we've accomplished in the last decade. Look where we sit tonight!"

I raise my glass of French red wine and Danni raises hers to me, smiling that beautiful smile that melts my heart and so often makes my mind stop racing. I look past her and see the lights of Paris below us. The breeze is mild and warm tonight, we are the only two people sitting at the top level of the Eiffel Tower, enjoying a romantic meal while violins play softly in the background. Two waiters stand far enough away to not hear us, but close enough should we require anything.

"I'm glad you like it, babe. It gets harder each year to find a better gift for you, and tougher to surprise you."

She's wearing a blood red dress, her hair curled and bouncing on her bare shoulders. Diamonds glitter around her throat, matching earrings dangling like cold fire from her ears. She gets more beautiful every day. I look around slowly, just soaking up the moment. Life is really about moments; they come too rarely and they leave too soon. We have had so many incredible moments throughout our lives, but I never want to take a single one of them for granted. I finish by allowing my eyes to come to rest on her. "Come dance with me, sweet girl." I stand up and walk to her, holding her chair while she gracefully stands up.

We move towards the little makeshift dance floor and start to dance. Nothing fancy, but it feels good.

"Happy early birthday, Trew." She kisses me. I still feel the electricity and the tingles, exactly like the first time we kissed.

"Sneaky girl," I say. "How's a boy to guess at his surprises when you don't even give them on the correct day?"

She laughs, "I will always surprise you, hun. Even if I have to spring it on you six months from the actual date."

I dip her and she giggles in surprise. "Six months from the actual date, huh?" I say. "So that means you're going to get me my Christmas surprise in June?"

"If that's what it takes."

We dance til the song ends, then go to the balcony to look out over the city. "It's magical, Danni," I say. "Thank you so much. It will make tomorrow seem like a boring, normal day in comparison."

"Oh, please." Danni raises her eyebrows at me. "Tomorrow is going to be a major celebration for the digital prophet, Trew Radfield. The man who has shown the world a better way to think about — well, about everything. People will line up outside just to catch a glimpse of you."

"A glimpse of us," I say seriously.

"Pfft, not us. Just you, babe. But that's exactly how I want it. I have lots of work to do and you're the man on the stage. I'm happy to do my thing from the sidelines."

"Yeah, it should be okay," I say doubtfully.

"Trew!" She laughs and slaps my chest gently, leaving her hand resting on me. "It's a birthday bash in a real German castle! There will be thousands of people there, and the event will be televised."

"I know. It's too much," I say with concern.

"It's fine," Danni says. "The movement has exploded. We have a worldwide following of how many now?"

"Millions," I say.

"Over forty million," she confirms. "We are helping so many people. They love you, and me; I know that, but you're the leader, the one who sees where we all come from, and where we all go. You've given the hopeless a reason to hope. You've fed the hungry by the millions, and you continue to inspire the world to be a better place."

"Did you ever think it would get this big, Danni?" I ask.

"No." She shakes her head. "I thought it would be much bigger by now. But my husband is a bit of a slacker. He prefers to spend too much time hugging and kissing his wife and ignoring the real important things in the world."

I pull her close and kiss her again, this time a long one. I wait until I'm dizzy before I stop, and I can tell she's dizzy too.

"You are my world, Danni," I say seriously. "If you weren't with me doing this, then I wouldn't have done it."

"I feel the same, Trew." She hugs me, then looks at me with sympathy. "It's just a shame that tomorrow you'll be an old man. Only a few good useful years left in you now that you're turning 40. I guess we should get you measured up for a home and wheelchair."

I laugh and reach out to grab her, but she dances away lightly. "Very funny, lady! You're almost as old as me. Maybe we can get a wheelchair built for two!"

"Almost, but not quite," she says playfully. "Besides, I'm going to live another 100 years after I turn 40."

"Really?" I ask.

"Of course," she says. "Remember those chicken cells that lived way longer than they were supposed to? Well, if a chicken can do it, then so can a human. It just takes belief, which I have plenty of. Add some talent and knowledge that the computer that runs this universe can be communicated with, and presto! It should be no problem."

"Hmm. I think you're on to something there, lover," I say seriously.

"Of course I am," she says. "What do you think? Want to join me? Live another 100 years? Can you put up with me for that long?"

"Yes," I say cheerfully. "I most certainly can!"

61

Trew - 40

Today was certainly busier than yesterday's intimate celebration, but I have to admit, this birthday bash wasn't as bad as I had feared it would be.

We flew from Paris to Germany late last night (early this morning, actually) and fell asleep together in our penthouse suite. Danni said she was getting tired of fancy hotels. I laughed at first, but then paused to consider it and then agreed with her. I promised her when we get home we'll hang out in our modest little 3,000 square foot cabin for a couple of weeks.

This morning we were up early to have breakfast with our family, who had flown in to be with us. We're so blessed to have all our parents still living and in good health. My sister brought her husband and kids as well; the little brat grew up into an awesome lady and her kids are wonderful. Of course, Stephanie and Raphael were there, too. My Dad always cracks jokes about Raphael and Stephanie looking horrible for their age and offering to share his beauty secrets with them. They look the same age as they did when I was just a little boy; one of the perks of being an Eternal. I wouldn't accept the job; the price is just too high, in my opinion, but they are part of our family and I'm glad to have them with us.

The afternoon was busy, moving from venue to venue, shaking hands and meeting with the thousands of followers who travelled long distances to celebrate with me but weren't able to come to the actual event. Even castles can only hold so many people.

The crowd at the castle was huge. The organizers brought in famous bands to play for us, and the meal was class A. The entire night I was on top of the world, smiling and holding hands with my bride. I could see that she was proud of me, and I glowed every time someone complimented her.

The big event ended with me standing up to say a few humble words. I'm not sure exactly what I said; there's a lot of times when I feel like I'm just the medium for some greater message that needs an outlet to voice it. At the end of my little talk, which lasted about twenty minutes, the crowd went wild, cheering and applauding. It's quite a rush to look out and see a large crowd of people who feel the same way about life, death, and everything in between as I do.

And that's it. Suddenly I'm standing here kissing Danielle, playfully smacking her bottom as she giggles and moves away from me to catch a limo to the hotel. Stephanie accompanies her; each of us are with an Eternal at these events, just to be safe.

"Okay, let's get this little meet and greet over with, Raphael. I love to mingle, but I'm so tired. Is it possible to wrap this up in less than an hour?"

Raphael nods, "That should be no problem, Trew. Consider it my birthday present to you if we get you out in time."

I smile and walk towards the elevator. People are all around us, gathered in small groups and talking. Some of them nod in my direction but they keep a respectful distance.

As I get to the elevator I look glance backwards at Raph. The crowd has gotten thicker and Raphael has fallen behind. He moves smoothly through the groups of people, gently touching them so that they move out of the way as he walks towards me. He looks up and smiles at me; I smile back. The elevator door opens and I get on, still looking at him. Raphael looks past me and his eyes blaze gold. His smile fades and as the crowd unintentionally slows him down, he yells out my name. The elevator door starts to close and I reach for the button to stop it, but a hand grabs mine in an iron grip, preventing me from doing so. I realize I'm not alone in the elevator, and as the door closes I lock eyes with a face I recognize. His eyes flash red and my legs turn to water.

I can't believe how calm I sound as I greet him. "Hello, Carl. Fancy meeting you here."

****

The room becomes instantly silent. Everyone takes their seat, every eye glued to the main viewer where Trew and Carl stand looking at each other in the elevator.

Michelle folds her arms to stop from shaking.

All eyes want to go to Brandon, but no one can look away from the screen.

"Sir," Michelle says.

Brandon's mind is racing as he watches the viewer. "I see. Please be quiet."

"Is this the robbery? He was supposed to be robbed at 40." Michelle asks, her voice quavering with concern.

"This isn't the robbery we purchased," Brandon said. "Now be quiet. Let me think. Everyone watch as if nothing in the world is more important to you."

"Nothing is," Nadine says in a quiet whisper.

****

Trew - 40

He stands looking at me, like he's the cat and I'm the mouse. I remain calm; I won't give him the satisfaction of losing my composure. Time is standing still.

Finally he speaks. "Look, kid, I'm not a real talker, and I get off at the next floor anyway."

Can it be just a bad coincidence that we are on this elevator together? Is it possible I can swim with a great white shark and walk away? I just nod at him.

"You turn around, the elevator gets to the next floor, and I walk off. Calm and quiet. Okay?"

I swallow and nod, slowly turning around with my back to him. Everything inside of me screams not to, but what choice do I have?

He presses the button and the elevator starts to move. All too soon it's coming to a stop. There is a ding to announce the door will open, and he whispers hotly in my ear.

"I'm sorry, Trew. This is too much even for a guy like me. But hey, we all have our bosses, right? And like you have convinced so many people, it's all just a Game, right?"

I nod quietly. He puts an hand on my shoulder to move past me. As he does I feel something hard hit me in the side, then a hotness starts to envelop me.

I see Carl walk past me, his eyes full of pity. Really? Can that be right?

Then I fall to the ground. I gasp for breath and suddenly I feel like I'm melting from the inside out.

I see a light in the distance, beautiful and warm. It seems to be calling to me...

I try to move towards it...

Epilogue

I really have had a great life. I think a large reason for it being so amazing is that I viewed it as good. I know there are times in my life that were tough, challenging, and even painful. Other people would likely have lived my moments and decided that it was terrible, then they would have let that bitterness and resentment shape how they viewed upcoming events as they occurred. I chose to be more positive, and I think it helped.

Each day in each person's life is filled with some good, some bad, and lots of filler. I think the secret to a happy life is to focus on the good, forget the bad, and move calmly through the filler without getting too bored.

My advice to everyone would be this:

When you encounter the happy, live in that moment for as long as you can. Smile and tuck it away in your memory to be looked at whenever needed.

When you encounter the bad, don't live in the moment. Let it pass as quickly as it can, don't focus on it, and whatever you do, don't grab onto it and tuck it away in your memory.

When you find yourself travelling through the filler, search earnestly for the happy moments. Realize that it is in the filler moments where both the happy and the bad float around, waiting to be noticed by whoever chooses to focus on them.

If that advice is too complicated to follow... just smile and laugh as much as you possibly can.

Trew Radfield - Excerpt from interview during his 40th birthday Celebration

No one moved in Zack's command centre. No one spoke.

"This wasn't part of the plan," Michelle said.

"I know," Brandon whispered.

"He was supposed to live for another thirty years, at least."

"Yes," Brandon agreed.

"He was supposed to..." someone said.

"Supposed to what?" Brandon asked.

"Lead the movement along."

"Lead the movement to where?" Brandon asked.

"Well..." Michelle said.

"Who the hell knows? Because there was never a movement built into our plan. In our plan he was supposed to become a world leader and help shape policies that would feed his country and lead them into a winning war."

"Yes," Michelle agreed.

"None of it happened. We couldn't stop it, we couldn't guide it. We had nothing to do with any of it," Brandon said. "She ruined everything."

Moments of silence passed.

"Where did he end up? In the rankings?" Brandon closed his eyes and rubbed the bridge of his nose.

"Just getting that now, sir."

Brandon sat patiently. His last look at the rankings placed Trew at just around 1,000. He'd done well to climb his way up, but there was no chance for success now. Brandon was confident when they had more time. But Zack's time was up.

"Number one, sir."

Brandon looked at Michelle to make sure he'd heard correctly. She was smiling as she held up the tablet to show the newest and final ranking for Zack.

"Well, I'll be damned," Brandon said, sighing with relief. So much depended on Zack finishing number one; now, against all odds, he'd done it.

The room erupted in cheering. Putting aside the drama of what had just occurred, this was first and foremost a Game, with big stakes riding on what they had just pulled off.

After a few moments of congratulating everyone, Brandon stood up and walked towards the door. "Okay, everyone, I'm going to check in on our boy. They will have started the exit process and he will be coming out in a couple of days. I want to make a statement to the press and make sure he's doing well."

"Sir!"

Brandon turned to look at Michelle. She was looking at the viewer again, her hand over her mouth.

"What is it?"

"They just found Trew, sir. Raphael is there. Look."

Brandon looked at the viewer and his heart turned to ice. Raphael was holding the murder weapon in his hand. It was a Sever Spike.

Zack wouldn't be waking up.

****

Well after midnight, Brandon was alone in an elevator travelling to the lowest level of the complex. He nodded to the security officers as he exited and walked slowly towards the door at the far end of the hall.

Brandon had spent the last several hours in front of the cameras, smiling and doing interview after interview in celebration of Zack's historical finish to his last play. During the chaos surrounding Trew's assassination, Raphael had hidden the Sever Spike, not that most viewers would have recognized it, but his quick thinking had allowed Brandon to keep Zack's permanent death a secret for a while longer. Tygon was celebrating like never before, they could wait a few days to hear the sad news. They would release a statement that Zack had experienced complications while coming out of stasis and died peacefully. Let the world have its day or two of happiness; it was all for the good of the Game.

Brandon nodded grimly to the nurses and doctors as they passed by. There were no happy faces on this level; they all knew the truth. Zack lay in the room at the end of the hall, his body kept alive by machines, for the moment, at least. Brandon had come to take care of this himself; he knew Zack would want it this way.

Entering the room, Brandon discovered that Zack had a visitor. He was standing at Zack's side, holding his hand and looking down at him with compassion. The 6 foot 4 inch tall man was dressed in an expensive tailored suit, his gold cuff links twinkling in the dim light. His golden hair hung slightly forward. When he turned to greet Brandon, it was impossible to miss the green eyes with twinkling gold flecks in them.

Brandon entered the room and stood across from the man, saying nothing as he looked down at Zack's body, its chest moving up and down rhythmically to the pace of the machine forcing him to breathe.

"You seem to be standing over dying people a lot lately," Brandon said.

"Indeed," the man said.

They stood quietly for a time.

"He played a hell of a Game," the man said.

"He certainly did," Brandon said proudly. "He was from the right stock. Orphans always seem to do well."

"Yes, they do. Terrible ending for him, though. Any idea who's responsible?"

"Carl mentioned a boss that he answered to, but that doesn't really narrow it down. It could be any of a number of groups," Brandon said.

Silent moments passed. Finally Brandon asked, "Can you help him?"

The man shook his head sadly. “I thought perhaps... but no, I cannot.” The man gently brushed a lock of hair from Zack’s forehead. “I must leave. I can’t be here long.”

Brandon nodded. “I know. Thank you for trying.”

“My pleasure.” The man came around to the other side of the bed and embraced Brandon in a hug. Brandon resisted for a second, then gave in and hugged the man tightly.

“Well, there we go,” the man smiled. “That alone was worth the trip.”

Brandon smiled. “It was good to see you.”

The man walked towards the door, Brandon looked down at Zack.

“Brandon?” The man paused at the door. “Don’t unplug him.”

Brandon’s face was puzzled. “Why not? He’s gone.”

“I know,” the man nodded. “But I was told that if I couldn’t help him to give you that message. Don’t unplug him.”

Brandon nodded.

The man smiled one more time as he started to walk out the door. “I’ll see you again soon, son.”

Brandon didn’t bother to look up as he replied. “I know, Father. Time’s running out.”

End of Book One...

15242534R00169

Printed in Great Britain
by Amazon.co.uk, Ltd.,
Marston Gate.